THE CURSE OF THE DACRON GEM

CASTLE SERIES, BOOK 2

J. H. WEAR

ISBN: 978-1-68046-842-7

Melange Books, LLC
White Bear Lake, MN 55110
www.melange-books.com

Published in the United States of America.

Cover Design by Ashley Redbird Designs

NOTE FROM THE AUTHOR

Writing this story has been fun, and I hope you enjoy reading it. I owe a lot of thanks to different people helping me in writing Castle: The Return to Domum, NOW CALLED The Curse of the Dacron Gem, too many to mention. Certainly, the efforts by the staff at Melange Books and the publisher Nancy Schumacher. My wife Lorrie has been a tremendous support during my efforts to write and has been instrumental in not letting me give up when I first tried my hand at writing. However, I decided I really wanted to dedicate this book to my father, John Wear, and my niece Caroline. Both passed away too soon and they are dearly missed. I wrote about heaven in this story, and I believe that's where they are now.

—Jack Wear

PART ONE

I pray not to save this life, but to save my next.

ONE

The three-quarter moon peeked between the clouds after the late-night rain. Buildings of various shapes and sizes pressed against the road, not leaving room for a sidewalk. Some stone buildings needed repair, though the two and three-storey structures looked like they had been standing for centuries and could last another easily.

The adjoining roads and lanes weren't even, twisting with rises and dips along them. Occasionally, they narrowed or widened as the buildings jostled for position. At intervals of about a block the cobbled road intersected with another, more or less, at right angles. Not all the roads had equal width. Some were wide enough to sport sidewalks while others were so narrow two people could barely pass one another. The late hour meant empty roads, except for one of the smaller side lanes where a small figure came out running.

Gilbert stumbled and slipped as he ran, trying to peer into the dark street behind him as he gasped for breath. The spirit that chased him didn't have trouble seeing him nor did it slip like Gilbert did as it glided through the air like an ill wind.

The dwarf regretted the six ales he consumed earlier that slowed his reflexes, truly regretted he didn't bring a protective crystal with him when he ventured out that night and now almost regretted the gem he stole from the headstone in the graveyard.

"Go aways! You's dead now, don'ts need no gem."

Gilbert, dressed in baggy brown pants and a leather vest over a green shirt, all rather worn and in serious need of cleaning, wasn't sure if the ghost could do him any real harm; some could, some couldn't. It depended on what power the ghost possessed, and he couldn't find out if this one was bluffing or not until it was too late.

Gilbert rounded the corner, sliding on the cobblestones slick from mud and rain. The ghost, dark grey in a human shape, passed through the outside edge of the brick building and was within ten feet of the fleeing Gilbert. The ghost let out a low moan resulting in a shriek from Gilbert as he looked back to see how close his pursuer was. The backward glance caused him tripping on one of uneven cobblestones and sliding hard on the palms of his hands. The ghost looked as unforgiving as the cobblestones as it floated in front of him wrapped in a cloak over a dark pair of pants and shirt.

Gilbert rolled on his back and pointed a dirty, stubby finger at his adversary. "Lets me be, lets me be. I's wants nothin' to do with yous!"

The ghost reached out with its arms; its fingers stretched in length as it neared Gilbert. The dark grey figure was partially transparent except for the centre which remained impermeable.

Gilbert let out a yell and rolled away. "Leaves me alones!" He scrambled back on his feet and ran again. This time he resisted the temptation of looking behind him and headed straight down the street. After two o'clock in the morning, most businesses or buildings were closed, though Gilbert tried the doors on two rooming houses. But there was still one definite possibility, the inn and the adjoining tavern where he had consumed his ale and came up with the inspiration to rob the tombstone. It was several blocks away and though Gilbert normally didn't do much physical activity he felt inspired to continue to run the rest of the way.

The door to the Greenrock Inn was unlocked, and Gilbert grunted with effort as he pushed the heavy black door open. Like most inns and places of business, the door had a pentagram painted inside a circle on the door. The symbol and similar ones prevented unwelcome spirits and creatures such as vampires from entering. Homes didn't require the symbol since they weren't open to the public and thus hadn't an open invitation for any spirits to wander in. Simple symbols could not stop all spirits. To protect against stronger spirits, a more complex symbol had to be drawn and, for added protection, be sanctified by a wizard. That cost money and not all proprietors were willing to do so.

When Gilbert ran into the inn's lobby and turned around, he could see the ghost stopping at the threshold, looking frustrated at its inability to move forward. Gilbert grinned at it and shoved the door closed.

"What be going on there?"

Gilbert whirled around and saw the innkeeper's son standing behind the counter. The boy, perhaps fifteen years old, was trying to stifle a yawn as he woke up from sitting on a wooden chair. The counter sat by the stairs which led to the three levels of rooms above. To the left of the stairs and the counter was the tavern, now quiet from the evening's festivities. It still smelled of spilt beer and whisky and a few chairs rested on their sides. To the right stood the dining room, holding a single long table of dark varnished wood with chairs on one side and a bench ran its length on the other. A kitchen and the innkeeper's residence occupied the remaining space behind the counter's back wall.

"Oh, nothin' lad, nothin' at all. I'll just be going up to me room now."

The boy watched him with scepticism. "What was it you closed the door on?"

"Oh that?" Gilbert casually made his way to the wood staircase. "Why me thinks that was just the wind blowing up some dust. Yes, indeed, just the wind." Gilbert advanced up the steps and ignored the final question by the boy.

"What wind? I saw something out there that wasn't dust."

Gilbert closed the door to his room on the third floor with a huge sigh. The room was square of about nine feet along the side and with a seven and half foot ceiling. The yellow plaster barely hid the wood beams behind it along the walls, and the ceiling had a series of cracks exposing the attic above. The only furniture was a small table holding an unlit oil lamp and a bed where the centre of a mattress was slowly sinking toward the floor. Gilbert quickly went to the window to lock the shutters, and after a wary look around, sat down on the edge of the bed. He used a flint to light the lamp and examined his prize.

The gem was translucent yellow-orange and perhaps an inch in diameter. In the centre a tiny blue centre sparkled with its own light. The gem, known as the Dacron gem, had been lost for over a century. The last known person to possess it was a weak warlock, Dacron Thomac. Thomac used most of his knowledge to extend his life to over two centuries. He lived in moderate wealth, survived several marriages, fathered a dozen children and generally made his life comfortable. Unfortunately, like many warlocks, witches and others who practiced magic to extend their life, Thomac neglected to extend magic to protect his mental well-being and gradually became mad.

Rumours of what the gem and its crystal centre could do concentrated on moving back in time or teleporting. Gilbert wasn't sure about the truth of the various stories of the gem, but he gathered enough information on Thomac to guess where he had hidden it. Thomac was jealous of his magic and his collection of enchanted items, choosing not to reveal their secret location as he approached his death. The Dacron gem he considered of special importance and vowed to take it and its secret to his grave.

Of course, after his death most of his enchanted items were found. Several thieves searched his grave for the missing gem to no avail and eventually the search for it was dropped. But Gilbert in a rare moment of measured thought when he was drinking considered the headstone itself might be the hidden spot for the gem. The gem was hidden underneath the family crest, a carved black stone attached to the headstone by iron bolts.

Gilbert pondered the use of iron bolts attached to the crest. Iron had the ability to dampen or neutralize magic spells and those iron bolts could hide the presence of the gem and its crystal centre. Inspired by this revelation Gilbert quickly downed his ale and hurried to the edge of town where the graveyard lay. He ignored the various spirits floating around and went straight to Thomac's final resting spot.

Spirits generally left their bodies behind to go to better places, but a few would stay near their burial ground for a period of time. Fewer still would stay for decades like Thomac's spirit did. His spirit didn't stay constantly at the gravesite, even ghosts get bored, but the noise from Gilbert working the crest and then the gem being pried loose aroused his attention. Just as Gilbert managed to dig the gem free with his knife, Thomac's spirit crossed the graveyard to defend his property. Despite being a warlock and knowing considerable magic, Thomac as a ghost didn't possess much power and would have to depend on fear to get Gilbert to drop his gem. When Gilbert ran into the inn, Thomac was repelled by the simple spell on the door and left enraged at the theft as he drifted back to the graveyard.

Besides not being sure what the gem was supposed to do, Gilbert also didn't know what spells could activate the gem. He pondered the gem in his hand and frowned, deciding even if he could find the correct spell it might not be safe to use it.

None of that really mattered. The reason Gilbert retrieved the gem—he didn't like to use the word steal—was to sell it to someone else. He had a few customers in mind, though some weren't available at the present time. Council Madoc, one of his better clients, was currently living in exile on Earth and was banned from the world of Domum until Lord Perry decreed he could return. Although Madoc was more inclined to barter for information, he would occasionally purchase some exotic items and the gem certainly qualified in that regard. It was risky for Gilbert to travel to Earth to find the warlock, and it would be more prudent to find a buyer on Domum.

Gilbert began to make a mental list of prospective buyers, mumbling adjectives attached to a few of the names. Gilbert gave a final peek at the gem and inserted it into a small pocket hidden on the inside of his shirt. He fell back onto the bed and the effects of the ale he consumed earlier plus the late hour pulled him into a deep sleep.

TWO

J on McKinney strolled from Mrs. Stewart's home to the O'Doul residence. Jon returned to the town of Ballymiller after he finished his master's degree at the University of Boston. He could have stayed at the Miller Castle, the castle he temporally inherited until the reappearance of his Uncle Gordon Miller, but the castle had only one bedroom equipped with the luxury of electricity. The rooms in the castle were drafty and prone to occasional visits from creatures from Domum.

Jon didn't mind most of the visitors, and he had even made acquaintances with some of them when he was in Domum. But they had a tendency to show up unannounced without regard to time of day or place. Gordon Miller seemed to be able to adapt to their intrusion, but Jon wanted more privacy and found a room to rent close by to where Liz stayed with her parents. She had returned to Ballymiller as well for the summer between semesters at university.

Liz and Jon had corresponded by phone, email and letters over the past nine months. At the end of his classes Jon flew back to Ballymiller to be with Liz.

The plane flight to Shannon airport wasn't overly taxing on him, but as he got nearer his destination, Jon became more agitated. The final leg of the journey on the bus seemed far longer than the first time he used it a year ago, though it appeared to be the same worn-down bus with the equally worn down driver. Several times he fingered the inside pocket of his jacket for the small felt-covered case and each time he grew more nervous.

With his sister Sandra's help he had purchased an engagement ring, sure of himself and Liz's acceptance. Now doubts had begun to form in his mind. Liz and Jon had shared an amazing adventure on Domum, barely escaping back to Earth after a harrowing battle with dragons and the insane Lord Bennett. Too soon after returning to Earth, both Liz and Jon had to depart for university classes.

Their correspondence was frequent and though they talked of love, there weren't the words of lifelong commitment. Sandra had given him encouragement. "Don't be stupid. She followed you all the way to Domum, didn't she? Right now, she's probably wondering what's taking you so long to propose." Jon agreed she had a point and told Sandra he wanted to wait so he could propose in person. So as the bus pulled into the town of Ballymiller, Jon sensed his hands getting clammy and perspiration forming on his forehead. The bus stopped at the same place as last time, across the street from the Demister Hotel and under a streetlamp giving off a garish yellow light.

Jon headed to the front of the bus and climbed down the steps to the sidewalk. He heard his name being called and before he could react Liz was there. He dropped his luggage and she hugged him.

Liz's girlfriend, Tori, stood back on the sidewalk and waited for them to finish their kisses before she stepped forward and gave him a hug. Jon took a few seconds to recognize Tori; she had dyed her brown hair blonde and grown it longer and shed almost a dozen pounds. She had offered to wait with Liz for the bus, not known for always being on schedule on its leg up to Ballymiller. With Jon carrying the two large suitcases and Liz the handbag, the three made their way to the Demister. Jon had decided to stay at the hotel until he could figure out better accommodations.

The three sat in the pub talking and it didn't take Jon long to recognize some regulars sitting about the room and the barmaid Charlene who remembered him as well. Jon also recalled the table he sat at when Liz first introduced herself and invited him to sit with her and her friends. He wondered if the Demister Pub would be an appropriate place to propose. It was where they first met, but he questioned the appropriateness of a drinking establishment. He decided he would have to give some consideration to where, when and how he would propose.

Two hours later, Jon felt the effects of the journey and the ale. Liz and Tori had to go to work in the morning and Jon escorted them home. Tori lived only a block away from the Demister and after walking her home, Jon tried to make the most of his time alone with Liz.

They talked about how much they missed each other and reminisced on their time on Domum, avoiding a discussion on a long-term relationship. Jon was reluctant to discuss it because he was tired, and Liz was of the opinion he should take the lead in that area. He did manage to kiss her several more times and after a few hugs reluctantly watched her disappear into her parents' home. Jon made his way back to the hotel, checking again for the familiar shape in his coat pocket. He stifled a yawn as he climbed the stairs to his room, opened his door and moaned as he saw the still unpacked suitcases on his bed.

———

Jon carried the ring in his pocket for the next several days, unable to summon up the place and courage to ask for Liz's hand in marriage. In the meantime, he searched for a place to stay, finding the hotel too expensive along with the annoyance of always having to buy meals. Liz's parents helped him find a rooming house. A widow in the neighbourhood was willing to rent out a bedroom and provide breakfast and dinner. Mrs. Stewart didn't normally rent out rooms but was assured by Margaret and Patrick O'Doul that Jon was a fine young man and would be staying only for the summer.

Jon knocked on the door at the O'Doul house and heard the shout of, "Come on in, Jon, door's open." The white painted house was over one hundred and fifty years old. The front porch had been rebuilt a few years back when the old one began to slant downward away from the front door. Otherwise, the house had not shown signs of aging with Patrick O'Doul maintaining both the home and yard with diligence.

As soon as Jon entered, he was met with a hug and a kiss from

Liz who, without her shoes on, had to stand on her toes to reach the six foot two, two hundred and fifty pound former college football player. Liz was average height but usually wore high-heeled shoes when she was around Jon. She was growing her hair long again, although it wasn't quite as long as when she first met him. After spending several weeks on Domum which had a shortage of washing facilities and shampoo, Liz decided to cut her hair. Midway through her year at university she decided she liked her hair longer rather than shorter.

"Have you eaten already? We're just about to have breakfast. We got up a wee bit late this morning."

"Oh, I ate already." He glanced toward the kitchen doorway.

"Come on then. I'm sure you can find room for a wee more."

"Well, your mom is a good cook." He followed his nose to the kitchen.

Liz and Margaret dominated the breakfast conversation about Sheila Bester's new baby and the upcoming baby shower.

As soon as Patrick finished his breakfast, he rose from the table and invited Jon to join him in the living room, carefully carrying a cup of tea as he did so.

Liz gave Jon a half smile as she rose to clear the plates from the table. Jon smiled back and followed Patrick out of the kitchen.

Patrick relaxed into the old armchair while Jon sat on the newer green fabric cloth loveseat.

"Liz's mom has known the family for years so everyone gets excited when a baby's born. Myself, I'd rather talk about the rugby matches."

"Me too."

"I saw some of your American football on the telly last week. Bit hard to understand all those rules and lots of wasted time, but in me younger days I betcha I could have played that game." Patrick often told Jon about his days as a rugby player and tried to understand what Jon did as a defensive back.

"I'll bet you could too."

"How's your uncle doing these days? I hear there're still creatures 'pearing around there."

"I guess there's always going be some of those. But Uncle Gordon is doing fine. He's working on how many worlds can occupy the same quantum reality. His words actually. I don't have a clue what he was talking about. Anyway, he's emailing stuff back and forth with Tom and Tuck about his theories."

"Nice young lads. Ah, I see Lizzy is putting on her shoes."

Jon turned and saw Liz standing by the door. "I better be going then."

"Sorry if me mom gets carried away with the new baby. She really likes babies and a new one is kind of exciting for her." Liz looked up at Jon as they made their way down the street.

"That's okay. By the way Uncle Gordon asked us to come by. Perhaps we could visit him first and then go for lunch. My mom was pretty excited when my nephew was born." Jon put his arm around her.

"You be already planning lunch after eating two breakfasts?" She reached over with her hand and patted his stomach. "You've put on a bit of weight since last year."

"Well, I haven't been able to work out much lately."

She laughed, "Perhaps you need to go back to Domum and fight dragons again."

"Lord, no. I'd rather go jogging."

Gordon Miller greeted them warmly, insisting they stay for lunch. Gordon informed them he wasn't troubled by visitors from Domum, though they occasionally took small items left lying around.

"Does my friend, Gilbert, come 'round still?" Liz took a sip of her tea and lifted a biscuit from the plate in the center of the dark oak table. Jon sat next to her while Uncle Gordon faced them on the other side. The table could seat eight as it was presently set and could be expanded to twelve by opening up the middle to insert leafs.

"Only once or twice and neither time did he take anything." He paused for a moment as he pondered. "At least as far as I can determine. He seemed to come over for just a visit, check what was going on, that sort of thing. He did inquire about Jon and Council Madoc and wondered if either of you might be coming back to Ballymiller."

"He didn't say if he was working for Lord Perry, did he? And was he still going out with Donna?" asked Jon, recalling the small woman. Gilbert had stolen an item from Liz's suitcase to give as a gift to Donna. Jon had pursued Gilbert and in the ensuing struggle, ended in going through a gateway to the world of Domum.

"Hmm, he did mention something about a girlfriend, but I don't recall her name. And while he didn't talk about Lord Perry, he did say he had better get back to work so I assume he was working for somebody."

"Did he by chance mention Tony … Lord Anthony by the way?" Liz injected her own question.

"No, other than he said everyone was fine."

Jon glanced at Liz when she asked about Tony and his own thoughts lingered about Nicole before returning his attention back to his uncle. He had traveled with Nicole around Domum as he searched for a way to return to Earth. During that time he fell in love with her, even becoming intimate. He was tempted to ask about Nicole but decided it wouldn't be prudent to bring her name up in front of Liz, who was aware only of what might have happened. He wondered himself about the friendship she developed with Tony while she was on Domum, but never questioned her about it. He was thankful Tony had safely taken Liz to Stone Retreat to meet him. He was also appreciative for Tony's help in rescuing Nicole from Lord Bennett during his desperate quest for power. "What about those gnome-like creatures I've seen around here? I saw a few at Domum, but I'm under the impression they didn't originate there."

"I believe you're right on with your thinking there. I've done some research on other possible worlds besides Earth and Domum."

"Just how many other worlds might there be?" Liz asked.

"Well, initially I considered there might be an infinite number of worlds. At least that was proposed by at least one theory. But I've discovered if two universes had the exact same natural laws, then it was impossible for them to occupy the same space. The weak electromotive force forbids it."

"So the laws of physics had to be at least a little different?" Jon grabbed another biscuit as he spoke.

"More than a little. You see, it turns out physical laws have to change in certain increment amounts. For instance, the speed of light, or the strength of the nuclear force, has to be at certain values. Something like quantum steps." Miller took a sip of his tea. "That means there are only so many possible worlds. As the physical laws change in steps, they soon are unable to support life and even the formation of stars and planets. We are left with a limited number of worlds like Earth that can exist."

"How many would that be?" Jon considered his own question. "It couldn't be too many. Even a minor change in the strong nuclear force would make the formation of worlds impossible."

"True, though there's a small counteraction of one force changing in step with another opposite force. In total I calculated there could be only about a dozen possible worlds or fewer which could support life." He paused. "Our life, that is. Some of these worlds could support life we're not familiar with."

"Does that mean all of these worlds can exchange visitors?"

"I suppose so, though it seems travel from some worlds is easier than others. It also appears smaller bodies, that is mass, require less energy to make the jump to other worlds. That's why leprechaun and gremlin size creatures are more common visitors than dragons or even people of our size."

Liz and Jon walked slowly down the street after their tea with Uncle Gordon. They discussed what he told them and wondered if Uncle Gordon was planning to try to see these other worlds. If he was, it was possible Uncle Gordon might try to draw them into his plans.

"Gee, I hope not, Jon. That was a bit too much adventure for me last time in a world in which people dominated. What would a world be like if gremlins ruled the roost?"

"I dunno. And I hope I don't find out."

THREE

"Lord Troy, you have a guest at the door." The tall blonde, Gwyneth, gave a smile as she paused. "Gilbert is waiting in the drawing room." She stood with her hands clasped in front of her as she waited for his response. Gwyneth wore a white gown with a loose gold chain belt around her waist, the gown almost touching the floor on her right side and rising to her hip on the left. The dress covered her left shoulder and arm while her right side was bare to her waist.

"Gilbert? I wonder what he might be up to now." Lord Troy chuckled. "Very well, I better see him." He followed the barefoot Gwyneth out the door of his library, staring at her half bare back as she headed down the red carpet in the hallway.

Gilbert was helping himself to a large glass of a gold-coloured liquid and chatting with a small framed dark woman with long black hair. She covered her mouth with her hand as she laughed at one of Gilbert's colourful jokes, looking at the entrance to the room as Lord Troy entered.

"I see you have been entertaining our guest, Marisa. Or is he entertaining you?"

"Oh! Freeman Gilbert is very funny, Lord Troy." She giggled again as she moved away from Gilbert to leave the room. Gilbert watched the bare-breasted Marisa shift her hips as she walked past

Troy and gave a backward glance at him as she left the room. She wore only a dark green wrap that hung low on her hips with a hem drifting around her ankles.

"Gilbert, my old friend! It is an honour you have come to visit me. How can I help you?" Lord Troy rested his right hand on a silver tipped black cane.

Gilbert stood in the centre of the large room, decorated differently from his last visit. The room featured a royal blue rug with the chairs made of dark wood and covered with yellow leather. The smooth finished rock walls used drapes and large paintings as a covering. The paintings depicted battles between men against dragons, werewolves or other assorted monsters. Some paintings also showed damsels in distress, waiting to be rescued. More than one painting showed Lord Troy Sussex as a warrior doing battle.

———

Lord Troy himself was not as large as indicated in the paintings or as young. He now looked to be in his early forties with his dark hair kept short. A small, thin moustache was his only facial hair.

Gilbert grinned at the tall, slim man. He heard Lord Troy was well over two hundred years old and used magic to keep his youth. Unfortunately, he had used the wrong wording on his spell, and to keep his aging at bay, he was confined to his castle and the adjoining property. "Lord Troy, it's always a pleasure to see yous." He tossed back the rest of his drink. He nodded toward the door. "Marisa is new, ain't she?"

Troy looked behind him at the retreating figure in the hallway before returning to Gilbert. "Indeed, she is, Gilbert. I purchased her only a few weeks ago. So far she is working out nicely."

"That is good, that is good." Gilbert poured himself another drink and wandered over to a chair to sit. "I was a wondering if yous could help me with a small question me has."

"Certainly, I can try. What concerns you?" Troy sat opposite him on a matching armchair.

"Wells, me was curious if yous knows anything abouts the Dacron gem."

"The Dacron gem? Presumed lost. Dacron Thomac guarded it carefully, and it was never found after his death. The gem was reported to have special powers, but most of the rumours are nonsense. Its true strength was something even stranger."

"Oh, an' what might that be?" Gilbert tried to feign casualness by studying his new drink.

"The gem could alter reality, at least that's what I've concluded from reading about it. You see, there're many possible outcomes from any action and most of the time the most likely outcome prevails. For example, dropping a glass goblet on a stone floor will cause it to shatter. But on rare occasion the goblet won't shatter, it will survive intact. In other words, a less likely outcome prevails."

"So, sometimes strange things happen."

"Yes, but that gem can cause those strange things to happen and the user can pick which possibility will prevail. If that gem is activated it can cause that goblet never to shatter, for someone to win every time in a game of chance, for lightning to strike two, three times in the same place, for an arrow to cause a tree to fall when it strikes…"

"To wins at games of chance!"

"Yes, just an example. This is a very powerful crystal and can cause abnormalities to happen."

"Games of chance, huh?"

"Yes, those too. But you see such a device can cause havoc, reality can be changed."

"Games of chance, you say?"

Lord Troy sighed. "Gilbert, this gem is more than just a way for someone to win bets. It's very dangerous." He paused and stared at Gilbert suspiciously. "Why are you asking me about the Dacron Gem? Do you know where it might be?"

"I heards rumours somebody finds it. He wants to learn what it does." Gilbert took a quick drink from his glass. "No, ol' Gilbert don't knows where it be, but maybe I can finds the person who does."

"I see. And who might that be?"

"Ah, just rumours I hears. Would you happens to know what kinds of spell would activate the crystal?"

"Ah, well, I suppose I could dig out that information in the library with a lot of work."

"That would be good of yous."

"Yes, but before I start digging for any information, I would like to see that gem."

"But I don'ts…"

"I heard what you said, Gilbert. But I really didn't live this long not to see through this game of yours. You know more than you say. I'll do research on the spell when you show me the gem."

Gilbert sighed. "Okay, okay. I sees if I can gets the gem. Might cost me a bit to obtain it."

"How much are we talking about?"

"I don'ts know. Hundred, maybe more, silver ferns."

"Hmm, that's a lot of coin. Though I suppose a fair price for such an artefact."

"I sees what I cans do, sees how much he wants."

"Okay Gilbert, I'll tell you what. I'll advance you a hundred silver ferns and you purchase that gem. And I'll give you twenty percent for handling the transaction. If it costs you more, let me know. And if you get it for less, I'd appreciate you returning the excess."

"Deal. See yous 'morrow or a couple of days."

———

Lord Perry sat at his usual spot in the library by the two large tables shoved together into an L shape. His two assistants scurried to bring him books and writing material as he worked. Lord Perry snapped his fingers, causing a gnant to scamper to the table.

"Rtze, bring me some tea and biscuits and enough for my assistants."

"Yesss, Lord Perry." The gnant quickly left the room. Gnants looked vaguely human, sporting large elf-like ears, a large hooked nose and a brown face covered with fine black hair, though some had blonde or red hair instead. Their hands ended with long fingers and thumbs with black short claws. A forked red tongue occasionally darted out between pointed yellow teeth and gave gnants a demon-like appearance. Gnants could walk upright slightly stooped, standing around five feet and shuffled along in an odd amble. But they became quick and agile when they used all four limbs to move.

Gnants were the original habitants of Domum and battled the human intruders unsuccessfully to remove them. The gnants didn't fight well together and lost heavily to the smaller numbered but better organized humans. After the gnants accepted an uneasy truce with humans a new culture and philosophy took over.

Tyreel Followers used selective breeding and education to change their race to be more sociable, certain that was the only reason humans defeated them in battles. Jon and a few other humans had befriended a few of the gnants, though a large portion of both humans and gnants had contempt and mistrust for each other.

Lord Perry enjoyed doing research in the main library, something he had found less time to do in the last few months. The tall but portly man had taken over the administration duties for Horstruff and the surrounding districts from Lord Bennett. Lord Bennett was missing, presumed dead, after an ill-fated attempt to take over control from King Charles.

His new role as administrator wasn't the only fallout from Lord Bennett's gambit. Council Madoc, who had warned Lord Perry of the uprising and convinced him to take action, had been ordered into exile to Earth. Council Madoc had been a supplier of information for Lord Perry and several other powerful figures. Unfortunately, his own quest for power, coupled with being a warlock, was a cause for concern to Lord Perry. Thus, Council Madoc found himself being treated with suspicion during the turmoil that followed the demise of Lord Bennett. Council Madoc accepted Lord Perry's decision without argument, trusting Earth would be only a temporary residence.

Lord Perry decreed gnants were to be treated as equals in the district of Horstruff and not to be killed or harmed without due reason. He also decreed gnants were subject to most of the human laws while inside his jurisdiction. The new laws caused a lot of grumbling among both humans and gnants, but it also reduced a lot of the more physical conflicts between the two races.

Lord Perry himself had gained more power from new alliances. The powerful family of Lord Kevin Graham had sided with Lord Perry since the onset of the challenge by Lord Bennett. In turn Lord Perry pushed the promotion of Graham's son, Anthony, from Sir to Lord. Anthony was engaged to Nicole Keaton, Jon's friend and companion during his adventure in Domum. Lord Perry felt indebted to Jon for his help in defeating Lord Bennett and granted him a number of concessions. One of these included giving Gilbert, with some misgivings, a job. Gilbert's duties to him varied but generally involved gathering information. Lord Perry was naturally concerned about the accuracies a thief would deliver but it was the safest job Lord Perry could think of giving him. It was better for him to be outside the castle working for him than inside where he could cause havoc.

Lord Perry studied the large open book in front of him. Each of the six hundred pages was covered with drawings and text explaining crystal technology, quantum mechanics and multi-dimensional physics. Unfortunately, the vague diagrams and text was written in a language unknown or long forgotten.

Lord Perry swung his attention to another book, smaller but also filled with diagrams and text. Some diagrams on the two books matched almost exactly. The text in the second book was comprehensible, and he used the information to try to decipher the text in the first. Understanding the language of the first book was essential to discovering the secrets of the crystals and Lord Perry felt he was making slow but steady progress. This latest discovery of common diagrams in two different books excited him. It was painstaking work comparing different works of his huge library, but he started to unravel the secrets of the ancients. Who had written the original texts was still unknown. It was a possibility they may have arrived from yet another world existing alongside of Earth and Domum and they may have not even been human or gnant.

Lord Perry's attention was broken by the arrival of Rtze and tea with biscuits. The gnant was staring at him and the open books.

"Rtze, you're a smart young fellow. Have you ever seen writing such as this before?" He indicated the large book with his hand.

The gnant scampered over to his side and peered at the book.

"That part isss alike what Rtze seen before when learning." The gnant touched one string of symbols with a black claw. "Not able to read ressst of page."

"So, on this page you have only seen one particular symbol or word?"

"True."

"What does it mean?"

"Conflict, argument."

Lord Perry nodded. "Yes, essentially that's what it means. The math calculations point toward a solution of infinity, hence the conflict. The rest of the calculations show a way around that problem. It is interesting you can read one word, and only one word, on this page. Never mind, have some tea."

———

Gilbert was elated. He had a hundred silver ferns in his pocket and hadn't given up anything for it yet, though not to bring the Dacron Gem to Lord Troy would have repercussions eventually, perhaps even rapidly. Lord Troy was Lord Perry's uncle, Gilbert's present employer. Besides the obvious danger in angering the administrator of Horstruff, Gilbert did have his own code of honour. First, he avoided stealing from people, preferring to "find" things unattended. This was partly due to evade the stigma of being a thief in his own mind and partly due to the danger of being caught by someone as he took an item. Stealing from someone he knew was worse, both ethically and by the fact he could be identified.

Thus, Gilbert was compelled to turn over the Dacron Gem to Lord Troy and not try to deceive him, at least not too much. The gem would be helpful in playing games of chance, a consideration that dawned on him during Lord Troy's explanation. Unfortunately, magic and spells were forbidden in games, and God help those caught using that advantage. To top off that danger there was Donna, Gilbert's girlfriend, who wouldn't be too pleased if he resumed gambling.

Still a hundred silver ferns were considerably better than he had hoped to achieve from the sale of the gem, and in addition was his commission for doing the transaction.

———

"Lord Perry, you wished to see me?" Gilbert dropped to one knee in front of the huge dark wood desk where Lord Perry sat doing paperwork.

He dropped his quill pen and frowned. "I did…yesterday. Where in hell have you been?" Lord Perry pointed his finger at Gilbert. "I only hired you because of Sir Jon's request I give you a chance to redeem yourself. Are you trying to make a fool of both him and me?"

"Oh no, no, no, Lord Perry. I's just ran into a spot of difficulty trying to get the right information for ye. Me just tried to make sure I's not making a mistake. Ol' Gilbert very thankful for job, yes indeed."

Lord Perry squinted at Gilbert and the silence lasted for several seconds. "Very well, I'll take your word this time. Now, just what did you find out about this dragon master, Sir Nolene?"

"Ah, Sir Nolene. Well, it seems he has learned the ability to train dragons…"

"Hence the name dragon master. Gilbert, I already aware he is a dragon master and I do understand what that means. Tell me something I don't know."

"Yes, Lord Perry, of course. Sir Nolene comes from the town of Waleington, in the county of Larope. He's a man of means and has a large stable of mature patiri dragons, maybe eight or nine. He sezs he wants newly hatched dragons to raise and teach, but there's more."

"Go on."

"Took me some time to finds this, but Sir Nolene also looks for men to join his army. Pay more than regular soldiers."

"How many men is he looking for?"

"Don'ts know, lots I guess."

"That's interesting information, Gilbert."

"Thanks."

"But it took you three days to find that out?"

"Uh, well, these men sworn to secrecy. Had to bribe a couple to learn truth."

"Where is this Sir Nolene now?"

"Gone to Homested."

"Well, we can't have mere Sirs raising their own private armies, especially one who is a dragon master. I shall have him summoned to come before me."

"Uh, Lord Perry, no disrespect, but he sez he bows to no man or king."

"We'll see about that."

FOUR

Council Madoc sighed inwardly at the young woman's enthusiasm, deciding it was a mistake to allow her into his dressing room. He had finished a simple magic trick which removed her bra without touching her.

"Oh, wow! How did you do that? I didn't feel nothing." She looked at her blue bra dangling from his hand. Carmen had long dyed blonde hair and stood five foot ten on her spiked heels. She grinned. "Betcha you can't take off my panties that way."

"Perhaps we can…"

"'Cause I'm not wearing any." She gave him a sexy smile. She had squeezed into a pair of black pants and the blue top that left her midriff bare. She placed her right hand on his shoulder.

"That's very interesting but it has been a long day. Perhaps another time?"

"Oh, I have some pills that will…"

"I do not use drugs, Carmen."

"Then maybe there's another way to keep you interested."

"I'm sure there is, but not tonight."

Carmen pouted. "Are you sure?"

"Quite."

"All right then." She turned and scribbled her name and phone number on a pad sitting on his table. "Call me, promise?"

"Certainly. Your bra?" He extended his hand toward her.

She used a finger to lift her bra from his hand and pushed it into her purse. "Until next time."

As Madoc ushered her out of his dressing room, he wondered how much longer he would have to live on Earth. Posing as a conjurer on Earth was easy, relying on his knowledge of magic to delight the crowds. He drew appreciative audiences for his shows and made a modest income as he toured various venues. The audience assumed he was doing spectacular illusions and while some tricks looked incredible, in fact they were easy for someone who understood how to do real magic. As a warlock, he found much of his powers reduced on Earth but not enough to hamper his show.

Council Madoc packed a small travel bag he used to carry a few props, such as rubber balls and coloured cloths. He could create those as well but didn't want to arouse unneeded suspicion. If anyone was curious on how he did his tricks, he could show them the tools of his trade. He took a last glance in the dressing room, one of three the small club had, before closing the door. He almost collided turning away from the door with a woman in the narrow hallway.

"Beg your pardon, miss. I didn't see your approach."

She stared at him a moment before responding. "That's okay. You're the magician, aren't you?"

"Yes, you are correct."

"You're good, really good."

"Thank you for the compliment." Council Madoc now recognized her as the singer. She looked different in her blue jeans, t-shirt and yellow tennis shoes after being on stage in a long blue dress singing Broadway tunes. He had noted she had a decent voice as he listened from the backstage, but the audience only clapped politely to her finish. Her wavy blonde hair bounced above her shoulders as she moved, and her hazel coloured eyes held a mischievous sparkle to them. Her curvy figure was shown well off on her medium height frame. "I enjoyed your singing as well, Miss..."

"Angela Perkins. Thanks, but you're one of the few that does. I'm trying to find a niche but without much success." She shrugged her shoulders. "Good thing my job as a waitress pays or else I'd be in trouble." Her grin showed off white teeth.

"I'm sure you'll find achievement soon enough. My name is

Madoc. It is an honour to meet you." He turned toward the exit door. The heavy metal door led to a small alley which gave him seclusion where sometimes he transported himself to his apartment rather than using a taxi. Out of necessity he had learned how to teleport himself on Earth something he rarely did on his own world of Domum.

He had taken two steps when she called out to him. "Hey, are you hungry? Like, it's late but I know of a couple of places that are open."

He turned back to her. "It has been a long evening…"

"True, but I don't like to eat by myself. I'll treat you."

"Very well, Miss Perkins, a small bite would be fine."

"Angela." She slipped her arm into his. "Italian or Chinese?"

Her Toyota had spots of rust on it but ran well enough as she made her way down the street.

"Do you have a car?"

"No, I don't drive."

"You don't drive? Did you lose your licence or something?"

"No, I never had one."

"Where're you from?"

"A part of Ireland."

"I should've guessed. You have a nice accent."

His cheeks grew slightly red. "Where are you from if I may ask?"

"I grew up in Leesburg, Virginia. I may have been spoiled because I was the youngest of two brothers and a sister. My parents have money and they treated us pretty good. What was your family like?"

"I have one younger brother."

She kept up a line of questioning as they shared a pizza and he hoped she wouldn't ask questions that might force him to lie to hide his true identity. She was fascinated he used Madoc as a first and last name. Council Madoc never revealed his full name. As a warlock, giving out his full name would give his enemies too much power.

"So where's your next gig?"

"That has not yet been determined. I'll be checking for possibilities in the morrow."

25

She grinned at him. "You have a different way of saying things. Kinda like old-fashioned."

"I don't mean to sound obscure."

"That's okay. Your accent sounds really sexy." She giggled as he blushed.

Council Madoc insisted in paying for the meal but agreed to allow her to drive him home.

"Look, I know this isn't any of my business but I'm friends with this hotel manager at the Hilton. I'll check with him to see if they need a new act."

"That would be most kind of you, though I assure you it is not really necessary."

"I'm glad to do it for you. What's your phone number? You do have a phone, don't you?"

"Yes, of course." He recited the number to her.

He shook hands with her and stood at the curb to watch the old Toyota drive off into the distance, slightly puzzled by what happened during the evening. He had met only a few women where he wasn't in complete control, but she seemed to test that power.

———

The apartment suited him due to its position away from power lines, cell phone towers and other major electrical transmitters. Council Madoc's apartment was sparsely decorated, without a TV, radio or stereo. He did have a landline telephone as a means for contact, but other than a few incandescent light bulbs and an electric stove, that was his only concession to electrical devices. Occasionally, Council Madoc would unplug his telephone and use candles instead of lights to help maintain uncontaminated aether. He could still sense the electronic noise from the cell phones, radio signals, electrical clatter from vehicles and a host of other electrical clamour spewing devices but at least it was more subdued.

His apartment was located in an older brick, two-storey walk-up on the second level. Other than kitchen appliances he avoided the use of metal, using wood furniture and covering the floors with rugs.

Warlocks on Domum were defined as those practicing magic not belonging to the witches' guild. On Domum, he belonged to a faction of warlocks that didn't approve of using magic to profit oneself and he carried those principles to. True, he was tempted to make a few easy dollars when he walked through a casino, but money was not a major consideration for him as he'd taken enough gold with him from Domum to do little if he so wished. He preferred to keep busy and practice his spells, which led him to choose to do magic shows under the name of the Great Madoc. His own natural appearance of height, slimness with dark hair and a small beard worked well as a magician.

He frowned as he opened the door to his flat, wondering if this was always to be his life. For someone who expected to live at least another two hundred years it was not just an idle question. He longed to go back to Domum, but he had given his word to Lord Perry he would not return until he was allowed to do so. Lord Perry didn't entirely trust him not to keep his bargain which made Council Madoc all the more determined to stay on Earth.

This week he didn't have to produce a show, allowing him to stay at home and relax. Until another venue showed up, he decided he could keep himself occupied reading. Some things Earth offered couldn't be matched on Domum, which included a selection of great literature and vastly superior wine. He also appreciated the music, in particular piano, but he declined to purchase the electronic equipment to reproduce the recordings.

The week passed uneventfully until Wednesday when the phone rang. He stared at the offending device, wishing he had just left it unplugged as he'd done yesterday. On the fifth ring, he picked it up.

"Hello. This is Madoc."

"Hi, it's me, Angela."

"Of course. How may I be of assistance to you?"

She giggled for a moment. "Uh, I don't usually, that is…let me start again. Are you interested in going for a cup of coffee?"

"Coffee?"

"Yeah, I can pick you up in an hour. If you're free, that is."

"I would be honoured."

She arrived at his apartment and knocked on his door, standing at the doorway and trying to see as much as she could of the inside of his apartment. She wasn't surprised it was rather Spartan but clean.

"Aren't you going to lock your door?"

He shook his head. "There is no need. No one will enter when we are gone."

She almost asked him why, but he had turned away and gestured for her to join him. She didn't say much as she drove but once they reached Starbucks, she opened up to him with a myriad of complaints. He listened how she got bumped out of a singing spot so "some idiot can swear on stage and claim he's telling jokes" and then "some jerk skipped out on a tab" on her job as a waitress. He tried to be supportive, but moments later she jumped to a new topic as he sipped his tea. She thanked him for listening, adding she needed to get some things off her chest and drove him back to his apartment.

"Here's my number, give me a call sometime if you want."

Council Madoc tried to give a noncommittal answer. He wasn't sure if she was just looking for a friend or wanting a relationship, something he didn't want to start until he knew how long he was to remain on Earth. She was different from most of the women he had met of Earth. She was more assertive than most women, but she did it with a style pointing toward intelligence. Most women on Earth found him good-looking, although he found them too young for him. But she made their connection appear in terms of friendship. She hadn't made any overt sexual moves toward him, but he sensed there was an underlying current of attraction between them.

——

The tan and green-striped wing-back chair by a window had become a favourite spot for him to sit and relax. The light through the white sheer curtains made it easy for him to read books, such as the *Collected Works of William Shakespeare*. Today, a half-filled bottle of red wine with a full glass sat on his right on a nearby table. He reached slowly for the glass with right hand as he turned a page of the book with his left. As he lifted the glass to his lips, the door chime rang.

He sighed heavily and glanced at the door, wondering if he should answer. It occurred to him it might be the newspaper girl collecting for the next month. He got up and pushed the intercom button.

"Yes?"

"Madoc, it's me, Angela."

He pushed the button to unlock the entrance door, wishing he didn't have to use the electrical device to open the front entrance. He waited a minute to open his apartment door to revealed her wearing a short black skirt and a T-shirt matching her yellow sandals.

"So you're home."

"Obviously."

"Are you going to make me stand out here or are you going to invite me in?"

"By all means." He stood to the side and gestured with his hands in a sweeping motion.

She stepped through the doorway and stopped in the middle of the living room, spinning around.

"Why do you even bother with a phone if you're not going to answer it?"

"The telephone is for my convenience, not others."

"Then how are others supposed to contact you?"

He sighed. "Maybe they aren't."

She put her hands on her hips. "Yes, well, I'm your friend and sometimes I have to contact you, convenient or not."

He noted the definition of their relationship without comment. "Obviously you have found a way to do so. My apologies for making you drive all this way to see me. What is this matter of importance?"

She looked at him carefully. "You never drop your stage act, do you? I mean you talk like you're an aristocrat or something and you wear the same clothes."

"It is the way I am. Would you care to sit down? I can pour you some wine or make you tea if you prefer."

"Wine? It's not even two in the afternoon. Oh, hell, why not?" She walked over to a cabinet in the dining room adjoining the living room and picked up a wine glass.

Council Madoc carried the wine bottle and met her as she crossed over into the living room, pouring the wine into her glass.

"Thanks." She sat down on a loveseat and sipped her wine. "Nice. Well, aren't you going to ask me why I came all this way to see you?"

He put his book on the coffee table and sat back into his easy chair. "So why did you?"

"Shakespeare? You're reading the collected works of Shakespeare?"

"He's a very good writer."

"No kidding? Hey, I got a phone call from Harold Spears. He runs the entertainment for the Hilton Hotel. He wants you to do your show on one of their stages next month for eight weeks! Isn't that great?"

"Yes, I suppose so. The hotel is a better venue?"

"Absolutely and they're going to pay you ten times as much as you're earning now."

"Hmm, I suppose that is good news. Thank you for negotiating a better situation for me."

"There are a couple of details. They want you to have at least one assistant to help you with your show…"

"I don't require any help to perform magic."

"Yeah, but if people are going to pay to see you, the hotel wants to put on a bit of a show. The set on the stage will be more elaborate and the assistant is to be used during the show. Make her disappear and reappear or saw her in half, that kind of thing. You can do that stuff, can't you?"

Council Madoc sat silent for several seconds before responding. "Yes, I can do those things and more. But I am concerned about having an assistant. I take great care my illusions must remain a secret."

"No problem. I have in mind the perfect assistant for you."

"And who would that be?"

"Me!" She gave a big grin.

"You?"

"Sure, I'm used to being on stage. I'm pretty and I won't reveal any of your secrets."

He stared at her smiling face for a few seconds and rubbed the bridge of his nose. "Very well, but there is one stipulation I do have. My talent is adversely affected by electronic devices and I will not explain why. Therefore, I will want to inspect the stage before agreeing to perform there."

"Fair enough, I can arrange that." She took another drink of her wine.

"Would you like more wine?" He rose from his chair with the bottle.

"Sure." She held out her glass. "Hey, you're not trying to get me drunk and take advantage of me, are you?"

"No, of course not." He carefully poured the wine into her glass as she held it out.

She grinned at him. "You could try, you know."

He almost spilled the wine as he poured causing her to laugh at him.

"Hey, I got a reaction from you! You're human after all."

"What else would I be?" He retreated back to his own chair.

"I dunno. Maybe like Data on Star Trek."

"Who on what?"

"Don't you ever watch TV?" She kicked off her shoes and curled one bare leg under her, twisting her body for modesty.

"No."

"Where did you grow up? Was it in some isolated village or something?"

"You could say that."

"God, trying to get you to talk about yourself is like pulling teeth. Ask me a question and I'll rattle on for ten minutes."

He studied her for a few seconds, noting how unreserved she was just sitting on the loveseat. He also considered it best if she talked about herself rather than having to answer her questions. "Tell me what you did yesterday."

"Yesterday? Lots. I got up at nineish, fed my cat, then had a coffee at Starbucks. They had a coffee mug on sale I almost bought but decided to save my money. Then I saw this guy, Spears, at the hotel. Then I went to the hairdresser to get a bit of a cut. Do you like it?" She held out the ends of her hair for him to see.

"Yes, it looks very becoming."

"Thanks. I don't like to fish for compliments, but you'd never say anything, anyway."

"I'm sorry if…"

She held up her hand at him. "That's okay, it's who you are. What else? Oh, I got a Brazilian done. That hurt a bit."

"A Brazilian?"

"If you don't know I'm not going to show you. Something only women put themselves through. Maybe if you're very lucky, you'll get to see it some day."

Council Madoc's face changed complexion slightly, turning a bit pink at his cheeks. "I believe I understand."

Angela giggled. "Hey, would you like to go for a walk? I need to get some stuff from the corner store down the block." She swung her legs down and slipped on her sandals.

"I suppose I could accompany you."

"Drink up then, time's a-ticking."

Council Madoc finished his glass and watched her as she headed toward the door. *What a fascinating young lady she is.*

FIVE

arisa opened one of the massive front doors in response to the doorbell. Each twin door stood nine feet high with the two tops forming a semi-circle.

"'Ello, Marisa."

"Well, hello Gilbert. It's nice to see you again so soon."

"Ah, I couldn't wait to feast me eyes on ye." He made a show of looking her up and down. Today she was wearing a dark blue wrap with a gold square trim on the edges. The wrap hung low on her hips and reached nearly to her bare feet. Other than a gold necklace it was all she wore. Her breasts matched her slim figure, smaller than average size.

She laughed. "Come with me to the back. Lord Troy is out in the back enjoying the garden."

Gilbert followed after her, his eyes taking turns from watching her walk to the various gaudy art objects and expressive oil paintings they passed. The castle didn't have straight hallways but rather curved around the main room, offering secondary entrances to it. In addition, other rooms and hallways sprang off to the side at regular intervals. Gilbert stopped to peer at one statue in an alcove, recognizing one figure as Lord Troy and the other as Patricia intertwined with each other. The nude, life-size white and grey figures impressed Gilbert in their detail.

"Do you like it?"

"Uh, well, just a wee taken back by their..."

"Animation?"

Gilbert nodded. "Is he really that large?"

"He is. Lord Troy said he wants to do a statue of me. I just have to pick what kind of pose I want."

"How abouts one with me?"

She giggled. "You're funny. Come on, this way to the rose gardens."

Gilbert spotted Lord Troy as he lounged on a red cushioned wood chair with a matching footrest, wearing dark blue pants with an open white shirt.

"Lord Troy, Gilbert is here to see you." Marisa strode toward where he was lifting a crystal glass to his lips.

"Gilbert, how nice to see you again. Do you have good news about the gem?"

As Gilbert looked around, the fragrance of hundreds of roses struck him as he took in sculptured gardens encircling the patio a short distance from the castle. The garden was the size of at least two football fields and a brick path wove around throughout it and to the patio. Fountains, benches, and gazebos stood around the gentle rolling hills of the garden. The colourful roses included several types of red, yellow, blue, white and even a pale green. On one of the white painted wood benches, a naked woman lay on her stomach sunbathing.

Gilbert studied the long blonde hair and the slim figure.

"Lord Troy. I do have news abouts the gem, mostly good." He walked over to an empty chair, stopping to peer again at the sunbathing blonde.

"Patricia, is that you?" Gilbert shouted.

The girl lifted up her head and then her hand to block the sun from her eyes. "Hello, Gilbert!" She sat up briefly to wave at him, grinning at him before resuming her tanning.

He stared at her a moment longer before sitting down. Marisa placed a dark ale in a tankard on the table in front of him and diverted his concentration from Patricia long enough for Lord Troy to get his attention.

"You said mostly good news, Gilbert?"

"Huh? Oh, yes, the gem. Well, this fellow wanted more for the gem than I thoughts was reasonable. But he sensed I's wanted it bad, I'm not as good as ye, Troy, at bargaining, no, indeed. But I's knew ye wanted it so me put in some of me own money to get it. I's hopes I's did the right thing, and ye won't think Gilbert a fool for paying a hundred and twenty ..."

Lord Troy's eyes didn't blink, maintaining the same concentration as before.

"...five silver ferns."

"Oh, that's not too bad. As you point out, I may have well been able to get it for less, but you did well to get it. Let's see you paid an additional twenty-five silver ferns, and I agreed to pay you twenty percent finder's fee..." Lord Troy closed his eyes in concentration. "So I owe you fifty silver ferns."

Gilbert nodded vigorously.

"I take it you have brought it with you?"

"Aye." Gilbert looked left and right carefully before slowly pulling the Dacron Gem out of his shirt inside pocket. "Here it tis."

"Bravo, Gilbert, bravo!" Lord Troy took the gem and held it up to the light, studying it. "You must stay for dinner, Gilbert, and this evening we can try some spells I have found. One may work and activate this thing."

"Of course, I's be glad to. I's always enjoy times here, Lord Troy." Gilbert glanced back at the sleeping Patricia.

———

Dinner was held on the second floor, rather than the usual dining room on the main. The weather was warm, and the upstairs room opened up to a large balcony where the fragrance of the rose garden filter in while providing a view of the countryside. The table was set with a series of forks, spoons and knives surrounding each large china plate.

Lord Troy and Gilbert sat on opposite ends of the long maple table with a candelabrum sitting in the middle. After setting the food on the table, the ladies sat at the table.

"Gilbert, you have already met Marisa and Patricia. These other fine ladies are Alicia, Lena, Gwyneth and Juliana."

"Hello, Gilbert," they all sang in unison. Marisa with dark hair and dark skin stood out along with tall Lena with her red hair. The rest were blondes and fair skinned. Marisa and Juliana wore only long skirts and sat on either side of Lord Troy while the rest wore revealing dresses.

"'Ello ladies." He raised his glass of ale in a toast.

Gilbert ate a fair bit of the venison, beef and lamb but less of the vegetables. After his third glass of ale, he entertained everyone with jokes and his tales of adventure.

"So you really had to save Sir Jon from those highwaymen?" Lena asked with a hint of credibility straining her voice.

Gilbert was oblivious to her interruption. "'Twas terrible, me tells you. Three of them and poor Jon not knowing how to use a sword yet. I's fights them off while yelling at Jon to holds his sword up higher to protect himself."

"That is indeed interesting, Gilbert, but perhaps it's time for us to withdraw to the library with a brandy and study this Dacron Gem." Lord Troy stood.

The library Lord Troy referred to was also located on the second floor and smaller than the one on the main floor but contained the older, more obscure textbooks.

Marisa carried a tray with two glasses and a dark glass bottle and set it on a table. She poured a generous amount of brandy into each glass and departed. Gilbert watched her as she disappeared down the hall and turned his attention to the glass of brandy in front of him. As he took his first swallow, he noticed the books left open on the table as well as a quill pen and paper Lord Troy had scribbled spells on. A worried frown appeared on Gilbert's face as he watched Lord Troy pick up the other glass of brandy.

Lord Troy and Gilbert had known each other for the better part of a decade. In the beginning Gilbert would bring Lord Troy the occasional piece of art or textbook he would hand over at the front entrance in exchange for money. Gradually, Lord Troy would invite him for a drink to discuss other items he was looking for. For Gilbert, it turned out to be a profitable arrangement. Lord Troy would often pay too much for a particular item and Gilbert enjoyed pulling a fast one over on one of the rich lords. He had to be careful. Lord Perry was a powerful lord who had little patience for those on the grey area of the law and in particular who would cheat one of his relatives.

Lord Troy was well known for his restrictions to his property and his preoccupation with the ladies. After a period of time, Gilbert found himself spending a few evenings visiting him and gradually developed an odd relationship with him. Gilbert bragged to his friends how he tricked Lord Troy into paying too much and laughed at his antics when it came to women. But Gilbert found he did enjoy appointments with Lord Troy and the women. The purchased slaves enjoyed life in his castle, often staying past their required contract time. He found though Lord Troy was gullible, he was also well read, kind and treated Gilbert almost as a friend. Almost, as their relationship hadn't extended to Gilbert being invited to one of his parties.

It was considered scandalous what Lord Troy did in his castle with his underdressed ladies and people often gossiped about what appeared to be going on in his castle. When he decided to host a party, rarely did anyone fail to attend who was invited and several others would hint or even send small gifts weeks prior to his social gathering in hopes of getting an invitation. Unfortunately, for Gilbert, the parties were the domain of the lords and other powerful people and Gilbert wasn't issued an invitation. Gilbert understood why. He knew he hardly belonged in polite company but still felt left out. Being invited to stay for dinner was a step forward. Gilbert had stayed for lunch before, but this was his first evening meal and now he was in Lord Troy's special library.

As Gilbert made eye contact with Lord Troy, he realized three things. One, he did like Lord Troy even though he was guilty of telling others what a fool he was. Two, Lord Troy did like him even though he considered Gilbert a thief and a ruffian. And three, maybe it was time for Gilbert to treat him as a friend and not to badmouth him outside the castle. As far as not taking advantage of his wealth, some things were just meant to be.

"Something on your mind Gilbert?"

"Huh? No, nothin' at all." He pointed at the page with scribbles of spells on it. "Are those the ones yous gonna try?"

"Yes, from what I've deduced from these books this should activate the Dacron Gem. At least one of them should, and perhaps more than one will work."

"Whatcha gonna try to do first with it?"

"Well, since I'm confined to my home and property, I'm hoping to do is to change the outside world to accept my particular spell so

I can do some traveling. This particular gem, not just a gem because it does have a crystal embedded inside it, would have a slow but powerful influence on the surrounding area. So to answer your question, I will first try to have the gem do some minor change in the surrounding area and observe the results. I wish to be cautious using spells I'm not familiar with, as a witness to my present predicament."

Gilbert nodded. Lord Troy was restricted to his own property because of the way he enabled a youth spell on himself. A minor change in the wording of the spell would have allowed him to retain his youth wherever he travelled. Try as he might he had never found a way around the spell, despite years of research.

"Aye. Well, here's ter ye gem and whatever spell that gives ye your freedom again, Lord Troy." He raised his brandy glass and then threw back the golden liquid.

"And to you, Gilbert, for your support." He raised his own glass in a salute and took a small swallow.

Gilbert poured himself another glass while Lord Troy studied the wording of the first spell.

SIX

Madoc and Angela walked down the concrete steps and down the short hallway. Producing a key she borrowed from the manager, Angela opened the steel door and peered into the darkness beyond.

"I hope the light switch is close by." She looked for a moment at the wall just past the doorframe. "There it is." She reached in and flipped up several switches, and after a few seconds passed, the overhead lamps changed from flickering to a steady bright light. Council Madoc stood back, letting her proceed onto the stage beyond.

The stage from the back to the front was open with the curtains normally separating it raised high above where they walked.

"Wow! It looks so big out here." She spread out her arms and spun around in a circle and stopped to point out where the rows of tables and chairs sat silently in the dark. "Can you believe how many people will watch your show here? This is great, isn't it?"

Council Madoc wasn't quite as convinced. "There seems to be a fair bit of disturbance…electrical noise. Would there be more electronic and electrical devices during the show?"

"I don't know. Maybe. Why?"

"I told you my magic doesn't work well under such conditions."

"How can that be? How can electric lights affect your illusions?"

"They're not just ordinary illusions. I use a different method to create the illusions and too much light will ruin the...the trick for the audience."

Angela squinted her eyes at him. "I'm not an expert on body language, but I get the feeling what you're telling me is a bunch of BS. Why don't you try a practice run and see if your illusions work first? Then we can worry about the stage lights."

A trickle of sweat began to form just above Madoc's left temple. He wasn't used to lying and the proposition of doing so to Angela made him uncomfortable. "Very well. I'll try a practice run first."

"Good. I'll set up a rehearsal for Thursday, if it's okay with you."

"That would be fine."

"For the rehearsal I can also practice being your assistant."

"Perhaps I could try this one rehearsal by myself."

"No way. I'm looking forward to doing this glamorous assistant thing."

Council Madoc pondered turning down the offer to work a show at the Hilton, but another part of him answered instead. "That would be acceptable." He closed his eyes for a moment, scolding his ego for wanting to perform in front of a large audience in spite of the danger.

———

On Thursday, Council Madoc and Angela returned to Hilton. He said little as they obtained the key to the stage and began to assemble the tables and props which helped him disguise his magic. He had several new devices made to help him perform tricks specified by the hotel to increase the show's appeal, including two closet sized boxes standing apart from each other.

"Do you need any help?"

"No, it is best I do this myself."

A few minutes later, the tables and props were set up to his liking. She stood a short distance away and crossed her arms, watching him carefully. He gave her a quick glance and placed a yellow plastic duck on a table and covered it with a white cloth.

"What's your favourite colour?"

She stared at the cloth covered duck. "Pink."

He removed the cloth with a flourish. The duck was now pink.

"Cool. Can you make it with blue polka dots instead?"

He nodded and covered the duck with the cloth again and mumbled a few phrases. "A blue polka dot duck." He removed the cloth to reveal a pink duck with blue polka dots.

Angela shook her head. "I don't see how…but that's the point isn't it?"

He performed a few more small tricks and then asked her to step in one of the small closet size wooden boxes. It was just big enough to hold her and Angela found herself in darkness, unable to make out any details when he closed the door. When the door was open again, she found she was now in the other box. At first, she felt disorientated and stood in front of the box, puzzled.

"How…? Man, that's some trick." She crossed her arms as cool air float down over her, rubbing her hands over her arms to get rid of the goose bumps.

"It seems to me the magic will perform well enough here. Perhaps we can make arrangements to sign the contract."

"Great." She smiled. "We're in show business together!"

She watched him sign the papers in the manager's office. He was older than most men she associated with and normally she wouldn't consider dating someone his age, though whatever his age was she had trouble guessing. But he had a style of dress with old world charm and an accent she found appealing. She found herself intrigued by him but there was something else about him that drew her to him, something she couldn't quite define, perhaps something sinister.

"I guess we're done here, Madoc. Want to go for a bite?"

He smiled. "Of course. You said you like a round dish called pizza. Why don't we go to a place which serves that?"

"I know just the place. It's close enough we can even walk there."

He gestured with his hand. "Then please lead the way."

Angela bit into a slice of pizza as Madoc cut the slice on his plate with a knife a fork.

"Can I ask you a personal question, Madoc?" She paused a moment, not waiting for his reply. "How old are you?"

He studied his pizza and looked up at her. "I'm two hundred and seventy-four years old." Then he smiled.

She laughed. "Jerk. I'm twenty-nine. Am I too young for you, like, if we dated?"

"You appear even younger." He gave her a smile. "What did you do before you became a singer?"

"Thanks. Well, my parents are well off and paid for me to go to attend university. I took education but after I finished, I wasn't ready to be a teacher. I guess I just didn't want to be stuck in a classroom. In the meantime, much to my parents' distress, I work in a bar as a waitress while trying to launch a singing or stage career. Everyone in my family is waiting for me to grow up. I guess they want me to settle down."

Angela reflected meeting men was not a problem for her but finding the right one was. She noticed she had a tendency to attract men who had little ambition and just wanted to have a good time. Not necessarily bad qualities she considered, but she would like to find someone who looked at life a little differently and was planning for a future. That drew her thoughts to Madoc. Not quite predictable, seemingly in control of his life and then there was definitely a dark quality to him. He was protecting a secret and a past, a mystery she found alluring.

———

Gilbert looked at Lord Troy.

"Nothin' happened."

"None we perceive, anyway. I'm sure I said the spell right. Perhaps the results are subtle or take time to make it known."

"Or maybe the gem don't work."

Lord Troy pondered that possibility for a moment. "No, the gem and the crystal contain energy, I can sense it. I'll try another spell. Perhaps the crystal is very sensitive to the right words."

"Maybe your book is wrong on spells."

Lord Troy shook his head. "No, I'm sure the book is right. I just have to make sure I say the spell right. I shall try again." He turned to one of open books lying on the table and flipped through several pages before landing his finger on a set of lines. "These words should do the trick." He began to recite the verses as Gilbert took another drink of brandy.

Gilbert looked around the room. "Don't see nothin' happening."

Lord Troy frowned. "I don't understand. There should have been some effect, some occurrence from the gem."

"Maybe in the morning we finds what's wrong. For now, let's have a few drinks. We cans invite some ladies to join us."

Lord Troy didn't seem like he wanted to give up yet but put down his pen. "I suppose you're right. I best sleep on this and try to come with a solution in the morning. Come and let's see what the ladies are up to."

————

The thumping on the door continued, each strike sounding like a cannon. Gilbert moaned and used the pillow to cover his head, squeezing the ends of the pillow around his ears. "Go 'way, leaves me be."

The oak door opened, and Patricia stepped inside, wearing a sheer white robe. She walked quickly to the bed situated in the far corner of the large bedroom.

"Wake up, you two! Wake up! There's a big problem outside, something's wrong."

Marisa lifted her head slowly and blinked at the light streaming from between curtains hiding French doors. "What's wrong?"

"Ohh, me head," Gilbert moaned.

"Take a look outside." Patricia pulled apart the blue curtains.

"Quiet, me head hurts."

Marisa rolled out of the bed and walked naked to the doors. She looked out and a few seconds later gasped. "What is that? What's happening? Gilbert, take a look at this."

"Later. I's don'ts feel good."

"Gilbert, now! This is important." Marisa turned back to the bed and began to pull off Gilbert's pillow from his grasp.

Gilbert groaned when Marisa ripped the pillow away and he slowly began to sit up. "Better be 'portant."

Marisa returned to where Patricia had now opened the doors to stand on the balcony as Gilbert tried to wrap a bed sheet around him. Muttering, he tried to get the blue silk sheet to stay tucked under his arms as he dragged it across the marble floor.

Patricia and Marisa distracted Gilbert as he made his way outside and didn't see past the balcony until he reached the stone railing.

Everything looked normal at first as Gilbert gazed around on Lord Troy's land. But when he looked beyond the hedges marking the perimeter of the property things were very different indeed.

"What happened to the trees and castles? Where they be?"

Where there used to be meadows, trees and homes of the moderately wealthy there was now an abundance of red, yellow and green plants. Tall plants and shrubbery had replaced trees while smaller undergrowth and grasses filled in the rest of the spaces. Something large was moving among the foliage, a yellow creature walking on four limbs, with a long neck. Gilbert tried to see and identify it, but it hid among the scrubs. "That wasn't there last night."

Marisa gave him a sharp look. "No kidding. What did Lord Troy and you do last night? What kind of spell did you two invoke?"

"Gilbert don't do nothin'. Lord Troy, he do all the spells."

"Let's go and see if Lord Troy is awake yet. Maybe he'll know what do."

The three returned to the bedroom with Gilbert still dragging the blue sheet behind him. Patricia waited while Marisa found her skirt, and the two women left the room after advising Gilbert to hurry up and get dressed. Gilbert waited until they left before getting dressed as quickly as possible. He wasn't sure if Marisa had noticed the tattoos covering his back last night. The ones on his chest looked unusual but didn't draw too much attention but on his back the tattoos had spells carefully written out. If Marisa saw them last night in the dark, she might not have recognized them for what they represented, but in the daylight, there would not be any doubt. They weren't illegal or dangerous but the fewer people knew things about Gilbert the better he felt.

Lord Troy woke up quickly to the knock on the door, put on a green robe and opened the door. "Yes, Patricia? Marisa, you too? Is there a problem?"

"Sorry to disturb you, Lord Troy, but have you looked outside this morning? There's something terribly wrong."

He shook his head and turned toward his room. "Which direction?"

"All around us." They followed him to a second room adjoining the master bedroom. Juliana stirred from the bed and yawned as she watched the three troop past the bed to the sitting room.

"What's going on?" She yawned again and slowly slid her feet to the floor as she sat up.

Marisa called out to her. "You better come and see for yourself."

Juliana started to walk to the sitting room, stopped and turned around to search for her skirt. She mumbled as she lifted up the bed covers and looked at the edge of the bed and spotted the long red skirt. She bent down to pick it up and received a pinch on her cheek causing her to whirl around. "Gilbert!"

He gave her a toothy grin. "Mornin', Juliana."

She gave a half smile back at him. "Trust you to sneak up behind me. What's going on?"

He beckoned her with a finger as he walked to where the others had congregated on a terrace. "Something strange has happened. Come see."

Juliana struggled to tie the strings of her skirt and hurried after him.

They gathered on the terrace staring off in the distance, not sure what to make of what they saw. The terrace ran along two outside walls of the castle and gave a generous view of the land around.

Lord Troy surveyed the change in the landscape beyond his property. The creature Marisa, Patricia and Gilbert saw earlier stepped into view for a moment. It appeared to be the size of a small elephant with a seven-foot long neck and a short fat tail. The skin glistened under the sun and appeared to be covered with scales. The head had large bat like ears and small eyes and was busy nipping at plants as it slowly made its way around the bushes.

"Did I do this?"

Patricia looked at him but didn't speak.

"I must have. What other explanation is there?"

"How come those plants didn't invade the castle's property?" Marisa asked.

"It must be the preservation spell I have on the property preventing change locally. But those spells I tried to use last night must have expanded slowly outward from the castle and caused this."

"Maybe yous better do backward spells, undos what happened." Gilbert slowly rested a hand on Marisa's hip.

"I'd like to do that, Gilbert. But those spells are vague and I'm not sure how to word a counter spell. There's also a problem of which spell caused this. I'd have to do a counter spell for each one." He crossed his arms as he studied the new landscape. "This is bad. I don't see Sir Roth's residence. It seems to have vanished much like the rest of the countryside. Patricia, could you ask Gwyneth to prepare breakfast and have it brought to the library?"

She nodded. "Of course, Lord Troy."

"Come, Gilbert, let's see what we can do to reverse this spell."

Gilbert eyed Marisa and Juliana wearing only skirts. "Perhaps it be best if I stay here with the ladies and watch..."

"No, Gilbert. I need your expertise in magic." He turned and headed out of the room.

Gilbert grumbled and followed him.

SEVEN

L ord Perry stared at the messenger. "Say again, there's some sort of disturbance of the ground and air?"

The messenger wasn't fond of giving difficult news to powerful lords, but he was obligated to relay the information as quickly as possible. "Quite so. There's a front of something moving through Horstruff."

"I better have a look." Lord Perry got up and moved by the messenger who followed him. Lord Perry used a corridor to enter a small dining room having a grand view of Horstruff. The room opened to a balcony and he stood, now with several servants and the messenger staring at the distant landscape and buildings making up Horstruff.

"What the devil…"

The area close to the castle looked normal enough, though there was a hurried movement of people all in one direction. Lord Perry had seen such a sight before, just before major battles when sometimes a whole village disappeared into the roads and woods beyond. Those who had horses used them to either carry themselves or their possessions. The wealthy used carriages to transport themselves as well as their valuables. Those on foot carried what they could, including crying infants.

He looked behind the scurrying movement and saw the border

between what Horstruff should appear like and a conglomerate of strange looking plants. The boundary itself was a blurred line, bending and curving like a wave on a seashore, rushing forward with the speed of a man's fast walk.

"Horse and carriage, immediately."

———

The driver stopped the carriage as close as he dared. Normally, it would be difficult to travel against a hoard of humanity trying to leave Horstruff but the town people were accustomed to giving way to nobles, and to Lord Perry in particular.

There were cries of "Turn back! Turn back, Lord Perry!" but instead the driver continued his hurried race down the street. As they approached the border, there became fewer and fewer people until it was all but deserted except for those too weak to run. Some prayed while others begged Lord Perry for help.

After the carriage stopped, Lord Perry ventured walked toward the disturbance.

"It looks like chaos, Lord Perry." A corporal in Lord Perry's personal guards stood slightly behind him.

"Chaos?" He watched the edge of the border, as a series of bubbles varying from as small as he could see to almost a foot in diameter. The transparent bubbles with their outline appeared as a distortion of the air and ground. The surface of the ground looked like boiling mud as it reshaped to a new configuration. "Perhaps, or it might be a new order. Those plants you see and look at that creature over there!" He pointed at a green and yellow spotted medium dog-sized animal carefully eating some plant leaves. "Have you seen that before?"

"Nay, Lord Perry, I can't say I have. Perhaps we should be getting back to the carriage?"

"Yes, in a moment. Those plants used to live all over Domum until Earth plant life forced them out. They still can be found in the remote areas of Domum. I suspect the plant eater was at one time a common habitant here. It looks like the natural life of Domum is trying to push us out." He pointed out a nearby stone structure, half of which used to be a small home. The other half had disappeared as the bubbles of distortion simply ate it away.

"The problem, corporal, is we may well find there isn't any place to run."

––––––

Lord Perry's carriage rumbled down the road leading out of Horstruff. They had been traveling for two days, passing many traveling on foot. Lord Perry sat in the bouncing carriage and pondered at what was happening, wondered what happened to all those caught behind the distortion. That included Lord Troy, and he considered his uncle must have been eclipsed by the distortion.

Lord Perry wondered how far and long they could travel before the distortion caught up with them. Sooner or later they would have to choose to head toward the mountains or the sea.

Travel over the mountain would be difficult and slow, faster if he left the carriage behind and just used the horses. The sea coast would be a dead end except he could commandeer a ship and continue on with their escape. He speculated their flight was only delaying the inevitable, and eventually they would be caught no matter how fast or far they travelled. He rubbed his forehead, wishing if only he knew how the distortion came into being, he might be able to stop it. So far he heard via the messengers several warlocks, witches and wizards had perished as they tried to stop the advancing wave.

He tapped on the roof of the carriage with his cane. "Driver, head to coastline. Corporal Jennings, send one of the guards ahead to procure a ship for us to travel in."

––––––

"Really Gilbert, I do dislike asking you do to do this but what other options are there?" Lord Troy spread his hands.

"Do nothin'." Gilbert clutched his tankard of ale with both hands and looked back at the six people watching him.

"But Gilbert, we could be stuck here forever if we do nothing," Patricia softly retorted and gave him a smile.

"Maybe better here forever than Gilbert gettin' killed."

Lord Troy closed his eyes for a moment before speaking. "Gilbert, I can't leave the perimeter of the grounds, and these ladies are not well versed in journeys without roads. Eventually we'll have to leave the castle to get food as our stores will not last forever. So far, we haven't seen any evidence of hostile wildlife, and we'll equip you the best we can."

Gilbert took another big gulp of his ale but didn't say anything.

Gwyneth tried to convince him. "All you have to do is travel to where the gate to Earth is located in what used to be Lord Bennett's castle. Once you slip through there, you'd be safer than you'd be here."

"If. Maybe gate not there, maybe it goes not to Earth from here."

Marisa stood up and put her hands on her hips. "Fine, stay here and do nothing and wait until we run out of food. As for myself, I'll travel to where that gate is. I will find some crystals to try to cross over to Earth to get some help."

Gilbert shook his head. "That be dangerous. Need special crystal to travel to Earth and you might be too big."

"Nonsense, you weigh about the same as I do. If you can travel there, so can I."

"Earth different from Domum, you be lost there."

"Better than waiting here to starve to death."

"We not starve. We cans hunt for food here."

"Isn't it dangerous to hunt for food out there?"

"Not if we prepare…" Gilbert blinked and then slowly released his breath. "You try to trick Gilbert."

"No, I wouldn't do such a thing to my friend. I'm just saying someone has to try to rescue us and if you won't go, I will."

Gilbert squeezed his hands into fists. "No, I'll go. Leave in the morning."

———

Morning came and a persistent knocking on the door woke Gilbert. Grumbling, he made his way to the second level dining room to have breakfast where he slumped in his chair and stabbed at slices of pork with his fork off a large oval plate. He scooped eggs on to his plate and began to eat.

Gilbert eventually looked around the table and nodded at the others just finishing up their own meals. Gilbert thought like he was being sacrificed to save the others on the possibility the gate to Earth still existed.

He didn't want to go; risks of any kind were to be avoided unless there was a potential of reward. To Gilbert, the risks of going to the gate were higher than the possibility of the gate existing. Still, he believed the others would see him as being selfish if he didn't and eventually might force him to go. He reluctantly agreed and now sulked as he ate his breakfast.

Lord Troy and the women dressed casually for breakfast, save for Marisa who not only was wearing her usual long skirt but also a blouse and a leather vest.

She noticed he was staring her and gave him a grin. "I'm going with you."

"You is?"

"I wouldn't ask you to go all by yourself."

Gilbert looked visibly happier. "That good. More fun, safer that way."

Both Marisa and Gilbert carried swords, knives and a backpack. Lord Troy also gave Marisa a special crystal to aid her traveling through the gate to Earth. Gilbert wanted to fill a sheepskin with brandy, but Lord Troy nixed that idea and he had to settle for water.

They left via the front door and made their way through the maze of six-foot high hedges Lord Troy had planted to discourage casual visitors. Guards protected most castles, but Lord Troy found a maze to his front door was an effective deterrent. Any unwanted visitors making their way through the maze then met magic spells from Lord Troy himself if he didn't want to see them.

After they made their way out of the maze, they saw a proliferation of plants of various colours. Some plants reached more than a dozen feet in the air using thick tree like trunks made of leaves intertwined with stems. Odd flowers and fruits hung from some plants, and Marisa stopped to sniff at the flowers. Gilbert grumbled at her, complaining she was delaying their journey.

"Hurry ups. We must keeps moving."

"We can spare a few minutes now and then. Do you think the fruit would be safe to eat?"

"Safe if yous want to die."

He plodded on ahead of her and she had to hurry to catch up.

Marisa had worked hard to convince Lord Troy someone, such

as herself, should accompany Gilbert on his journey. She cited safety in numbers, making sure Gilbert actually went through the gate to Earth and how it wasn't fair to send him out on his own. Lord Troy took his time deciding but eventually told her she could join him. Marisa wasn't too worried about any danger. The idea of freedom, however short, was too enticing.

She had been a slave since she was fourteen after becoming an orphan. After being sold from one household to another and later to a tavern, she eventually ended up in Lord Troy's castle. She'd had more than one chance to get out of slavery, after she spent five years working in a tavern and had fulfilled her contract, she became a free woman. Unfortunately, she managed to get herself in difficulties with the law a short time later and ended up back in court. Lord Troy purchased her, and she resigned herself to another five-year contract as a slave.

He was different from most owners and he made it clear what he expected of her. He offered her a choice to go back to the court and be purchased by someone else if she desired. But she had both seen and been in far worse situations and decided living in a castle was better than working in a tavern. She also had seen people like Gilbert, and though he was a freeman, he didn't live as well as she did.

For now, she was happy to follow Gilbert out into the strange world of colourful plants and odd animals. So far, there wasn't much in the way of predators, just the occasional wolf-sized creature covered with green and yellow scales. She also observed a group of small dragons flying overhead. Dragons were often creatures to be feared but to Marisa they represented a moment of familiarity in a strange world.

They worked their way among the foliage, brushing away stray leaves, insects and, a few times, birds smaller than a hummingbird. Gilbert didn't do much talking, and it was up to Marisa to carry the conversation. She chattered away, and he responded with reluctant grunts before he turned around and admonished her.

"Could ye quitcha jabbering? There might be somethin' out here tryin' to eat us."

"Nothing big lives here. Every animal we've seen is small. No trees, just these oversize plants."

"So far."

She sighed and took to just looking and plucking the odd flower as they made their way to where a gate was supposed to exist. She glanced back behind her to study a green flowered plant with red leaves. A blur of something black and furry ducked behind a bush a hundred feet behind them.

"Gilbert?"

"What now?"

"Something is following us."

"I knew it. Ye talkin' has done us in." Gilbert turned around and crouched on one knee, raising his sword in the process.

"It's just one small animal."

"Could be more. Surrounding us."

"Don't be silly. Why would they do that?" She walked past him to continue the journey.

"Hey! I's supposed to be leadin'."

Whatever following them was keeping a safe distance. Occasionally, Marisa and Gilbert would check around, but the creature was quick to hide behind a large plant or bush.

"Whatever it is It seems we don't have to worry about it. It's only curious about us."

"Maybe. It might be a gnant."

"A gnant? I guess they could be in this strange world…what did Lord Troy say? An alternate world?"

"Yeah, he says that. But it has something to do with that Dacron Gem. I's don'ts know why he was so keen to use it."

"Him? Wasn't it you who tried to get him to look up spells to activate it?"

He waved his hand at her. "Sure, to learns about it, not to actually use it."

"Gilbert, that's nonsense. You're at as much fault as he is for this mess."

"Fine thing, blame me while I risk me neck to go to Earth."

"Gilbert," she whispered, "I see two of those creatures now. They're gnants."

"Getcha sword ready, they gonna attack!"

EIGHT

Council Madoc looked a second time at Angela.

"Is there a problem?" She gave him a smile, pleased with his reaction.

"No, I suppose not. Just I wasn't expecting you to dress in such a fashion. Not there's any wrong with it, just unanticipated."

"Madoc, this is show business. I better dress the part." Angela put on her top hat and stood wearing a tuxedo jacket, fishnet stockings, black shorts and high heels. "What else should I wear?"

"Nothing. That is, I don't have an alternate suggestion."

She giggled. "Good. Shall we go through our dress rehearsal then?"

"Of course. Perhaps we can start with the floating body first."

Council Madoc wasn't pleased at first in having to use an assistant on stage. There was a chance she would be able to discover he didn't use illusions to do tricks but rather used real magic, despite using some standard illusion props.

But now he was enjoying the company Angela provided. He also understood if he was to become successful at his stage career, and he wasn't sure how long he would be forced to stay on Earth, he would have to be more than a one man show. Adding a charming assistant had become a necessity. He had come to realize how lonely he had been for an intelligent companion and Angela provided a welcome relief from other women he had spent time with.

The practice run proceeded well, with only minor mistakes when Angela had a case of the giggles. She promised she would be all right during the show and promptly burst into another series of giggles.

The day of their first performance came to be. Council Madoc found himself pacing as he studied the routine he was going to use on stage in the dressing room. He was confident Angela would be fine, although she constantly talked as they drove over.

Angela stood on stage, behind and to his left, as he motioned with his hands. Council Madoc mouthed a few words and suddenly fire leaped in the air following his hand movements to sudden gasps from the audience.

Angela held her smile as she watched him finish the first part of his fire illusion. How he performed his illusions, she wasn't even able to hazard a guess. She had helped him set up the equipment and hadn't noticed much in the way of secret latches or compartments. During their practice he had made her float on her back at table height. *Something* pushed up on her as she lay suspended in mid-air. It was something not hard, more like lying on an air mattress in a swimming pool. She tried to push her hands down below her and found the lower she moved her hands the stronger the resistance became. It was strange, like it wasn't an illusion but rather she really did float in air. She wanted to ask him how he did it but understood magicians carefully guarded their secrets.

In a few minutes, she would step forward and he would use her in the floating woman illusion. She was nervous in front of the large audience, but fortunately she only had to lie still as he produced his magic.

Angela rested on her back on a cloth-covered table, trying to watch the show without moving her head. Madoc walked around the table, gesturing with a wand. Then as the crowd grew quiet with anticipation, he pulled the table slowly out from under her. She remained floating at the same height as the table as he waved his arm above, below and around her.

The audience burst into applause as he placed a hand on her shoulder and slowly spun her around in a circle.

He held up his hands for silence and suddenly spread his fingers toward her.

Angela heard the crowd clap and cheer enthusiastically as flames burst around her. At first, she wanted to scream, but she calmed down as she realized the surrounding fire didn't seem to be generating much heat. She took a slow deep breath to calm herself and considered the one minor problem she had with her costume, willing the button on her tuxedo jacket to hold.

Suddenly, the flames disappeared, and he tilted her to a standing position by lifting her shoulder. She felt gravity return.

It was the final illusion and a few minutes later she stood next to him to take a bow on stage. The air around them was cool, almost as if an air conditioner was working above them at the maximum.

After the performance, Angela said, "You should have warned me about the flames." She sat across from Council Madoc, drinking coffee after they had emerged from their dressing rooms. The hotel coffee shop was open twenty-four hours and catered to late night guests and also the performers of the various clubs in the hotel.

"I decided at the last moment to add flames. There wasn't enough time to inform you."

"I could've been burnt."

"No, the flames weren't hot to the touch."

"Not hot? How can flames not be hot?"

Council Madoc pursed his lips for a moment. "Please trust me. I wouldn't allow you to come to harm."

Angela didn't speak for a few moments, watching his eyes carefully. "Okay, let's say the flames wouldn't have hurt me. But you better find a way to tell me if you're improvising during the show. I almost screamed when I saw all those flames around me."

"You are quite correct. My apologies."

She slumped into her chair, crossed her arms and smiled at him. "You know, the way you talk and with your accent, it's impossible to stay mad at you. Have you always been so damn polite and formal?"

"It serves me well to be that way." He stood up. "It's getting late. Perhaps we should call it an evening."

"Okay. I'll give you a ride home."

"I don't wish to cause you any inconvenience. I can easily find my own way home."

"It's no trouble. Come with me and you can tell me how flames can't be hot."

———

Council Madoc closed the apartment door behind him, feeling troubled. Angela had kept up a steady line of questions and opinions as she drove, not allowing him much opportunity to speak, and fortunately, to answer. As soon as she had stopped in front of his apartment, he thanked her for the lift home and pulled on the door handle to open it, intending to leave rather than worry about answering any more questions. But before he could unfasten his seat belt, she quickly leaned over and kissed him on his cheek.

Now safely in his apartment he touched his cheek where she had planted a kiss and the remains of her lipstick.

"This is getting dangerous," he muttered to himself.

———

Angela drove rapidly down the street and, noticing her speed, slowed down to closer to the speed limit. She drummed her fingers on the steering wheel when she stopped at a red light, switching her radio from one station to another.

"He must wonder if I'm a blooming idiot! Can't I just shut up sometimes and let him talk? Oh, no, not me. Ask him a question and then continue to talk before he has a chance to answer. And then I kissed him on the cheek! God, talk about mixed signals. What was he supposed to think about that? That I'm a scatterbrained blonde? Well, he'd be dead right on there."

Angela was loath to admit why she was attracted to him. She told herself his voice and mannerism attracted her, and he was polite and intelligent. But what also really drew her to him resided in his dark features. He looked a bit sinister, and with his formal clothing, she speculated there was something menacing about him.

During the show, Angela had felt completely under his control as she floated. He stood slightly behind her, his hands extended as part of the illusion and his cape spread out. The lights behind him made him appear almost as a silhouette, a dark shadow with upraised arms. To her, he suddenly looked intimidating, and she had the illusion she was about to be sacrificed in front of the audience.

Her heart was pounding as she cast a quick glance at the audience, noting the tuxedo jacket which fitted so well standing up didn't quite do the same job when she was horizontal, with the bottom half tugging at her waist from the single button. The exposure of her legs and hips didn't bother her so much as the worry the button may suddenly give way and add too much excitement to their opening night. After a moment, she decided the button would hold and just as she tried to breathe out and relax when the flames rose around her. She almost screamed.

Now she had trouble concentrating as she drove home, wondering if she could come up with some excuse to see him the next day.

———

The ship, The Blue Moon, made decent time, leaving Lee Harbour and entering the Dorn Sea. Lord Perry sat in the front room, normally used by Captain Taff Lloyd. Despite the captain's obvious annoyance at being forced to use smaller and less accommodating quarters, he quickly bowed to the new owner and ordered Seaman Pettie move his belongings.

Lord Perry muttered to himself as he worked mathematical calculations on the side of a large map that included Horstruff. "Four days, no more." He shook his head.

The captain frowned at being summoned to Lord Perry's quarters, which used to be his. He tapped on the door and waited for permission to enter.

"Lord Perry, you commanded my presence."

Lord Perry watched the captain's face. "Yes, yes. Come inside and close the door, please."

"Very well." He turned and closed the door slowly and stood stiffly in front of the desk.

"It's obvious you're annoyed I took over your cabin and you're not even allowed to complain about it."

The captain pursed his lips, noting to contradict some lords meant death.

"But what I have to tell you will make such a complaint seem minor. Our world is coming to an end."

"To an end, Lord Perry?"

"You may not believe me, that is your prerogative."

"Oh, no, Lord Perry…"

Lord Perry held up his hand. "Please, I'm not blind to the fact others have an opinion. Hear me out and judge for yourself accordingly. This disturbance we are running from has no doubt been initiated by some careless use of magic by some damn fool. Domum is reverting back to a world where people and animals from Earth never had a chance to cross over. A small change in Domum's deep past has caused it to divert from the world we see now. How this was done I cannot exactly say, but according to my calculations, if we assume the disturbance started near Horstruff, then it will completely circle the rest of the globe in less than four days time. We can run from it in one direction, but it is also approaching us from the front." He shook his head. "It is terrible news, but I thought I should warn you. You may tell the ship's crew or not as you see fit."

"What will happen to us then?" The captain was dumbfounded by the news and though the news was incredible, it was being delivered by Lord Perry. He accepted the news as a fact being given by the highest authority.

"When the disturbance overtakes us, we will simply fail to exist. Not only that, we will never have existed according to this new Domum."

"Our souls, Lord Perry?"

"I cannot say. If we have never existed, perhaps our souls never existed either. Nevertheless, I plan to pray."

The captain stroked his chin. "I shall do likewise. But is there nothing we can do?"

"To fight this terrible spell, one would have to do so where it was created and understand how. But obviously it is out of our reach now. All we can do is pray for a miracle."

———

The ship sat still in the middle of the Dorn Sea. Its sails had been taken down, and now it floated along the gentle currents of the water. The captain had waited until yesterday to inform the crew, seeing little point in causing a possible panic among his men. The sailors, for the most part, took the news well, knowing when they decided to live a life on the seas death was never far away.

Behind them, the wave of disturbance moved closer to within a few metres. In front of them, a similar turbulence approached them. Captain Lloyd leaned on the railing at the bow of the ship. Lord Perry stood close to him observing the end of his world.

"You have brave men to face this with such quiet."

"Thank you. Those born to the sea understand we have little choice in our lives, that the wind and fate will decide how we shall live and how long."

"Yet you pray. So perhaps you believe you can influence your fate."

"Good point, Lord Perry. Though now I pray not to save this life but to save my next."

Lord Perry turned to see the disturbance touch the stern of the ship. The sailors stopped to watch, several dropping to their knees in prayer.

"Then I shall hope there is indeed another ocean for you to sail. May God have mercy on us all."

"Indeed." He was silent for a moment before continuing. "I have no complaints about this life, only wish it could have been longer. It has been an honour to meet you, Lord Perry. I have heard you are just and fair to those under you and I have seen this to be true."

Lord Perry nodded. "It has served me well to be fair to others. Like you, my life has been rewarding." He pointed with his right hand. "Interesting how the ship just disappears without listing or reacting to the loss of rudders."

Part of the ship was indeed disappearing and though the stern was open to the sea, the water didn't rush in, held back by the front of the disturbance. The sailors on deck didn't run, though most backed away from the small bubbles of change. Some stayed on their knees and prayed as the disturbance washed over them, not crying out in either fear or pain.

A few minutes later, only Captain Lloyd and Lord Perry stood as they faced the wave.

Lord Perry took a quick glance at where the captain stood. "The tradition is for the captain to be the last man aboard his ship in times of distress." He took a step forward toward the disturbance. "Good luck, Captain. May we meet again someday, somewhere."

Lord Perry reached out a hand toward the wave of bubbles, pushing his fingers into the curtain. There wasn't any sensation at all, no tingling and without pain. He stood there, trying to keep his eyes open without blinking to see if there was anything to see in his final moments. A mist of white fog came and suddenly blackness, quickly followed by light. Amazingly, he found himself floating, finding he could now see in all directions, if seeing was the right word. If he thought about a direction he could look there, as if he had a 360-degree vision.

Lord Perry wondered if he was still caught in the disturbance or if he was dead. In either case, he found himself moving in one direction, the same direction as the others on the ship, he noticed. The direction was hard to determine as he didn't have any sensation of up or down, and there wasn't anything around him to give guidance. Some sailors had begun to disappear, the air around them giving a slight shimmer. He had seen that shimmer before when someone went through a gateway to traverse to another world. He wondered what world he was traveling to or was this just the last dream of a dead man, an illusion his mind making up to give him peace. Lord Perry concentrated on moving in a different direction than the others and soon began drifting backward.

The surrounding grey dissipated slightly, and he discovered he was above the ocean, although the Moon was no longer in sight. He concentrated on the shore and began drifting toward it.

The shore was where he expected it to be but to his disappointment it was of the new Domum with strange plants and animals. He slid past and through the plants and most of the animals ignored him though a small gargoyle ran from him after baring its teeth.

"So, you can see me. Maybe I am still real in a way. You, my frightened friend, have confirmed rumours gargoyles can see spirits. No wonder we value your ability to protect our homes."

Then a voice came to him. It seemed to be all around him and inside his head. The deep voice spoke gently to him, "Lord Perry, you may wander if you wish to do so. But there is nothing of your old world here. It's time to come home."

He looked around and saw a crack in the sky above him where light poured out. "Home? My castle?"

"Nay, Lord Perry. Your original home, the home where you came from and all life and matter come from."

Lord Perry felt a gentle tug on him toward the sky. He could resist it if he really wanted to but understood the speaker was right. Other than his own curiosity, there wasn't any reason for him to stay. The thought of going home appealed to him and now there was a distant memory of being there. "I am coming, Father."

PART TWO

Gilbert is not meant to be the one to save the world.

NINE

Gilbert reluctantly admitted Marisa might be right; the gnants seemed more curious than wanting to attack. But Gilbert wasn't about to trust them yet.

Before the world had changed into this new version, he was all too familiar with gnants. They could be at the very least antagonistic to people, sometimes violent and occasionally murderous.

The gnants resented and resisted the human invasion to Domum but couldn't stop the conversion of their world to one similar of Earth. Hundreds of years ago, gnant scientists, Adapts, had pushed the boundaries of magic and crystals resulting in a rift opening between Earth and Domum. Creatures from both worlds flowed through the new doorway. Earth plants, animals and humans adapted and quickly took over their counterparts on Domum. Domum life fared less well on Earth. After the doorway was closed, Earth life prevailed on Domum but the dragons, gnants and the multicoloured plants died out on Earth, leaving behind only fables they once existed.

Try as they might gnants couldn't force the humans to leave, with many battles fought to reclaim their land. Gnants, not normally social creatures, often attacked the humans as badly organized clusters, usually without weapons and relying on magic to win the day. Humans used weapons, armour, horses and battle plans to defeat gnants over and over again. A truce was finally declared and the thoroughly defeated gnants came close to being completely exterminated in the largest landmass on Domum. The geographical features on Domum reflected Earth in many ways, but being smaller than Earth, some landmasses became mere islands.

It was only in the North America counterpart in Domum the original native life prevailed, protected from Europe and Asia by the oceans. Gilbert had seen paintings of North America in Lord Perry's castle and recognized this new landscape looked very similar to what he was seeing now. It seemed to Gilbert the gnants following them might not have seen humans before and not sure how to react. How long that would last, he didn't want to speculate, and he certainly wasn't as optimistic as Marisa they didn't mean any harm now or later. He kept his hand near where his sword hung from his waist and was prepared to go down fighting if they attacked. He knew gnants preferred not to make use of weapons, finding their own claws and teeth more than sufficient for most fighting. It gave a sword-wielding human some advantage, especially with range. But the quick gnants tended to attack from a crouching position which gave little opportunity to strike them.

Marisa was taking a much more relaxed attitude, keeping her sword in her backpack as she strolled among the plants and bushes.

Another gnant joined the others in tailing them, making Gilbert increasingly nervous.

"Marisa, me don'ts like all these gnants arounds us."

She glanced around. "Yeah, they seem to be growing in number. So far, they're not showing any hostility. I doubt if we can do much about it in any event."

Gilbert pointed with his hand at a distant hill. "Let's go there, give a view of the area. Maybe we find an easier path to gate."

She looked at the hill. "You sure? Can't we just keep walking this way? The gate's gotta be in the same place?"

"Same place, sure. But what if there be something along the way we should knows about."

She shrugged her shoulders. "Okay, you're the leader."

"Best you don'ts forget that." He strode off in front of her, not noticing she rolled her eyes skyward.

The journey up the hill wouldn't normally be difficult, but the ground was wet from overnight rain, making the path slippery and muddy. Gilbert found it easier than the taller Marisa and waited for her at the top as she cursed about getting mud on her skirt and hands.

"This better be worth it. I've got dirt on my skirt."

"It'll wash off. I's got dirt on me pants and I's not complaining."

"Yeah, but you always have dirt on your clothes. Me, I like to keep clean."

The gnants had followed them up the hill and though they didn't seem to have any problem climbing the greasy slope, they kept well back. The hill didn't have many tall plants or bushes, and they seemed to prefer not to be caught in the open.

The top of the hill gave them a good view of the surrounding area and where the gate was supposed to be located. The vegetation didn't change much wherever they looked except near the river where it grew denser. Before their world had changed Domum, the land in front of them had contained the town of Horstruff and near the centre of it resided the castle formally belonging to Lord Bennett. Lord Bennett's castle contained the gateway to Earth, and on Earth that gateway led to Gordon Miller's Irish castle similar in shape to Lord Bennett's.

In the new version of Domum, Gilbert and Marisa gazed on a collection of scattered mud huts, the homes gnants preferred to live in. None of the huts stood close to one another, indicating these gnants still weren't highly social creatures. On the previous version of Domum, gnants tended to be even less social and a large cluster of huts was rare These gnants seemed more tolerant of each other's company, though still not wanting too much companionship.

Near the centre of the gnant's village stood a brown and green building, right where Lord Bennett's castle and the gate would reside. The building looked odd, not exactly like a large hut but more of a rectangular shaped building. It stood perhaps twenty feet high with a dome roof, covering thirty feet wide at the front and forty feet deep.

"What is that building?"

"Dunno. Looks like something special to these gnants."

"You mean like a temple?"

Gilbert shrugged his shoulders. "Coulds be anything. But it be near the gateway, must have something to do with that."

"What do you think it's made of?"

"Gnants make huts out of mud and sticks. Probably the building is made of mud and these stupid plants."

"Well, you were right to check here first. Now what do we do? I doubt we can just walk down there to the gate."

"I's don'ts know." He sat down on the damp ground. "I's thinks about it."

Marisa walked around on the small hilltop as Gilbert sat, mumbling to himself occasionally. The gnants stayed close by and she saw some of them hiding behind the larger plants. She was enjoying her stroll outside the castle and guessed it would be a long time before she had this much freedom again. Lord Troy was a kind, if eccentric, owner. He rarely ordered his slaves to do anything, phrasing most of his requests as if they had a choice to accomodate him. He did have the women walk around largely undressed but gave them a selection of garments from which to choose. Marisa's previous owner had her wear a slave's collar most of the time to remind her of her status.

Now, she was trying to enjoy every moment of her outing, knowing her liberty was to disappear at the end of Gilbert's task, probably for a very long time.

Gilbert got to his feet. "Okay, let's go. Ol' Gilbert gots a plan."

She followed a short distance behind him. "What is exactly this plan?"

"Shh. Can't tells you because the gnants might hear."

"Gilbert, these gnants wouldn't understand English. We're the first people they've come across."

"Maybe. But Gilbert don'ts trust thems anyhow."

"Oh, for…you just like keeping secrets, that's all."

"You just follow me, a plan is in me head."

"Well, I hope the plan doesn't get lost in that void up there."

"Hey, you just remember who the leader is. You still a slave, show proper respect."

Marisa pursed her lips. What he said was right; she was still a slave. Lord Troy had allowed her to leave the castle, but she was then placed under Gilbert's charge. It didn't worry her at the time, just getting away from the castle for a short time was wonderful, but the reality of Gilbert being her master even temporarily was now giving her second thoughts. Still, she didn't have much choice; she could hardly go running back to the castle after asking to go on this adventure. The other part was Gilbert getting to gate and going to Earth to get help was their best chance of returning Domum to the way it was. And Marisa wasn't confident Gilbert could do so by himself.

They made their way down the slope with the gnants scattering to find new locations to hide. Marisa guessed now at least a dozen gnants were following them. She didn't suspect the gnants meant them any harm. On the world of Domum that disappeared just a few days ago gnants were hostile to humans but that wasn't always the case. When humans first appeared on Domum, the gnants appeared curious and not unfriendly. It was only after the humans began to take over huge areas the gnants used to hunt that skirmishes and finally war ensued. Marisa's theory was as long as she and Gilbert didn't do anything to provoke them, the gnants wouldn't harm them. They were the first humans these gnants had met and shouldn't feel any hostility toward them.

Gilbert continued to lead the way. Marisa was annoyed he refused to tell her his plan or even their route. As a result, she had to follow him as he plodded among the vegetation. A few times she guessed the direction he was heading, and she tried to walk ahead of him. Gilbert would then abruptly change his bearings, leaving her staring at him in frustration. After she trailed him for a short time, he would change back to his original route.

"Gilbert, you're being childish. Do you really have to be in front every step of the way?"

"Why do you say childish? Cause Gilbert short? You don'ts like a dwarf leading?"

"No, that's not..."

Gilbert turned around and waved a finger at her. "I tells you, me was happy you come at first but then me sees you just wanted to go outside. Sure, I's knows you slept with me cause ye hadta but I's thought you likes me. I's was wrong, but now I's reminds ye that yer just a slave and though Gilbert just a dwarf, you better listen to me!" Gilbert shouted out the last sentence and turned around to continue his walk.

Marisa was silent for a few minutes as she followed him. She considered it did appear like she was just using him. She knew dwarfs had a difficult time on Domum and rarely had opportunities for positions of power. Besides their small stature setting them apart from others they also had their own set of beliefs based on an assortment of spirits. While called dwarfs like their Earth counterpart, they appeared similar in that regard only in height. They were proportionally much like the taller humans in hands and limbs with only their heads slightly larger in ratio to their bodies.

In Horstruff many of the dwarfs resided as a group in one of the less affluent districts called Vegrandis. The community had developed its own shops and taverns, most of them operating out of former homes. Of course, the dwarfs and their businesses had a tendency of migrating around the district making tax collection by the authorities difficult. Horstruff as a whole left Vegrandis alone. There usually wasn't any problem for normal sized people to wander around in Vegrandis and dwarfs certainly moved freely around Horstruff. But there existed unspoken boundaries.

Most children stayed in schools until the age of fourteen, but dwarfs taught their children in their own schools, usually in one of the converted homes. Their education was slightly different from Horstruff's, focusing more on survival skills, magic spells and history of their people. Marisa admitted the dwarfs were not always treated fairly and a few of them had resorted to stealing to put food on the table. That included Gilbert who was well known for his trades and business transactions, though his efforts went well beyond the need just to make a living. He was a rarity among the dwarfs, spending considerable time outside of Vegrandis.

Neither the taller humans nor the dwarfs entirely trusted him. Many on both sides had reason to be unsure of his motives but they did respect him. He was not known for his bravery but certainly could fight, downing many a bigger opponent. He also knew people in positions of power and influence and was able to get through doors barred to many of the other dwarfs.

All in all, Gilbert had managed to rise above many obstacles to be accepted in Horstruff and beyond as an appreciated citizen.

Marisa slowed her pace as she considered how she had treated him. It was true as a slave she was required to do what a guest wanted unless Lord Troy indicated otherwise but that didn't mean she disliked having to sleep with Gilbert. He was in fact better than most men in her bed; he didn't take her for granted and was determined she was satisfied first. She could see how Gilbert would think she was just using him to get off the castle. Marisa wasn't just using him to get out of the castle. *Well, I suppose a bit.* But she did like him and decided she better make amends to him before it got out of hand.

Marisa sat on the ground. "Gilbert, stop! I twisted my ankle." She grabbed her right ankle with both hands and watched him.

Gilbert stopped for several seconds before slowly turning around and staring at her. He looked annoyed.

"Please, it really hurts." She made a show of grimacing.

He frowned and walked back to her. "How did ye hurt it?"

"I stepped on a stone or something."

He crouched down by her ankle. "It don'ts look sore."

"It hurts all the same."

He touched her ankle with his hand, and she made a small gasp. "Careful."

"Gilbert say small spell to help."

Gilbert mumbled a few phrases while holding an open hand above her ankle.

"There, that better?"

She moved her foot around in a small circle. "It does feel better." She slowly stood up using his shoulder for support. "I can walk if I'm careful."

"You sure?"

"Can you walk next to me for a while in case I slip?"

Gilbert nodded. "We walks slow."

Marisa kept her hand on Gilbert's shoulder for support as she limped slightly alongside him. Marisa didn't like being deceitful, but it seemed the easiest way to patch things up with Gilbert. She knew from experience the fastest way to get men to change suddenly from being argumentative to being sympathetic was for a woman to be injured, or at least pretend to be. Crying helped too, but she didn't want to go overboard to get his attention; she might have to use that later. She figured it was now time to make up with him before Gilbert started to lose his compassion for her. Once her ankle got supposedly better, he might become angry with her again.

"Gilbert, I'm sorry we got into a fight. I didn't go on this journey just to get out of the castle. I really like being with you."

"That true? I's likes you too."

"I guess I got a little excited when we left the castle. I'm not free like you and didn't know what to expect when I got away. You understand, don't you?"

"Sure, I does."

"Then you're not mad at me anymore, are you?"

He shook his head. "How's yer ankle?"

"Oh, much better now, it hardly hurts at all."

"That good, 'cause I didn't really use a magic spell on yer ankle."

"Oh."

"But we be friends just the same."

Gilbert led Marisa in a long walk avoiding the gnant's collection of huts. Several gnants still followed them but they seemed to be losing interest, especially as they moved farther away from their village.

"Can you tell me your plan now?"

Several seconds passed before Gilbert answered in a whisper. "Don'ts want them to know what we up to, that why we walk far away first."

"What are we up to?"

"We goes a ways thens head to the river and swims across."

"Swim across? Why?"

"Gnants not swim, can't follow us."

"Oh. I forgot that. You're pretty clever, Gilbert."

Gilbert gave a smug smile. "Gotta use me noggin or I's don't live long."

"We should stop soon, have a break."

"Sure..."

"Gilbert! I see a dragon!"

Gilbert looked to where she pointed in the sky. He first saw one and then two dragons, their bodies the size of a large dog. "Lupus dragons. There be more, they hunts in packs. Quick, lie down on ground, maybe they don'ts sees us."

The lupus dragons normally hunted in groups of five to twelve, with two of the dragons the parents of the other dragons. After the siblings reached four years old, they would leave the group to try to form their own pack. Dragons were formidable predators and a group of them with their toxic fire breath could take down almost any prey. But dragons could be considered bullies; stand up to them and they would often turn away to easier meals. The social lupus dragons didn't want to lose any member of their pack and avoided creatures that could fight back.

Gilbert heard dragons depended on their hawk-like eyes to spot quarry. By lying still, the dragons might not see them as live food. Most types of dragons would only eat fresh kill.

Marisa and Gilbert lay frozen on the ground as the dragons wheeled above them.

TEN

Angela took a final bow with Council Madoc and together they stepped back behind the curtain. Angela squeezed his hand briefly and let it go.

"Good show. The audience really liked what you did."

"Thank you."

They walked toward the dressing rooms.

"Are you going to add more acts to your show?"

"More acts? Why?"

"It's just you're always improvising or changing something in the show. And I wondering if you'd like to try something new."

"I improvise to improve the acts I do have, not to add a new act."

"A new act or two would be good. Change things up so the audience won't know what to expect."

"Perhaps you're right. I will try…"

"I've a couple ideas you might be interested in. Nothing too fancy but a bit different from what you've been doing."

Council Madoc looked at her anxious, smiling face as they came to a stop in front of her dressing room. He concluded she definitely had something she wanted added to the show and he should give in gracefully and hear her out. "Why don't we discuss your ideas tonight at the eating establishment in the hotel?"

"Sure, I'll change and catch up with you at your dressing room."

———

Council Madoc cut into his steak as Angela waved a piece of fish with her fork as she talked.

"How about if you have me in this cage, made of clear plastic or iron bars and tied up or chained. The audience will see there's no way I can get out of those chains or the cage. Then a sheet drops over the cage to hide it and a few seconds later when the cover is raised…Voila! I'm gone." She beamed at him as she put the wavering fish piece in her mouth.

Council Madoc chewed on his steak slowly as he considered it was certainly something of which he was capable. But he wondered how he would accomplish that bit of magic without her discovering his secret. She looked so enthusiastic about the act he would have to be careful how he worded his reply. "Well, it certainly does warrant merit of consideration. However, I would have to obtain the necessary equipment." He paused as reached for his wine. "What are you proposing would happen after you disappeared?"

"I could come strolling out from behind the curtains. Can you check for such the equipment? I think it would look really neat. I would need a new costume, such as a prisoner's uniform. Or, even better, as a sexy slave girl."

"I will give some consideration on the matter."

"Okay, but just picture the effect. I would be wearing this little slave girl costume, blindfolded and chained up inside this cage. Lots of lights and music as I try to break free. Then suddenly this black canvas drops in front of the cage. When it's pulled away, I'm gone and a few seconds later I walk on from the side of the stage."

"Blindfold?"

"It would add to the element of me being helpless."

"Perhaps we can check on the availability of the equipment."

"That would be great. Thanks." She gave him a huge grin.

Council Madoc considered a blindfold would prevent her from seeing how he was using magic. He also knew she wanted a bigger part of the show and wearing an eye-catching outfit while inside a cage would certainly draw the attention to her. He didn't begrudge her need to be seen more on the stage and understood this was her chance to be a star. He would just have to make certain she couldn't learn of his way of performing those tricks.

Angela continued to talk. Council Madoc watched her and heard her, but he didn't listen. He wondered why he even would agree to her proposal. Was it a quest for power, recognition for a part of ego he needed to show how good he was at magic? But no, he decided. *The ego is here; I know it well. It isn't pushing my decision. It is her. Somehow, I do care very much about her happiness.* He wasn't sure whether it was as a friend or as a potential lover. But if being in the limelight would make her happy, then he wanted to make it happen.

The risks existed, he understood that fully. Normally, he tried to avoid risks, carefully calculating the odds of success before committing himself to a plan of action. As Council Madoc, adviser to lords and other powerful people on Domum, there was enough danger in just telling the truth. His charade as a magician had its hazards and now he was pushing the envelope of detection because she wanted to have a bigger part in the show. He took another drink of his wine, noted the hint of the spicy end of the Pinot Noir, and turned his attention to what she was saying, enjoying the odd inflection of her voice.

"… So he had to be drunk or something, so I called the manager over and it turns out this guy is his cousin. Well, now, that was crazy situation. I didn't want to serve him anymore, but the manager didn't want to piss off his cousin."

Madoc smiled and nodded. Angela was one of those people who could take a small incident and turn it into a whole story. She was also one of the few people he didn't mind she almost constantly talked. He avoided using too many words, wanting to make sure his meaning and advice was clear and concise. In addition, there was little point giving more information than was necessary. Advice and information presented a saleable commodity and any knowledge about him was a guarded secret. The less said, the better.

In the meantime, he was content to listen to her and try to figure out how to perform the trick she wanted to try without revealing his own abilities.

———

The cage was six feet wide and eight feet long. It stood seven feet high with a solid wood floor and ceiling. Bars spaced eight inches apart made up of the rest of the cage, including the front door that was hinged to swing outward. The cage, painted black, looked formidable and impossible to break out of. It was one of Madoc's few illusions: the cage was actually made almost entirely of wood and plastic, not iron, and the back corner was hinged so a small opening was available. The only metal used was for the hinges and the lock on the front door. The construction of the cage in wood would not affect Council Madoc's powers as a metal one would.

While the cage was being constructed, Angela spent the time looking for a new costume, finally selecting one needing only minor changes. The modification was done with the help of a girlfriend adept at using a sewing machine.

Madoc and Angela practiced several times until she perfected opening the hidden door at the back of the cage and sprinting to the back of the stage, with the cover over the cage hiding her exit. There she continued to walk through the backstage until she could reappear from the side of the stage.

The next step in the rehearsal was for Madoc to tie her arms and legs using a length of rope. The thick rope first secured her wrists behind her back and wrapped around her body before being knotted. Angela was blindfolded as she stood still in the centre of the cage. Madoc and Angela counted off ten seconds in unison, the time for the canvas to cover the cage. He uttered a magic spell and the ropes loosen. She whipped off her blindfold and scurried out of the back of the cage to the backstage, meeting up with him seconds later.

"How was that? Fast enough?"

"Yes. When you made the reappearance from the side of the stage, I would estimate less than one minute elapsed from the time the canvas covered the cage. It should be a good illusion for the audience."

"Great! This is going to look really cool."

He nodded. "I recall you said you planned to wear another costume for this event."

"Yup, it's ready. I'm going to make you wait until our live show before you get to see it."

"Why? Is there something special about it?"

"Of course, there is. I just want to surprise you with it." She grinned happily at him.

Madoc sighed. He didn't like information being kept from him but she seemed to enjoy keeping him off balanced and surprising him. "Is it like your other costume? The abbreviated man's suit?"

"Abbreviated man's suit?" She giggled. "No, this is definitely more feminine."

————

The show started normally with Angela wearing her tuxedo jacket. She was now used to the flames being in proximity and didn't worry about getting burned. After she finished the floating act, she disappeared to her dressing room, running the entire time, while Madoc performed tricks of making coloured balls appear and disappear inside an egg carton. Just as he finished making the egg carton and balls disappear, two stagehands pushed the cage onto the stage. He turned and swept his hand toward the cage as Angela reappeared from the back.

Angela had indicated to him it was going to be a slave's outfit, but it certainly wasn't any slave's garments he had seen on Domum.

On Domum most slaves wore what their masters gave them or what they could afford out of a meagre allowance. If a slave was attractive enough, they might be given finer clothes. Some, such as those at Lord Troy's castle, wore hardly anything at all but they certainly wouldn't be allowed out in public dressed the way Angela was dressed. The other thing Council Madoc had trouble getting use to was the footwear women chose. On Domum, almost all shoes were flat and similar to sandals. What Angela wore for shoes hardly qualified as for a slave. The red shoes had thin leather straps wrapped around her ankle and the spiked heel lifted her several inches above the floor. The shoes shocked him less than the rest of her outfit.

The glittering red bikini didn't hide much of her assets and would have qualified as a bathing suit except for the sheer, loose fitting pant legs and sleeves. The cuffs of the legs and arms had the same glittering material as the bikini.

Council Madoc found he was holding his breath and slowly released it. He wished Angela had showed him what she was going to wear. He would have tried to convince her it wasn't necessary to show off so much of her body. But it was too late now as he moved toward her to escort her to the cage.

She looked pleased with herself and smiled as he led her.

"Do you like it?" she whispered.

"Yes, it's very... unusual."

"Good, I was worried you might think it was too extreme and I wanted you to like it. It's not over the top is it?"

He knew he could hardly criticize her with the show still on. "No, no. It's fine, Angela."

She put her wrists behind her back and he quickly wrapped the rope around them and around her torso. With the same rope he began to circle her legs, which was when he noticed her bikini bottom had less material at the back then the front. He stopped for a moment and carried on with the rope, ending in a knot. He decided he knew too little about Earth women and their fashions to decide if it was "over the top" as she put it or not. On Domum she would have been arrested if she appeared in public dressed like that.

———

Angela could sense his uneasiness as he tied her up. That was okay as far as she was concerned. If she dressed in a thong bikini, it was meant to make men react the way they thought about her. Especially Madoc, who always seemed to be too calm and collected.

Madoc turned her around so the audience could see the rope looked secure and left the cage, locking the front door behind him. The canvas cover dropped in front of the cage and suddenly the ropes fell off, landing at her feet. She quickly tore off her blindfold as a wave of cold air hit her. She shivered slightly and slipped out of the rear of the cage, hurrying to the back.

A few seconds later, the cover was lifted, and the empty cage revealed. The audience applauded and increased their enthusiasm when she walked onto the stage from the side.

Angela took her bow with the Great Madoc and walked off the stage. She changed into her street clothes with mixed feelings. She was happy with her performance and the chance to be in the spotlight. But there was something working at the back of her mind. For one thing, she wasn't certain Madoc approved of her costume. He didn't say anything to her, yet she had a feeling he thought her outfit was too revealing. She mused that was true, but it wasn't any worse than what others wore during stage shows and she was comfortable with her costume. She wanted him to act pleasantly surprised, not shocked. It was something she would have to talk to him about. She considered he just didn't like her getting as much attention as she did and wanted to keep the spotlight on him.

There was another troubling thought working its way up from her subconscious. Every time Madoc did magic involving her, a waft of cold air descended on her. His illusions were not what she expected; other than the second hidden door in the back of the cage, there didn't seem to be any deception. It was troubling she couldn't understand how the tricks were accomplished and coupled with the mysterious bit of cold air made her wonder there was more to his magic than just illusions.

None of those troubling thoughts caused her to back away from working with him; to the contrary, she found this made him even more fascinating.

———

Angela dropped in again on Madoc's apartment two days later in the afternoon. He didn't act surprised anymore at her unannounced intrusion at his apartment, or the fact she helped herself to a glass of wine and sat on the loveseat.

He put down a copy of *The Infinite Book* on the coffee table, carefully putting a bookmark inside the pages first.

"Good book?"

"Interesting. Unusual premise. Do you read much, Angela?"

"When I have time." She kicked off her sandals and folded a leg under her. Today she was wearing shorts and a sleeveless shirt. She noticed his eyes glance quickly at her legs.

"Can I ask you something? Actually, I have a couple of questions."

"Go ahead. I will answer them if I am able to."

"Okay. First, do my costumes bother you? I mean, I get the impression you find them too revealing."

He was silent for several seconds and he looked down. Then he met her eyes. "It is not for me to judge. Where I come from such clothing would be considered inappropriate. But this is a different world, that is culture, and I want to assure you I have not changed my opinion of you because of what you and others wear. In short, if you are comfortable wearing such outfits, that is fine with me."

She cocked her head to her side. "Good, but I would wear something else if it bothered you."

He shook his head. "Please don't, it is fine."

"Great. How about if I went topless?"

He looked stunned for a moment and opened his mouth.

She laughed. "I'm kidding you. I wouldn't do that."

Madoc smiled and looked relieved. "You had me fooled there for a moment."

"Can you tell me where you're from exactly? Somewhere in Ireland doesn't quite cut it. I mean, in most places in Ireland they would wear the same stuff we have here and have TVs. So where did you come from?"

"I cannot tell you exactly, except to assure you it was from a place you would call Ireland. But it is isolated from what you think of as Ireland. I suppose you would consider it somewhat backward."

"Hmm. You keep holding back information. Are you a fugitive? An axe murderer on the run? Like you only use Madoc as a name. Don't you have any other names? Is Madoc your real name?" She grinned at him, trying to tease him to tell more.

"You're very inquisitive. Aren't you concerned you might be right?"

"Na. But you sure don't say much about yourself. Ever been married? Are you married? Kids?"

"No. I have never married. And, alas, I haven't any children. Why all these questions?"

"Just curious. Besides, you aren't answering most of my questions." She took a sip of her wine. "Hey, you aren't gay, are you?"

He considered her question a moment, trying to remember what gay meant. "No, I'm not."

"It's just I haven't seen you with any other women."

"You're not with me all the time; therefore, that is a rather poor deduction."

"Whatever. Say, would like to go to the bar where I work tonight? Like, we could go for a bite to eat and a couple of drinks."

"Well, I don't know…"

"Com'on. What else have you got planned? I promise I won't keep you out too late."

Madoc shook his head. "You are rather persistent. I agree then."

"Great. I told the other waitresses about you and they're dying to meet you."

"What did you say about me?"

"Just girl talk." She got up. "I'm going home to change. I'll pick you up around seven."

He stood as she got up, not entirely comfortable on what just transpired.

ELEVEN

Liz cuddled up to Jon on the bench seat. He took a big swallow from his pint of beer to wash down the last bite of his dinner. The Dockers Pub was only partially filled with patrons; the evening was still early, and the younger crowd had still not made their way in yet. Liz and Jon sat near the back to obtain a small amount of privacy, something they found in short supply. Liz was staying with her parents while Jon rented a room at the Stewarts'. Both places made serious open affection to one another difficult. Jon was wondering if he was going to have to rent a hotel room for them to get intimate.

Jon pushed his plate away and wrapped his arm over Liz's shoulder. He gave her a squeeze, causing her to turn toward him where they exchanged a series of kisses. His hand massaged her shoulder then dropped down to her waist where he slipped his fingers under her T-shirt.

"Your hand is under my bra. Someone will see."

"No one's looking."

"Don't be so sure. Hey, I've got to go to the loo."

"Okay." He withdrew his hand from under her shirt, sighing.

He sat patiently sipping his beer when Liz came back. He noticed Liz approach the table from the far side of the bar, walking slowly between the tables. Liz sat next to him again, and he immediately put his arm around her again.

"Drink up. Let's go for a walk. I know of a couple of secluded spots we can go to."

Jon took a couple of big swallows of his beer, holding his pint for another drink.

She laughed. "I didn't mean for you to chug it down. I'm not about to throw my drink back. You Americans can be a bit eager at times."

"Okay, I'll slow it down." He slipped his hand down to her waist.

"No fondling. Others can see us just fine and I don't want to cause a scandal." She took a drink of her gin and smiled and waved at one of the other tables.

She readjusted the dark blue cotton shirt, straightening the bottom over the multi-coloured mini-skirt. She thought she would have to stop Jon from sliding his hand up her thigh when they first sat down, but he surprised her, leaving her legs alone and concentrating on her torso. Usually, he wasn't so intent on what he wanted, but it was clear his patience for time alone with her was running low. His desire for her increased her own appetite for some seclusion and she recalled a few places in previous years that offered some privacy.

Jon finished off his beer while Liz shook her head at him. "Bit of a hurry, are we?" She finished off her gin and tonic. "Okay, let's go."

They walked quickly toward the exit with Liz preceding Jon. She smiled at the waitress as she cleaned a table, but a ringing phone caused her to dash to the bar.

Jon pushed the door open and allowed Liz to precede him when the waitress called out, "Jon McKinney. Might there be a Jon McKinney here?"

Jon and Liz froze, looked at each other, and returned to the bar.

"I'm Jon McKinney."

"Phone's for you." She held up the receiver.

Jon walked over to the phone and spoke as Liz stood by the doorway. He glumly hung up the phone and hurried back to Liz.

"That was Uncle Gordon. He said something has happened to

Domum and wants us to go to his castle right away, like immediately." Then he added quietly. "Damn it to hell."

"Come on, this probably won't take long. Uncle Gordon sometimes gets a little excited. I'm sure it's nothing, then we can get back
to business." She gave him a small hip check as they walked and
gave him a grin.

———

"So, you see, when I hadn't heard from Gilbert, or for that matter
any of the Domum inhabitants, I decided to take a look through the
laboratory apparatus. Actually, some leprechauns and gnomes have
come to visit, but they are uncommunicative at best and have been
no help whatsoever to my inquiries. You know how …"

Liz and Jon exchanged looks.

"Uncle Gordon, what did you see in the lab?" Jon decided he
better try to get his uncle back on the topic.

"Oh, that was most astonishing. The land had changed
completely! There wasn't any town, just a collection of these grasses
and mud huts gnants occupied. At least a hundred of them. The
huts, not the gnants; there were even more of them. I didn't see any
humans or any sign of human activity either."

"Perhaps you weren't viewing Domum?" Jon asked.

"I thought of that. I reviewed the settings and ensured they were
correct. Also, it seems likely there would only be one world where
gnants inhabited. And dragons too, I saw several creatures in the sky
that looked like dragons. I'm positive the world I was seeing was
Domum."

"Maybe it was another part of Domum then."

Gordon Miller shook his head. "I considered that possibility. But
I checked the shadows at their noon and determined it was close to
the same latitude as before unless I suddenly was viewing the
southern hemisphere." He stopped to think for a moment. "No,
that's not a reasonable proposition. Besides, the only way my apparatus can work is in the immediately area of the same location of
this castle on another world."

"Could we see this new Domum?"

"Of course, how silly of me not to have offered right away." He
stood up quickly and began to march up the stairs to the laboratory.

The lab was the same as how they had last seen it. The equipment was on three different heavy wood tables with power cables running around the room from a conduit installed a few months ago. The one-inch metal conduit ran from the room, out through a hole in the castle outside wall and back to the power generator located in the backyard. Tom Markus and Tuck Richards, the two university graduate students, had done the work. Liz and Jon's sister, Sandra Draper, originally convinced the physics students to help them set up the apparatus when Jon disappeared. They had remained friends and continued to work with Gordon in developing the theory on why it worked.

Gordon switched on the equipment and after a minute the monitor changed from showing snow to a fuzzy image of green and brown. He adjusted several knobs and a picture of Domum appeared. The image had the effect of looking at a hologram. The focus was good near the centre, but the outer edges appeared soft. Still, it was easy to see this was a world composed only of plants, bushes and gnants.

"No Horstruff in evidence." Liz whispered out loud, her thoughts suddenly on Sir Anthony 'Tony' Graham. "What could have happened to all the people there?"

Jon's heart sank. He knew many people in Domum. One, Nicole Keaton, he had fallen in love with and who had later become engaged with Tony Graham.

"I have been working with Tom and Tuck on this situation and they conclude this Domum has replaced the one we knew. How or why, I cannot say. But according to our best theory, and it is the most probable one, is the Domum we know doesn't exist anymore. More to the point, it never did. Something has changed the past of Domum and this is the only one that exists now."

"You mean all those people are gone forever?" Liz covered her mouth with her hand, her eyes wide with fear.

"But can't we change what has been done, revert it back to the old Domum?" Jon asked.

"Maybe, if it's some phenomenon that we can comprehend. If it was human caused, or gnant caused, then there might be a way. But it may also be a natural occurrence, something their world goes through occasionally. Of course, in such a case, the same phenomenon could occur here."

"But we haven't seen any evidence of that, have we?" Jon noticed the warning light blinking on the control panel and pointed a finger at it.

"Oh, yes, thank you." He toggled a couple switches and the picture on the monitor vanished. "I don't know of any evidence but then again there wouldn't be? If the Earth only came into being a year ago, we wouldn't know of any previous Earth because all our memories and geological history would be of this one."

Jon scratched at his chin. "But what if one of us was on Domum when Earth changed? Would we still exist and have memories of the previous Earth?"

"Yes, because we would be outside the sphere of change. And we could return to Earth with our previous memories, though we would find a very different Earth than the one we knew."

"Interesting. Because here on Earth, we have at least one individual from the old Domum, Council Madoc. And if this change on Domum came from humans or gnants, then as a warlock, he may be able do something about it."

Gordon raised a finger in the air. "A splendid idea! Splendid! Good thinking there, Robert, I mean Jon." Gordon occasionally forgot Jon had changed to using his middle name rather than his first. The change had saved his life when Lord Bennett tried to use magic on him by using a spell on him using the name Sir Jon rather than the name he was christened with.

Gordon suddenly rushed out of the room, leaving Jon and Liz to stand looking puzzled. His voice carried on from the hallway, growing fainter as he talked. "I have a way of contacting him. He left me this crystal device. I've left it in my desk."

"We might as well follow him." Jon led the way out of the third floor laboratory.

By the time they had reached the main floor they could hear him rummaging around in his desk, a drawer being opened and closed and another opened.

"Here it is! I've found it!" Gordon came out of the room holding a small brown leather bag. "This bag contains the crystal device to contact him."

"Great." Liz spoke for the first time since the shock of Domum suddenly changing and all the people she knew gone. "How does it work?"

"Oh, Madoc implied it was a magical device, but I believe it just makes use of entangled pairs of photons. You see if we affect…"

"Uncle Gordon, I meant how do we use it to contact Council Madoc?"

"Oh. Well it's a rather simple procedure. One simply shines a bright light on it. Council Madoc has a corresponding crystal at his end that will react to the light. My understanding is if we direct a red light on this crystal, then his will emit a red light, thus alerting him to respond to us."

"Sounds simple. What light should we use?"

"I have a trouble lantern with a flashing red light at the end. It should be sufficient to get his attention."

Jon looked at the flashlight. The lamp used a six-volt battery and had a normal light on one end and a smaller red light on the rear. Gordon had switched on the red light that blinked off and on in front of the oval-shaped crystal. The crystal, three inches by one and a half, was almost flat with a yellow tinge to it. The red light was placed within a foot of the crystal, both sitting on the kitchen table.

"Now we wait?"

"I presume so. Council Madoc said he would contact me. He didn't say how long that would take."

Liz crossed her arms, feeling the coolness of the open door in the kitchen. The castle had become warm during the afternoon and the narrow, five foot high exit seemed to have been added as an oversight but served well as a method of allowing air circulation. "How was he supposed to contact you?"

"To be honest, he didn't specify that either."

Jon shrugged his shoulders. "I guess we just wait and be patient." He eyed the fridge along the wall. "Anyone hungry?"

TWELVE

Gilbert and Marisa kept their heads down as they lay on the grass. One of the dragons cautiously landed on the ground about thirty feet away, legs stiffly holding up its body while its wings slowly beat the air. The dragon's head, twice the size of a large dog with a wide snout swivelled around with horse-like ears that twitched as the forked red tongue tasted the air. The lupus dragon's body had a thin covering of long black hair over reptilian skin and was almost five feet long with an equally long, thick tail.

Gilbert raised his head slowly and watched the dragon move its head around before fixing its gaze on Marisa and him. One six-clawed foot took a hesitant step toward them as the dragon lowered its head level with its shoulder.

"Gilbert, it sees us!" Marisa whispered.

"I's knows."

"It's coming towards us!"

"I's knows that."

"Another two dragons have landed!"

"I's knows that too."

"What are we going to do?"

"I's don't knows."

Marisa clenched her teeth and hit his shoulder with her fist.

"Gilbert, we have to do something. You're the man, do something manly."

Gilbert stared at her and back at the approaching dragon. He rubbed at his shoulder. "Okays, Gilbert thinks of something."

"Hurry!"

"I's gots a plan."

"Well what is it?"

"We stands up."

"Yeah? And then?"

"Scream and throw rocks at them."

She hit him again on the shoulder. "That's a plan?"

"Ye gots a better one?"

"If I die, I'm going to kill you." Marisa stood up and screamed. She picked a stone and threw it at one of the dragons.

Gilbert yelled. "Throws rocks at the first dragon that's landed. He be the leader." He joined her screaming and throwing rocks.

One dragon that just landed took to flight again. Two more dragons stood behind the first dragon while a fourth stood off to the side. The first dragon, the male leader, took one more hesitant step toward them. Slowly it moved its hind quarters forward and as its back became arched, the tail became stiff and extended far from its body.

Gilbert recognized the posture as a dragon about to attack by launching itself toward them while spraying them with a mixture of hot acid from the twin fire glands inside its mouth. The attack would be the signal for the other dragons to follow. "Scream louder."

Marisa gave a horrifying death scream as Gilbert reached for his knife hanging on his belt. He hefted the knife in his hand and grabbed the blade. Gilbert took aim carefully, looking for an opening to hit. The dragon's head was mostly a tough hide over thick bone. Gilbert knew a knife was not likely able to cause much damage on the head, but where the neck joined the shoulder there was a considerable muscle and blood vessels.

The dragon tensed its shoulders when Gilbert let his knife fly, sinking the blade just above the collarbone. The dragon screamed and leaped into the air straight up, wings beating rapidly as it clawed at the knife with its front paw. The other dragons quickly lost their interest in the prey and flew off, leaving Marisa and Gilbert screaming. Moments later, the knife fell to the ground with dark red blood oozing from the blade.

"They're gone! Gilbert, you did it!" She bent down and kissed him on his cheek. "My hero."

Gilbert didn't react for several seconds, his face without expression. Then slowly he began to look around and a grin formed on his face. "I's did it, didn't I?" He first touched his cheek where she kissed him and began to laugh before dancing around in a circle. He shook his fist in the air and shouted at the dragons. "Bewares, you buzzards! Gilbert not takes any gruff from yous."

A few minutes later Marisa helped Gilbert find his knife, and they restarted on their journey with Gilbert complaining about his shoulder where she punched him.

"Honestly, you're such a baby at times."

"I thoughts I was a hero."

"You are, you are. Just an aggravating one at times." She gave him a big smile as he eyed her suspiciously.

Later on, Gilbert pointed to near a spot where they had hiked. "We best make camp here." He pointed at a small patch of ground nestled at the bottom of a hill.

"Looks as good as any to me." Marisa was tired and just wanted to stop walking.

"Hard to see us when we set up the tent. We be safer that way."

Marisa wasn't about to argue with him. Her earlier conviction this new Domum was safe was given a big jolt by the attacking dragons. In the old world of Domum, lupus dragons rarely attacked people, having learned humans were not easy prey and could become predators on short notice. These dragons had no such experience and didn't fear humans. Now, she wasn't certain what else was harmless on the old world could be dangerous here, including gnants. At first, she thought Gilbert was paranoid and overly fearful of the unknown, a small man who told boastful tales. Now, she saw him as her protector and an experienced traveller. He didn't appear as small anymore.

Marisa helped him stretch the canvas cover between the fibrous tree-like bushes, hanging a sheet along the ends for closure. She then followed his example of tossing leaves and plants over the canvas as camouflage.

"You rest, Gilbert. I'll make something to eat with the provisions."

Gilbert looked only too happy to sit down and relax. The dragon fight had taken a lot of energy out of him and after the initial adrenalin rush, he began to feel increasingly lethargic. He began to doze off when Marisa gave him a bowl of steaming vegetables and pork and a mug of tea.

After dinner, Marisa watched Gilbert as he poked around in his backpack and produced a roll of dark brown string. He walked to the perimeter of their small camp and tied the string around the bushes and plants so it ran taut about two feet above the ground. He squatted down in front of the string and mumbled a few phrases. Gilbert struck the string with a finger, causing the string to produce a loud humming sound. Satisfied he turned back toward the tent.

"You put a magic spell on the string?"

"Just a wee one. Anything touches me string will cause a noise."

Marisa yawned. "Is there anything else you have to do? I'm ready to go to sleep." She thought after calling him her hero he would be after his compensation in the tent. Being a slave under his control she couldn't lawfully refuse him in any event, though in practice she knew she could turn him away. Gilbert might be a bit of a scoundrel, but he wasn't one to force his will on others. Marisa believed she was giving him fair notice; if he wanted her tonight, he better finish with his business of securing the campsite.

"All but done. Just one more spell for inside the tent."

Marisa nodded, watching Gilbert head inside the tent. It was getting darker rapidly as the setting sun sent long shadows across the campsite. The moon was a thin crescent and wasn't likely to give much light during the night. Marisa gave one last look around and began to undress, finding it easier to do so outside than in the small confines of the makeshift tent. She folded her clothes in her arms and entered the tent.

The first thing she noticed was how much darker the tent was than she expected. It took her several seconds for her eyes to adjust to the lack of light and find Gilbert sitting on the ground on left side of the tent. She slipped over toward him, moving carefully in the dark.

"Hard to see in here, Gilbert." She sat down next to him and put her hand on his shoulder. Her hand went right through him, causing her to scream.

"Quiet, you wake up the spirits. I's over here."

She looked over to where the voice came from and followed it by crawling over toward the other side of the tent. As she crossed the ground, Gilbert suddenly appeared to her, sitting on the right side of the tent.

"Gilbert, is that you this time?"

"Tis I. I's puts a spell inside the tent to makes it darker and then adds a mirror spell."

"Clever. The mirror spell made me see you at the other side of the tent."

"Help make us safe tonight.

"I could use some safe." She sat next to him.

He turned to her. "Marisa, I knows you wants me, but I needs to get some sleep tonight. Maybe tomorrow night." He curled down on the ground and pulled a blanket around him.

Marisa didn't know whether she was relieved he didn't want sex or amused he thought she wanted him. Right now, it didn't matter to her. She curled next to him with her own blanket and fell asleep.

Her dream of walking alone down an endless hallway in someone's castle was disturbed by a humming sound. In her dream she turned her head to try to find out where it was originating but the sound seemed to all around her. Her eyes opened to the noise of metal scraping the ground, the humming sound still prevalent.

"What, what's going on?"

"Quiet," Gilbert whispered back as he readied his sword. "Somethin' has touched me string."

Marisa looked around, but only darkness prevailed in the tent, save for the opening allowing a grey light to enter. Her dream had evaporated, but she didn't feel anymore secure knowing where she was.

The humming noise faded away, leaving only silence. She watched Gilbert slowly rise to a crouching position, his sword raised to attack. Marisa felt defenceless, her sword and knife at the far end of the tent. She held her breath as she listened to her own heartbeat.

THIRTEEN

M adoc followed Angela hesitantly into the bar. The brick building housed three businesses; a gas bar, a dry cleaner and the Ryder's Pub. Beyond the double set of wood doors, the pub had tried to establish an English style of décor, using oak on its tables and chairs. The floor was made from dark slate slabs with the walls covered with horse racing posters from long ago eras.

Angela greeted several of her co-workers with hugs and a big grin. The bar manager, a short stocky man with sandy-coloured hair, gave Madoc only a short gaze before returning to the bar. The two other women working gave him longer appraising looks. Madoc sat at one of the tables with Angela, looking around the bar as he did so. Compared to the taverns in the world of Domum this one was quieter, cleaner, better lit and didn't have obvious drunks sleeping at their table. At the back corner, a pool table attracted his attention as he tried to deduce the rules of play.

A blonde waitress, Traci, wearing blue jeans and a short red top, stopped at their table. "How's it going, Angie?"

"Good. This is Madoc. Madoc, Traci."

"It is a pleasure to make your acquaintance, Traci."

Angela giggled. "See, I told you. That's how he talks."

Traci grinned back. "It's nice meeting you too."

Madoc wasn't surprised by their comments after hearing Angela remark on his manner of speaking before. He waited until Traci asked what he would like to drink and asked for a glass of red wine, remembering not to ask for it to be uncut like he would in a similar bar in Domum.

"House wine okay?"

Madoc considered. In Domum he would simply ask for the best. But here he wondered if that was the accepted way of doing business.

"Give him that New Zealand wine, Soljans. He'll like that."

After Traci left, Angela said, "The house wine isn't too good. Most don't care but you have a pretty good taste in wine."

"Thank you. I appreciate your help."

The wine was good, and Madoc soon ordered a second glass. The bar was getting populated and louder. Several patrons watched a football game on a large screen TV with music replacing the audio of the game. Their table was invaded by two women and the bar manager. Angela introduced Marc, Cindy and Catherine. Catherine, with dark hair, quickly brought the conversation to Madoc. "Hey, I understand you do magic tricks."

Madoc nodded. He didn't like the term magic "tricks" but understood Catherine didn't mean any harm in her question. "Yes, I perform magic."

"Can you do a trick for us? Please?" She gave a pout.

Angela jumped in. "He came to relax, not to do a free show."

Marc added his feelings. "He needs his props. Hard to do tricks unless you're prepared ahead of time."

Madoc frowned. He knew he could back out of doing any magic, but he didn't like it when Marc said he needed props and time to prepare. "Refill my wine glass and I shall do a little magic for you."

For Madoc it was a simple bit of magic. But he knew the electronic noise in the bar would interfere with his ability to do anything complex. Still, he impressed the others when he put a full glass of beer in the centre of the table, covered it with Cindy's jacket, and made the contents disappear. Marc was less pleased as it was his beer that disappeared.

"Can you make it reappear?" Marc picked up his empty glass.

Madoc was enjoying his triumph. "Put the glass back and cover it with the jacket again."

Marc did as was requested and, after Madoc muttered a few phrases, was invited to lift up the coat.

Marc lifted up the coat and looked at the glass now filled with a dark liquid.

"Coffee! You filled my beer glass with damned coffee!"

The others laughed at his look of disbelief.

Traci shook her head. "How in the world did you do that? The coffee is even hot. That was great."

Madoc bowed his head. "Thank you."

Marc was scowling, but a waitress brought him another glass. "Relax. you don't pay for your drinks, anyway."

"Waste of beer."

Angela watched Madoc give the half smile of satisfaction. She thought he would make a great poker player, magic aside, with his ability to hide his feelings. Still, give him a few glasses of wine and have a couple of women fawn over his tricks and he showed a glimpse of his emotions. That was good; she was wondering if he was made of ice sometimes. As she watched him, cool air drifted past her neck. She was getting use to the cool air every time he performed his magic but was getting curious as to its cause. Angela took another drink of her rum and Coke, sucking on the straw slowly. She watched Traci as she draped an arm on his shoulder, trying not to frown.

Madoc noticed the bar had become noisier, though not much louder than the taverns on Domum. The music was something not common in the drinking establishments on Domum, though occasionally there would be a lone singer with a stringed instrument. The singer usually sang songs of great battles or lyrics praising the king or lords. He was quite enjoying the evening and the attention he was receiving, especially from the ladies. The wine was having a mild effect on him, but if he used a simple spell the alcohol's influence would disappear.

Madoc looked around the table and noticed Angela had not returned to the table after going to the washroom. He scanned the bar, looking for her.

———

Angela felt slightly left out as Madoc garnered the attention. She doubted he even noticed when she left for the washroom, and instead of going back to the table, took a detour to the pool tables. She said hi to a couple men she knew as customers waiting to take a turn at a table and found herself talking to Trent. Trent was just over six feet tall, had a heavy build and was approaching forty. He kept his thinning black hair under a Pittsburgh Steelers' baseball cap, complimenting his running shoes, blue jeans and a grey golf shirt.

"Come on, Angel, let's hit another bar."

She shook her head. "No, I'm with some friends here."

"Screw them. You an' me, we can have a good time together." He put a hand on her waist.

"Trent, I'm not leaving with you." She tried to push his hand off her waist, but he was resisting, grinning at her. She looked around for Marc. The bar manager was usually pretty good at spotting trouble, but he had gone back to the kitchen to get a food order straightened out. If she asked for help from the other patrons in the bar, a fight could break out.

"Hey, don't play hard…" Trent stopped speaking and looked behind her.

She was suddenly aware of it too, a power pushing at her. She spun around as Trent's hand fell to his side. Madoc was standing there, fixing his eyes on Trent.

Angela wasn't the focus of Madoc's irritation but there was still a brush of the dark energy radiating toward Trent. She looked at Madoc's eyes; they looked dark and focused at Trent. She turned her attention to Trent, who was taking a step backward. His face had turned pale as he muttered apologies. "Sorry, man, I didn't mean nothin'… sorry…"

"Go!" Madoc pushed the palm of his right hand toward him.

Trent turned and almost ran away, his forehead glistening with sweat.

Angela turned back to Madoc. "What the hell did you do to him?" She reached out and squeezed his hand. "Thanks, but I can handle things myself."

"You're welcome."

"Now tell me what you did there. Something was there, what was it?"

Madoc had hoped Angela wouldn't have felt the brief bit of magic he directed at Trent, but the electronics had caused the aether to dissipate the spell. He scolded himself for overreacting when he saw Trent getting too aggressive with Angela. On Domum a woman could be at risk in a tavern without male protection, but he reminded himself this was Earth with different rules. Though he decided Angela probably could have handled herself on Domum.

"It is difficult to explain."

"Try me."

He sighed. "It was a trick I used to make him believe I was bigger than I was. He became scared, that's all."

"Oh, BS. Tell me the truth or just don't say anything."

He followed her back to the table, wondering if he should say anything. Being told he was a liar didn't sit well with him and he wanted to tell her the truth. Or at least a truth she would accept without giving his true nature away. Madoc took another glass of wine when he sat at the table, pondering his dilemma.

Angela was looking straight ahead, listening to the others talk. Cindy was telling Marc what a jerk Trent could be at times, and though they couldn't see exactly what had happened from the vantage point of their table, they appreciated Madoc had told him off.

"Angela, I'm sorry for interfering with you over there. Where I come from, ladies sometimes need help from unwanted advances. I forgot where I was, and I know you can handle situations yourself."

She tightened her lips, looking slightly mollified. "Okay, apology accepted. But what did you do there?" She looked right at him, challenging him.

Madoc met her eyes. "Mind control. I made him feel fear."

She narrowed her eyes at him. "Like you hypnotized him? Pretty neat trick if you did it that fast."

"It's the best explanation I can give you. I don't know how to explain it otherwise."

"Okay, I believe you. This time."

Madoc and Angela left the bar as two o'clock approached. Angela started her car and looked at him.

"Look, my place is close to here and I'm thinking it would be best if you crashed there. That way I won't have to drive you home and then backtrack to my place. But I don't want you to get the impression there's anything more than a place for you to sleep. Okay?"

"Fine. However, I won't have any trouble finding my own way home."

"Cabs aren't always easy to find at this time. You can sleep on my couch, that's not a problem." Angela gripped the steering wheel tight and, as she noticed Madoc watching her, relaxed her fingers.

He shrugged his shoulders. "Very well."

Her apartment, a six-story affair that at one time might have been for the upward mobility, now looked dated with its pastel sidings but featured rather large suites. A small elevator, an oppressive box that stifled any conversation, reached Angela's fourth floor unit. When the elevator doors opened, Angela let out a torrent of conversation with Madoc quietly following her footsteps.

"My place is a mess. Well, not really a mess but compared to your place it's a little disorganized."

"No need to explain, Angela."

"I know, I know. I just don't want you to think I'm some sort of a slob. I'm not." She dug into her purse for her keys as she stood at her door. "It's a bit untidy, but clean."

"I'm sure it's fine."

The furniture in the apartment wasn't old, most of it purchased only a few years ago. There was a rosy-brown coloured carpet in the living room and tiled floor in the entrance and the kitchen/dining room. The black wood end tables matched the coffee table, covered with magazines, a pocketbook and a pizza box. A can of Coke sat on the floor below a TV.

Angela immediately began to push the magazines into a single pile. "Sorry, I guess it is a bit of a..."

He touched her arm, causing her to stop. "It's not necessary to put everything away. Your home is meant to give you comfort, not to cause you distress."

"Okay, it's just that..."

He leaned forward and kissed her gently on the lips. Angela gasped for a moment and wrapped her arms around his neck and kissed him back.

———

She felt awkward in the morning, planning to arise early, fixing herself up and making him tea and breakfast. Instead she slept in until almost eight and found he had already made tea. What was even worse he was relaxing in the living room reading one of her magazines, Cosmopolitan, with the front cover offering to reveal several new sexual positions.

She said hello quickly, and almost ran into the bathroom where she studied a worried face and messed up hair in the mirror.

"Damn, damn, double damn!" She muttered under her breath. "I better get my act together. He must think the world of me now."

Madoc looked unperturbed as she bolted from the bathroom wearing a towel to the bedroom again to get dressed. When she emerged from the bedroom in a pair of black jeans and a short pale yellow T-shirt he stood waiting for her with a mug of tea. "I believe you prefer a scoop of white sugar in your tea." He extended the mug toward her.

"Thanks." She took the mug with a shake of her hand.

"Are you all right?" He peered at her, his forehead creasing in concern.

"Yes. No. That is, I'm physically all right. Other than the hangover." She studied the tea in her mug. "But, I think you think that I...that I'm..."

"Why don't we sit down in the living room?"

She allowed him to lead her to the couch where she sat rigid with the tea mug wrapped in both hands.

"Now, tell me what you believe I'm thinking."

She sighed. "I didn't ask you to stay here tonight to go to bed with you. That just happened. I had too much to drink and I really like you, and I was miffed at the other girls in the bar for flirting with you, and when I get upset and angry I drink too much, and then I do something stupid..."

He held up a hand. "Please, I'd prefer to think you being angry and under the influence of drink wasn't the only reason you slept with me. I think you're an extraordinary woman."

She blinked her eyes at him. "Really? You think I'm extraordinary?"

"I said so, didn't I?"

She punched him on his shoulder. "Then why didn't you say so before I got all upset at you in the bar?"

"I didn't have the right opportunity."

"Lousy answer."

He sighed. "Is there no pleasing you?"

"Breakfast. I'm hungry. Do you want me to make something or do you want to go out to eat?"

He cast a glance at her kitchen where several dishes waited in the sink. "Allow me to buy you breakfast."

She grabbed her purse and opened the door. "That's a smart choice."

Angela chatted as she drove down the quiet streets. "I just wish guys would say how they feel. Like, it's not just you not letting me know how you felt about me but men in general just figure the girl is supposed to know."

Madoc was quiet as he listened to her but finally spoke. "But you didn't tell me how you felt. Perhaps we're both guilty of hiding our feelings."

"No way." She shook her head. "It's in the rules. Guy has to chase the girl and has to express his affection for her first."

He tilted his head as he looked at her. "What rules are those? I've never heard or seen any such rules."

She parked the car. "Trust me, they exist. But only women get to make them up and we only tell them to men when we see fit." She jumped out of her car and waited for him as he slowly exited.

"Such a set of rules could only lead to confusion."

She smiled as she took his arm. "Then you better stick with me so you won't be so confused."

Madoc poked at his fried eggs with suspicion as they sat in Turk's Grill. "These eggs are certainly well-cooked."

"You should've ordered the pancakes. They're good." She shovelled a fork into her mouth, the pancake dripping with syrup.

"Perhaps you're right. After we finish breakfast, it might be best if we go to my residence so I can change."

"Sure. Say, how long have you thought of me as an extraordinary woman?" She grinned at him and took a drink of her coffee.

He stared at her before answering. "I'm not sure of the exact moment but it was early in our business relationship."

"Business relationship?" She giggled. "I love the way you talk."

At Madoc's apartment Angela followed him into the suite and

plopped herself on the couch while he entered the bedroom to change. She kicked off her shoes and sprawled out on the couch, yelling at the ceiling as she talked to him.

"Hey, are we hanging out together today? Or do you have something you have to do today by yourself?"

"Hanging out?" A pause. "If you mean if we can spend time together today that would be fine with me."

She got up off the couch, laughing. "You really should get a TV so you would learn how to speak here." She moved to the cabinet sitting in the corner of the living room. Two books lay on top, a finished book on Shakespeare and a paperback version of *Moby Dick* with a bookmark inserted near the middle. The door on the lower part of the cabinet was ajar, and she swung it open. She pulled out a large leather-bound book, the pages inside cut unevenly along the sides. It looked to her like a book made a few hundred years ago, although the paper didn't feel or look old. Inside the words had been written out by hand with the few diagrams similarly drawn. She couldn't decipher the words, but after studying them a short time, decided it appeared to be Latin.

Difixus meus sententia quod meus visum
Ut ego animadverto aedificium edificium superstes
Permissus thine fulmen intra thine saxum atque materia
Exsisto privatus super meus ut energia.
Verto firmus tergum in navitas
Quod planto in aedificium edificium abolesco.

Angela began to read the words out loud, seeing if sounding them out might reveal their meaning.

Madoc ran out of the bedroom without his shirt on. "Stop! Halt at once!" He reached out and tore the book from the grasp of a startled Angela. "You must not finish that spell...that is, sentence, that is..."

FOURTEEN

"Spell? That's a book of spells?" She looked at him and at the book. "Are you saying these are actual spells that do magic?" She took a step back from him. "Do you use those spells in your magic shows?"

He held up his hand. "Please, don't be frightened. These spells may not work here and you're unlikely to be able to incite them."

"But you use those spells in the shows?"

Madoc thought for a moment. Lying now would be too transparent, and his reputation on Domum demanded he always told the truth. "Yes, that is true."

She took another step back from him and deeper into the living room. Angela looked around the room, looking for either a weapon or a way to escape.

Madoc frowned while taking a step toward her. "Angela, try to …"

"Stay back! I—I know how to fight." She raised one fist in the air and tried to assume a threatening pose by jamming one leg in front on the other.

"Oh, dragon's breath. What do you think I'm going to do?"

"I don't know. I found out you use real magic, and you'd want to keep me silent."

"I doubt a dozen gags could keep you quiet." He sighed. "Look, if you want to leave, leave. No one will believe you I use real spells. But if you want to wait here while I resume dressing, we can then go for a walk and I'll explain a few things to you."

She considered his offer for a few seconds. "Okay, I guess I can do that. You're not trying to trick me, are you? Because if you are…"

"I'm not trying to trick you." Madoc returned to his bedroom, carrying the book.

"You better not." She watched him disappear into the bedroom. "Hey! What do you mean a dozen gags couldn't keep me quiet? That is so untrue! I mean, I can be quiet if I want to."

They walked down the block toward where a Starbucks Coffee Shop was located.

"So you say you're from Domum?"

"Yes, it's a world smaller than Earth but has many of the same features. It lies on a parallel plane with Earth but to travel to it requires special knowledge."

"And real magic exists there?"

"As well as here. It's just magic is much more prevalent there, partly because of knowledge and partly because of the lack of interference with the aether there by electrical devices."

"Oh. Is that why you don't have a TV?"

"It's a good enough reason. Though being honest, I'm not sure of the fascination with it. What I would really like to have is a device that plays music but that gives off too much electrical noise."

She walked with him without speaking for a few minutes then spoke again. "So, what is your plan? Are you planning to go back to Daman…?"

"Domum."

"Domum then. Were you planning to tell me when and if?"

"Please don't take it personal…"

"Personal! We slept together last night! You, you, you just suddenly disappear off the face of the Earth and I'm not supposed to take it personal?"

He took a deep breath. "Allow me to try again. I was ordered exiled to Earth and I now await a signal allowing my return. It may come tomorrow. It may never come. Yesterday, if the signal arrived, I would have told you I would not be returning. Now, well, let us just say things have changed between us. Please understand Domum is my home. It is where I live. Here on Earth I only exist."

"You haven't given Earth a chance yet. You're trying to live as if you're still on Domum."

He considered her words. "Perhaps you're right."

"You know I am! You're scared if you get too comfortable here the signal will never arrive. Newsflash: that signal is going to come whether you're happy here or not."

"All right, I understand your point."

"Good. Now tell me all about Domum. What kind of shopping can you do there?"

It was Madoc's first cup of coffee. He was startled by the taste and tried to subdue it by copious amounts of sugar and milk. Angela laughed as she drank hers black.

"I suppose it's an acquired taste."

"A lot of things here are. Want to share a bear claw?"

He stared at her.

"It's a pastry." She grinned and got up from their table and went back to the counter. When she returned, she gave him half of the pastry on a plate.

"I love these things."

"They're rather sweet."

"I have a sweet tooth. Tell me, on Domum where do you live? In a castle?"

"I have more than one place of residence. And yes, one of them is a castle, though a modest one."

"A modest castle? Is there such a thing?"

He frowned. "I assure you while I have considerable wealth on Domum I do not flaunt it." He paused and tore a chunk of pastry from the bear claw. "Besides, one doesn't taunt fate by having a castle that rivals royalty."

Angela giggled. "So you could afford a bigger castle but don't want to make the king mad?"

"Not just the king. There are his lords one has to consider. Besides, outside appearances can be deceiving. The interior of my castle has more to it than would be indicated from looking from the outside."

"Secret rooms?"

"I suppose you could say that."

"I'd love to see it. Take me when you go back? Just to visit I mean."

"If it's possible. I may never have a chance to go back."

"Come on, be positive." She touched his arm and gave him a smile.

Angela still wasn't sure if she believed him. True, there was the issue of the magic spells. It appeared he really did use magic spells. Either that or her imagination had gotten the better of her. But even if he could do some real magic spells, it was a big jump he came from another world. She decided real magic did exist, and he'd found a way to tap into it. As far as the world of Domum was concerned, maybe he was just a nut case. But now at least she didn't feel she was in danger being with him and last night had changed their relationship.

"Tell me how magic works for you but not for others." She slipped her hand in his arm as they returned to his apartment.

"Magic." He considered the subject before continuing. "Magic is the ability of focusing one's mind to alter objects. All objects, all matter is composed of the same very small particles. The particles are just arranged differently to give different characteristics."

"You mean particles like atoms or molecules?"

He shook his head. "No, these particles are much smaller than that, much smaller. They're actually not really particles but bundles of energy that act like particles."

"How do you know that if they're so small?"

"This information was passed down by the ancients, but I have used magic to amplify their size to the point where I can see them. What appears to a solid surface is actually a collection of vibrating points of energy."

"Okay, so how does magic fit in here? You think and presto! The magic changes things?"

"A mind has much energy but most of it is uncontrolled. I, and others, have learned to focus a wave of energy at these energy particles to cause them to vibrate differently and thus change their composition. When one says certain phrases, it helps focus the proper energy of the mind."

"That book of spells."

"Correct. The other thing is one cannot have any doubt the magic will work, or it will fail."

"You mean even if I said the right words and concentrated real hard, I couldn't do magic if I didn't believe it would?"

"That is correct."

"So why were you so upset when I was reading out loud your spell book? I didn't believe or even know what would happen."

"Ah, but I did. Just hearing those words could cause my mind to focus enough there was danger to both of us."

"What was the spell I was reading going to do?"

"An explosion of energy is the simplest way of describing it. The apartment building would have ceased to exist."

"Oh. Hey, how come there's this blast of cool air after your magic tricks?"

"Magic takes energy. I borrow the energy from the air around us and it sinks down. The easiest magic is to make ice out of water as one simply pulls energy out of it and places it somewhere else."

"Oh. Can you teach me to do magic?"

"I can try. But it takes a lot of practice and, like I said, a belief that you can. To do what I do takes decades of study and work, plus an inborn ability to manipulate magic. I am what is called a warlock and my power frightens even lords on Domum. Hence my exile here."

"You're a warlock?"

"Yes. Please don't jump to conclusions. A warlock on Domum may not mean exactly the same thing on Earth."

"Meaning you're not an evil demon bent on taking over the world." She laughed. "I feel better already."

Madoc sighed. "Angela, I'm trying my best to explain to you who I am. I hope you understand I'm also trying to adapt to your world."

"Like drinking coffee? Since you're living here, it's not just my world but yours too." She reached for his hand. "We can share it together."

"Maybe we can," he replied.

As they walked, she asked him what a warlock did mean on Domum.

He considered her question for a moment before answering. "A warlock on Domum means a witch who does not belong to the main coven of witches. The witches are a guild on Domum and have a strict code that governs their use of magic. I refuse to follow their laws for a variety of reasons. One is simply because I will use black magic against those who threaten me. Due to the nature of my work, there are some who will use whatever means to discredit me. I am sometimes forced to use methods to defend myself."

"So because you will use black magic you are a warlock?"

"On Domum, yes. Here on Earth it means something different."

They reached his apartment and Angela proceeded ahead of him. "How come you never lock your door? Aren't you scared someone will come in and steal your stuff?"

"No one will enter while I'm gone. I've placed a spell on the apartment preventing unwelcome guests from entering."

"What happens if they do?"

"They cannot. They become too physically ill to enter."

"What happens if I try to enter while you're gone?"

"Nothing. If you don't intend me any harm, there won't be any effect on you."

She shook her head. "Quite the burglar alarm you have there."

She waltzed into the living room, spun on her heel and turned to face him. "So now you have told me everything, does that change our relationship?"

"I believe you are making a presumption I've told you everything. Domum is a much more complex world than I can describe in a few sentences, and there is more to myself as well."

"Oops, sorry, I didn't mean it that way. I meant now that I know you're from Domum."

He bowed his head slightly. "Apology accepted."

"Good. Our relationship?"

"As in our magic show? Or between us?"

"Both. Jeez, Madoc, do you think just maybe I see you differently now and wonder if you do the same?"

"I suppose you do. I don't see you any differently. I would still like to work with you and get to know you better."

"It's like pulling teeth to get you men to say something half-ass sensitive. Thank you, that's all I wanted you to say."

He resisted giving a sigh. "I believe I shall make myself some bread and cheese. Would you care for some?"

"Bread and cheese? Is that some kind of Domum delicacy? Sure, I'll have a bite."

Madoc went to the kitchen. He unwrapped a French loaf and

began to cut off thick slices. He heard Angela walk around the dining and living room opening and closing drawers and doors of various tables and cabinets. "What're you looking for, Angela?"

"Nothing. Just snooping."

Madoc took a block of cheese out of the fridge and returned to the table where the bread was. "I don't have much for you to pry into and some objects you won't be able to find any discernable use for."

"I know. That's what makes it fun."

Madoc frowned. If anyone else was poking around his belongings, he knew he would be upset, but somehow, she managed to make it seem fairly benign. He began the task of cutting up the cheese.

"What's this thing?" She entered the kitchen holding up a flat piece of crystal. "It's blinking off and on like it's an alarm or something."

The knife fell from his hand, clattering on the table as he watched the crystal flash a red glow. He slowly drew a long breath and whispered. "It's the signal. I'm being summoned."

FIFTEEN

Marisa looked at Gilbert crouched with his sword held high and at the front of their tent where the canvas flap was slowly pulled to the side.

The outline of a clawed hand held the edge of the canvas flap and two yellow eyes peered into the darkness. The black dots in the centre of the eye weaved back-and-forth searching, and suddenly the tent flap was closed, leaving Marisa and Gilbert alone in the darkness.

Marisa released her breath. "What was that?"

"Damn gnants. Theys better stay aways." He slowly lowered his sword. "Gilbert no likes thems prowling arounds."

Marisa fell back on her back. "Whatever. As long as they stay away so I can get some sleep." She closed her eyes for a few seconds and opened them again. Gilbert was still staring at the front of the tent. "Are you going to just sit all night looking for gnants?"

"Maybe."

"Don't be stu...so, so protective. Lie down and go to sleep."

Gilbert glanced at her and slowly reclined.

"I's will sleep lightly."

A few minutes later, his snoring kept Marisa awake.

In the morning, Gilbert looked for tracks and disturbed vegetation around the campsite.

Marisa finished packing her belongings into her backpack. "See anything?"

"Nothin'." He began to roll up the string tied around the front of the tent. "Just some marks in the mud."

"Footprints?"

"Claw marks. Demon gnants, no doubts."

"I think they're just curious, Gilbert."

"Maybe yes, maybe no. I's don'ts like taking chances."

They continued their journey, not sure if they were being followed. Gilbert and Marisa occasionally looked for anything following them, but there wasn't any telltale sign of pursuit. That meant nothing to Gilbert who challenged Marisa to prove they weren't being followed.

"They's sneaky, clever demons. Maybe they makes themselves invisible."

She rolled her eyes skyward. "Gilbert, then we might as well be worried about being followed by ghosts."

"Ghosts! Didja see something?" He whirled around looking into the vegetation.

"No, of course not. Stop being so paranoid. And put your sword away before you hurt yourself."

He slowly slipped his sword back into its sleeve. "I's ready to fight yous. Best stay aways," he called out to the bushes and slowly resumed his walk.

The sun raised the temperature quickly in the morning under a clear sky. Gilbert grumbled how hot it was and wished he had a cold ale.

Marisa, for the most part, followed just behind him, knowing Gilbert liked to be in the lead. It didn't bother her too much; she was taller and could still see past him as they walked. He didn't keep a straight path, weaving around the small plants and tree-like bushes.

A low groaning noise broke the silence of their walk. Gilbert immediately fell to the ground, pulling out his sword as he did so. Marisa didn't react as fast, casually dropping to one knee with her hand on the hilt of her own sword.

"What made that noise, Gilbert?"

"A monster of some sort, ye cans be sure of that."

"Okay. What kind of monster?" She stood up and looked

around. "That sound seemed to come from that direction. I'm going to take a look."

"You'll get eaten!"

"I'll be careful. We need to find out what it is."

"I goes with ya." Gilbert crouched behind Marisa as she slowly made her way to the top of a small rise. After a minute, he summoned up his courage. "Waits, Marisa. I's should be the one leadings."

She stopped and turned, watching him nervously take the lead.

The low rumbling growl caused him to freeze as lupus dragons circled overhead. The lupus dragons circled once more and departed, flying in a single file away from Gilbert and Marisa and the noise.

"Whatever is making that noise was able to scare off those lupus dragons."

"Ye speaks true." He took a big gulp of water. "Stays here. Gilbert will 'vestigate."

She noticed his hand trembled as he replaced the cap of the water skin. "I better go with you in case you get in trouble."

"Nay. I's be safer by meself. Troy be most upset if ye got killed." He paused. "If I's not come back, you go and tell Lord Troy that Gilbert died bravely." Gilbert crawled over the rise and slowly disappeared as he made his way toward where the growl had come from.

Marisa sat on the ground and waited. She knew Gilbert was right about being safer by himself. He knew how to remain undetected as he moved between bushes and rocks. She was tempted to look over the rise herself, but if whatever was out there spotted her then Gilbert would be in danger.

Minutes passed. Marisa shifted position on the ground, wondering how Gilbert was doing. She began to consider how long she should wait before investigating and, regardless of what he indicated, she wouldn't abandon him. Gilbert was clearly frightened by the prospect of investigating the growling and she admired his courage in going forth.

"I's back!"

She grinned at him as he sneaked back to their side of the rise. "What did you find out?"

"Biggest dragon me ever see! It be huge, bigger than a fornido dragon."

Marisa wondered if Gilbert was exaggerating. The fornido dragon was the largest of the dragons, greatly feared solitary hunters. Marisa had seen one only once, and even at a distance it had made the hair on her arms stand on end.

The monster was over fifty feet long with a head too big even for its huge size. The oversized wings supported the weight the blue body with yellow and red markings on its skin. The sight of it gave her nightmares afterward.

"How big is it?"

"Come see." Gilbert had a smile on his face.

She crawled after him and stopped with him behind a tree-like plant. She peered past him at a dragon squatting on its four legs as it ate. The dragon wasn't quite as long a fornido dragon; the tail wasn't as long as the fornido's, looking short and stubby in comparison. However, what the dragon lacked in length it made up with an enormous girth, looking like a huge football with a neck and tail. The dragon was dull in colouring, sporting mostly brown and yellow except for its head, which was dull green. The head of the dragon was about eight feet long, about the same length as its neck, and it was attacking plants. The great jaw opened and locked on one of the tree-like plants, shook it free of the ground, and began the slow munch of the whole plant.

"It's a plant eater!"

"You be right. Instead of using dragon fire to break down flesh, it uses fire to dissolve plants."

She nodded, considering it made sense in a way. The acid of the two glands making up the dragon's fire might also be used to break down the tough fibre of the plants. The huge stomach would allow for more time to reduce the whole plant for digestion. "I would guess it can't fly even though those wings are pretty big."

"True. I's saw it spread its wings once; they too small to lift it. Maybe use it to scare off lupus dragons."

"I doubt it can even walk very fast. Of course, with its size I'll bet it doesn't have to worry much anything attacking it. That has to be the biggest and ugliest dragon I've ever seen."

They made a wide circle around the dragon, not wanting to test the creature's mobility in case it did notice them and continued their journey.

Marisa and Gilbert looked behind occasionally but the gnants seemed to have lost interest in them. The plant life didn't change much, continuing with clumps of the multi-coloured leaves. Among the plants, small rodents scurried about.

Marisa's long legs allowed her to keep up with Gilbert easily, but he did appear to be tireless. His stride might be small, but he made up for his constant pace and he never stopped to rest.

"Gilbert, why don't we take a break? I'll make something to eat out of the provisions."

He continued to walk. "A bits more, Marisa. I's wants to gets to the top of that hill." He pointed at a close by hill. "I's wants to take a looks around theres."

———

Marisa put some cheese between slices of dark bread as Gilbert scanned the horizon. She watched him survey the landscape and stood staring at one area in particular.

She handed him the sandwich and followed his gaze. "What are you looking at? Something wrong?"

He shook his head as he took a bite of the sandwich, looking deep in thought.

"What aren't you telling me?"

Reluctantly he pointed at a patch of land looking similar to the rest of the countryside except it rose slightly higher. A small stream cut through it as it wiggled its way to the river. "That area there's where Vegrandis used to sit. I's wondering how Donna is doing." His voice had a strain to it.

Marisa nodded as she put her hand on his shoulder. "We can only hope for the best, Gilbert, and carry on with our task." She walked a short distance away and sat down to rest, giving him some privacy with his thoughts. She knew Gilbert didn't like to reveal much about himself but must have felt burdened with the knowledge he had a part in the destruction of their old world.

———

The river running through the centre of Horstruff looked to be exactly the same in this new world. On closer inspection, Marisa and Gilbert noticed the water was cleaner and with fewer debris floating along. In the water they also noticed the foot long water dragons. Water dragons were rarely seen in the river that ran through Horstruff. The creatures spent almost their whole life in water though they still could move about land on their webbed paws and using their lungs. Their wings, however had become stunted and used like fins in moving about the water.

"When are we going to swim across?"

"In the mornin'. Let's catch some fishes for dinner in the means time."

———

Marisa woke up first and stuck her head out of the tent flap to peer around. A rustling noise in among the densely packed plants drew her attention, but she didn't see anything. She assumed it might be a gnant watching them but wasn't too concerned. She looked back in the tent at the still form of Gilbert and decided she wouldn't tell him about it as he tended to be a bit paranoid about the creatures.

She put a few dry stems and leaves from the plants in the same blackened pit where they had made a small fire to cook the fish the previous night. Marisa collected a few stumps and broken limbs of the tree-like plants near the tent, picking them up reluctantly with her fingers. The fibrous limbs and stumps were much lighter and porous than normal wood, inviting insects and worms to live in and devour the interior. She shook one of the stumps loose, sending a shower of small creatures tumbling to the ground. She grimaced at a couple of pale lime green worms that fell and curled into the vegetation below.

A few minutes later, she had the various pieces set in the fire pit. The next step was to wake up Gilbert, needing his expertise in magic to make the fire actually work. Dry, real wood she could have handled by herself, but this vegetation normally would have made any flame sputter and die.

After tea, Gilbert stood by the river and stared at the far shore.

"See anything?"

He shook his head. "Nay. We might as well gets started."

Gilbert tied a rope around the canvas bag holding their tent, tying the other end around his waist. He stuffed his sandals in his backpack and made his way to the edge of the river.

"Are you going to swim like that?"

"Sures. How else do I's gets this stuff across?"

"I mean you're going to wear your pants and shirt? Wouldn't it be better if you took them off?"

"Too much trouble. See yous on other side, last one across has dragon's breath." He jumped in the water and began to swim across with a great deal of splashing.

Marisa shook her head and proceeded to take off her clothes, rolling them up carefully before putting them into her own backpack. Wearing only her backpack she slid into the water and with barely a ripple made her way across.

Gilbert continued to splash as he swam. At the halfway point he saw her backpack float past him. He looked again and tried make out her body under the water. A moment later, her head broke the surface. She gave him a quick smile and disappeared under the water again. Gilbert tried to catch her, increasing his efforts. When he reached the three-quarter mark of the river, he heard her call out to him.

"Hurry up, dragon breath!"

He looked at the shore. A naked Marisa with water gleaming on her skin was standing, waving at him. Gilbert stopped swimming as he looked at her and dropped under the water. Moments later, he came up sputtering and coughing before resuming his journey.

"If I's wasn't pulling the tent."

"Don't make me laugh. I can swim circles around you."

She lay on the ground, letting the sun dry her as Gilbert stood behind a large plant trying to squeeze water out of his pants and shirt. Marisa's clothes were only slightly damp in areas and she spread them out.

Marisa was torn between laughing at Gilbert when he disappeared under the water when he saw her on the shore and rescuing him. When he came up a few seconds later, she decided to hold back her laughter lest he got upset with her again. Gilbert didn't want to let her see him undressed, but she didn't have any qualms about letting him look at her as she took in the sun. In a way, she was flattered she could distract him so easily. She noticed Gilbert had chosen a plant to hide behind but still afforded him a view of her. She decided not to make a big deal about it.

Eventually, Gilbert got his clothes dry enough to the point where he could wear them again.

"You should have rolled them into your backpack like I did."

"Maybe yes." He watched her as she put on her skirt. "If yours clothes still damp, you cans leaves thems off as we walk."

She looked at him. "You want me to walk naked while you hid behind a plant when you took off your shirt? How very generous of you."

"Just a suggestion."

"And not a very good one." She put on her blouse.

Marisa followed Gilbert although she knew the destination, the point opposite of the gnant's temple-like giant hut. He would frown if she stayed too long in front of him and eventually scold her for being disobedient. Gilbert was right about one thing; the gnants hadn't crossed the river to follow them and didn't seem to be anywhere in sight on this side of the river. Of course, she knew they might just be hiding among the plants, but it seemed more likely they preferred the other side of the river.

"Marisa." His voice was low.

"What?"

"We be followed."

She looked around but didn't see anything. "Are you sure?"

"Sure. Far back, on our sides. They not gnants."

"Dragons?"

"Don'ts know, hard to see them."

"Do you think they're dangerous?"

"Maybe, maybe not. Gilbert don'ts like being followed."

"So what do we do?"

"We walks towards river; maybe it don't likes water." He paused as he looked behind them again. "We be all right, Marisa."

Marisa trailed after him, noting Gilbert had increased his pace considerably.

SIXTEEN

"Summoned for what?" Angela looked again at the crystal as it blinked off and on. "Domum?"

"Perhaps. The signal was generated by Gordon Miller. He owns the castle in Ireland I told you about."

"The counterpart on Earth?"

"Correct. He was kind enough to promise me to send a signal if he heard any news from Domum he deemed important."

"So now what?"

"I will have to transport myself to Ireland and see what Gordon Miller needs to talk to me about."

"Transport yourself to Ireland? You can do that?"

"It will be difficult; I will have to meditate and focus to use my magic for such a distance. It is also tiring, so I will need rest afterward."

"So, you are going to transport yourself just to see what this Gordon Miller wants?"

"Yes."

"And it's difficult to do?"

He nodded. "Greater distances require greater use of energy."

"Okay then, if you just need to talk to Gordon Miller why don't you just use the phone?"

"The phone?"

She pointed toward the living room. "That thing sitting on the table you sometimes unplug. It does have its uses."

He stared where she pointed. "But I don't know how to reach him using the phone."

"Well, aren't you lucky I'm here because I do."

"You can do that?"

"Believe me if there's one thing this girl can do its use a phone. Watch and learn." She paused. "It strange using a land line phone. I just have a mobile."

Angela pressed the zero button on the phone, getting the operator to connect her to Gordon Miller in Ireland.

"Here, I got him online." Angela passed the phone over to Madoc.

"Mr. Gordon Miller?"

Angela walked over to the couch and sat down, listening to Madoc's side of the conversation. Eventually, he hung up and turned toward her.

"Well?"

"It appears Domum has changed or perhaps vanished." He closed his eyes for a moment. "I now will have to go to Ireland to investigate what happened."

"What do you mean Domum disappeared?"

"I don't fully understand it myself, but Gordon Miller informed me when he viewed Domum through his special apparatus, he saw a very different world than the one I left."

"Maybe he wasn't seeing Domum or made a mistake."

"Perhaps, but he assured me there was little possibility of that."

"So you're going to Ireland to do what? If Domum doesn't exist what's the point?"

"I don't know if there's anything I can do. Regardless, I have to investigate myself."

"When are you going?"

"In the morn. In the meantime, I'll have to prepare as if I'm not returning." He studied Angela's face for a moment. "I'm sorry, Angela. I do not have a choice in the matter. If Domum is in danger, I must do what I can regardless of my own personal preferences."

She bit off her first retort before it left her lips. She looked away and stared back at him. "Take me with you."

He hesitated before he spoke again. "Are you sure that's wise? You have a life here and I cannot assure you of when you may return-if you can return."

"It may not be wise, but it's what I want to do."

"Domum is froth with danger, in particular for women. I cannot in good conscience assure you I will be able to protect you if you're thinking I can take you there. You may wish to reconsider your decision."

"I still want to go."

He bowed his head. "Then I concede to your request."

The next morning, he prepared a small breakfast and once again asked her if she still wanted to go with him. Her answer didn't waver and soon he prepared to teleport them to the Miller Castle.

Teleportation wasn't at all what she expected. She supposed she had a vision of Scotty pulling some lever and she would dissolve in a cloud of light and reappear. Angela watched as Madoc wrapped his arms around her and spoke Latin phrases as he concentrated, his eyes focused far away. The world around them became hazy and transparent. Slowly they began to drift across the room, passing through a table and an outside wall. Their speed began to increase and within a few seconds the world around them became a blur, the colours muted in their transparency as they raced across the city and the countryside.

Angela clung to Madoc as they reached the coastline and passed over the water. She didn't feel the wind as they crossed the ocean, but she could smell the salty, wet air. When she looked down, she noticed they had risen several dozen feet above the water but didn't feel any push against her feet. It was like floating in the air only at a high speed. From what she could tell, their speed was increasing; they caught up to and left a cruise ship behind in mere seconds. In fact, the ocean itself was becoming a blur and when she looked up at the clouds flying behind them it was like watching a high-speed film.

Minutes later, the ocean changed to the brown and green ground of Ireland. Angela noticed their speed not only began to slow down, but their path curved over the countryside, as if Madoc was searching for a landmark. The ground was a blur as they travelled but she perceived a reduction in speed as they weaved their way toward Ballymiller.

They finally came to a stop just outside of the Miller Castle, standing in the back yard. Angela felt dizzy as she stood on the grass, holding on to Madoc's arm for support. She also felt odd in a way she couldn't explain.

"I feel kind of strange."

"I know."

"Really weird. Like, like I'm hollow or something."

"I know. It'll pass in a few seconds."

"Are you sure? Because I feel really…" It hit her like a jolt of electricity, making her knees buckled for a moment. Suddenly, she felt normal again. "What the hell was that?"

"Your soul. It took a few seconds to catch up to us."

"My soul? You mean…"

"There was nothing to worry about. Your soul will always find you and always knows where you are. It just can't travel quite as we do." He gestured toward the back door of the castle. "Shall we proceed?"

She stepped toward the door. "You should have warned me about this soul thing. What if it got lost? Then what would happen to me? Did you think of that?"

"That would not have happened." He knocked on the door. "Trust me. I'll make you aware if you're going into a dangerous situation."

Gordon Miller opened the door and ushered them in, rambling about what may have happened to Domum.

Madoc listened patiently and surmised they still didn't have enough facts to determine what happened. "I will review all the details later, but perhaps you will allow me a rest. The transportation to here is rather taxing."

"Of course, of course. You may use my room. It has a comfortable bed but also there is little natural light in it."

While Madoc rested, Angela introduced herself to the others, which included Jon, Liz besides Gordon Miller. She found them easy to converse. She indicated to them Madoc and her were more than just friends.

Less than an hour later, the group sat near the fireplace in the living room. Gordon Miller decided to light the fire to remove the chill in the evening air. He chose a large wingback chair closest to the fire while Liz and Jon shared the loveseat. Madoc, after having a short rest and a bite to eat, joined the others. He sat in an armchair next to Angela faced toward the coffee table. The chairs were of mixed design, some leather-covered while others sported a dark cloth covering. The one common theme to them was their large size and swallowed up their occupants save for Jon.

Angela noted everyone seemed to act like old friends though Madoc also held their respect and they referred to him as Council Madoc. It was explained to her it was a title he used on Domum that implied he was a gentleman who gave advice to the wealthy and lords. She also became aware his manner of dress which seemed so odd back home looked appropriate in the dark, cool interior of the castle. He also seemed to gain strength and power in his new surroundings.

Angela noted how Liz clung to Jon on the loveseat but wasn't sporting an engagement ring. It appeared to her Liz expected Jon to propose soon and part of her display of affection to him was to warn her he was taken. Madoc was not entirely ignoring Angela but was obviously concentrating on Gordon Miller's narrative as he stumbled through sequence of events leading to him sending out the emergency signal to Madoc.

Gordon had supplied refreshments of tea and an assortment of crackers and cheese that Jon consumed half by himself. After the tea was finished, they proceeded to the upstairs laboratory where Jon helped Gordon turn on the apparatus. The equipment came slowly to life as switches were flicked on; lights flickered from red to yellow to green and the humming noise increased.

Angela stood well away from heavy wood tables, not sure of the safety of the equipment. Liz slowly walked over and joined her.

"When it works, it gives quite a view of another world."

"Did you travel to Domum?"

"Yeah, I was stuck there for a few months. It was quite an adventure."

"I'll bet." She watched Jon as he calibrated an oscilloscope displaying a waving green line slowly coming to a stop. "Things pretty serious between you and Jon?"

"Pretty serious. Are you and Council Madoc partners?"

"No, at least not yet. He doesn't reveal his feelings easily."

"No, that's not his style. Be careful, he wants to return to Domum as soon as he's allowed."

"I know. I told him I'd like to visit Domum."

"If you were with him, I'd guess you'd be safe. Myself, I've had enough of it to last me a while."

"Is it dangerous?"

"Depends on where you are. In the town of Horstruff it's safe enough but outside of the town you can encounter dragons and some rather nasty characters."

"We have a picture!" Jon called out to the two women.

Angela peered at the monitor. The image wavered occasionally and seemed more in focus in the middle than the edges. The view appeared to be from the window of the castle and looked down at a distance at the surrounding landscape. Mud huts dominated the centre of the picture with green, yellow and red coloured plants filling in the open areas. Taller plants shaped much as trees intermingled between the huts and the smaller plants. What gave Angela a start were the creatures walking among the huts. From a distance, they looked vaguely like skinny chimpanzees though with less hair. Their faces had human-like features but with elf ears and large hooked noses.

"What are those things?"

Madoc answered. "Gnants. They coexist with people on Domum to some degree. That is, in the old Domum."

"What do you think happened here?" Jon pointed at the mud huts. "This Domum looks like people never existed on it."

Madoc frowned. "That may be exactly what has happened. The why or how is the unknown."

"I'm receiving a warning light. I'm afraid I must shut down the equipment for a period to allow it to cool off." Gordon toggled several switches, and the equipment came to a whining close. "I've thought of a theory, well, actually a couple of theories, why we're seeing a different Domum. If you wish, perhaps I could elaborate on them."

"Please, if you have some information on what has happened to my world."

"First, we may be looking at your Domum, that is the Domum you're familiar with, but in the far past or the far future. Earth and Domum may have come out of sync along a time line and are no longer tied with each other. We'd need to look at Domum's night sky to verify this possibility of course.

"Another possibility is this Domum has changed because of magic induced changes affecting its past leading to this situation. However, this could also be a natural occurring event; one would have to assume then it could happen on Earth as well. There is no evidence for or against this theory, as our memories would be changed as well.

"One last possibility is this Domum is not the one you came from. We may have several Domums, and therefore Earths, and one Domum will at times take precedence over another in relation to our Earth. Over time, the original Domum may return in contact."

Madoc stood silently as he looked from Gordon, to the now dark monitor, and back to Gordon. "Is there a way of determining which possibility is the right one?"

"Well, the time theory could be easily verified by checking the position of stars against records I have of them from several months ago. You see, I took photographs of the images of Domum when I first…"

"Uncle Gordon what about the other possibilities?" Jon sensed his uncle was about to go on a long trajectory from the original conversation.

"Oh, of course. The theory of several Domums and as a consequence of the theory, several Earths… how many would be hard to determine."

"Uncle Gordon?"

"Oh, yes. The multi-world theory is legitimate, basically an offshoot from quantum mechanics. One theory is every time a choice can be made, whether on the subatomic level or on the human conscious level, both can occur and the universe splits so each choice exists. But such a theory also prohibits ever seeing or visiting such a world."

"So maybe that theory isn't so good?" Liz spoke up.

Gordon thought for several seconds. "No, it doesn't appear to meet our parameters. Still, it is a good theory."

"But not maybe for us. What about the theory of magic and what did you say? Something about a new world happening on its own and giving us new memories as well?"

Gordon frowned. "I have to say I'm not too fond of that theory. You see if we want to push such a theory to the extreme, we could say we only have a false memory of Domum, including Council Madoc believing he used to live there."

"So that leaves magic as our culprit?" Liz looked at Madoc.

Madoc nodded. "I suppose it might be possible to use magic, but it would require the use of a specific device. Certain gems and crystals have extraordinary power to alter reality. But why someone would initiate such a spell is beyond comprehension."

Gordon summed up the situation. "It appears none of the theories are entirely satisfactory. However, one of them must lead us to the truth and it may well be someone has used magic to create this new Domum."

Madoc took a drink of wine before continuing. They had retired back downstairs to discuss what to do next. "I suppose I'm inclined to support Sir Jon's proposition reluctantly. If I, or anyone else, went to Domum now, we don't know if we would trigger another event. We need to obtain more information, possibly using Sir Gordon's looking device."

Gordon looked at the rather glum face of Madoc. He decided he wouldn't correct the "Sir" title erroneously bestowed on him for the time being. Jon at least was allowed to carry the title of Sir when he was in Domum, and since Madoc came from Domum, he naturally extended the title to him on Earth. "Let us give ourselves another week to try to find out what happened. If at that time we are still unsure what to do, it might be worthwhile for one of us to go to Domum to do some exploring."

That seemed to mollify Madoc to some extent. "That seems like a reasonable compromise. How often are we able to use your looking device? Are we able to point it to a different direction?"

"My rule of thumb is ten minutes on, one hour off. As far as looking in a different direction, that is problematic. First, the end of the device must look out a window or opening of some sort; there is little benefit at looking at a wall of our castle. Second, to move the device to look elsewhere would require moving those heavy tables and equipment and do a rather tedious task of calibration. The calibration can take hours to perform correctly, I'm afraid."

"So we are unable to obtain a different view without a lot of work?"

"Essentially, yes. However, it has been my experience even the one view we have will often produce additional information if one is patient."

Madoc did not reply for several seconds as he looked away from Gordon and toward the fireplace. When he spoke, his voice was quiet and solemn. "Then I shall be patient."

Gordon looked at Madoc's worried face. "The truth is I'm not only one who is familiar with the way the equipment operates. I shall present the problem to those two young men you met the last time you were here, Tom and Tuck. Perhaps they will have a solution to this difficulty. Young minds can be quite inventive." He looked at his watch. "I shall phone and perhaps leave a message for them on their voice mail."

————

Angela leaned back on the wall, crossing her arms as she stifled a yawn. "This is getting so boring. We wait around, for what? A few minutes of TV?"

Liz shrugged her shoulders as she stood next to her. "I know, I agree with you. But it's important to find out what happened to Domum. Council Madoc is pretty worried."

"I'm not saying it's not worthwhile. I want to help Madoc find out what happened. But I don't understand what I'm supposed to be looking for." She looked at her watch. "It's almost two o'clock in the morning back home. I hope something happens soon."

"Probably not. Why don't you crash in the spare bedroom?"

"Maybe I will." She yawned. "I better tell Madoc I'm disappearing."

Liz watched her approach Madoc, trying to guess how intimate they were. To her Council Madoc was an aloof, powerful warlock who seamed too distant to be capable of romance. She watched as Angela spoke a few words to him and gave him a short hug and kiss. He returned her kiss and watched her as she turned and left the room.

Liz wasn't positive but there appeared to be a longing in his eyes as she left, not something she expected from a man who sold secrets to lords and kings.

————

The images were consistent with each other; gnants could be seen moving about the mud huts, occasionally having short-lived arguments with each other. Madoc finally agreed with Gordon and Jon they should try again tomorrow after they all got some rest and a bite to eat.

Liz waited for Jon to shut down the equipment, watching Madoc as he pondered the fate of Domum. She walked up to him and touched his arm.

"Hey. Tomorrow's another day to figure this out. You need some rest."

He waited a few seconds before speaking. "You are right, of course. I just wish I knew what I should do and how much time we have to correct this problem."

"Tomorrow we'll try again. Angela is in the spare room. I assume you two are…?"

"Your assumption is correct." He paused. "Thank you for your help and advice."

She gave him a smile. Maybe there was something between them. Maybe, she mused, Council Madoc was capable of romance. Liz turned her attention back to Jon, wondering when and if he was going to propose to her. "Come on, Jon. I'm getting tired too. Let's get some rest."

"Uh, you go ahead. I'm going to make myself something to eat first. I'm getting a bit hungry."

"Again? Maybe you should marry a refrigerator."

He looked at her puzzled, wondering what brought on that comment.

SEVENTEEN

"Marisa, we goes to the river!" Gilbert gave one more backward glance at whatever was following them and made a sharp turn between the foliage.

"What did you see?" Marisa didn't have much trouble keeping up with the shorter Gilbert, although she found her own backpack cumbersome as it bounced on her shoulders now she was trying to run.

"I's thinks they's..." He puffed a few times and resumed speaking "... getting ready to attack."

"What's getting ready to attack?"

"A type of gargoyle..." again he stopped to gather his breath "... called silva lacerta."

"I've never seen one of those before."

"Don'ts live here on old Domum. Hurry, I's sees the river."

Without pausing, Gilbert ran the final distance to the river and ploughed into the water. Marisa followed suit, stopping with him when the water reached his neck.

"Okay, now what? Won't they follow us into the river?"

"Maybe, maybe not."

"What kind of answer is that? Why did we run into the river if you didn't know?"

He continued to watch the riverbank. "Looks, we not see no

signs of thems on other riverbank. I thinks they can't swim too good, not liking water."

Marisa watched the bank with Gilbert. First one, then two more appeared. Finally, five of the gargoyles stood at the river edge. Two of the largest appeared to be parents of the smaller ones standing slightly behind them at the riverbank.

The silva lacerta had an onerous diet, including scavenging and going after a fresh kill. Like dragons, gargoyles had evolved into several species. This type of gargoyle was the largest and had lost the ability to fly, only using their wings to allow them to take large jumps.

The largest of the group was a male, looking much like a lion without fur but with wings situated on its shoulders. The creature's front limbs were shorter than the rear with all four paws sporting seven claws each. The body was covered with long wispy brown hair over a yellow reptilian skin, save for the triangular shaped wings that had both hair and feathers. The four-foot long wings waved slowly as the gargoyle watched them with small blue eyes. Hesitantly, it placed one paw into the water and quickly withdrew it. It whined a high-pitched squealing noise.

Marisa shuddered and stepped back until only her head stayed above the water. It was a struggle to keep her balance from the gentle flow of water, her backpack with trapped air making her even more buoyant.

"Gilbert, how sure are you they aren't able to go into the water?"

"Pretty sure. Theys haven't gone in yet."

"I don't know if it makes me feel much safer."

After another minute, the gargoyles turned and walked back into the plants and bushes.

"Gilbert?"

"What?"

"Nice thinking about going into the water. You saved us again."

He grinned. "I dids, didn't I?"

"Don't let it go to your head. You guessed. A good guess, but just a guess."

"Yessir, you cans trust ol' Gilbert to gets yous out of trouble."

"One compliment and now I have another monster to contend with."

"Monster! Where?"

"Just an expression. So do we just stand here until we turn into fishes?"

"Let's walk in the shallow end of the water for a whiles until we's sure they's gone."

Their progress was slow and Marisa contemplated her clothes were now so utterly soaked they might never get dry again, and it made a mockery of her careful preparation of protecting her clothes when they first crossed the river.

"Gilbert, it's going to take forever if we have to walk the whole way in the river."

"I's cans see that Marisa, but I's got a plan."

"A plan? What would that be? Walk along the shoreline?"

"You reading me mind?" Gilbert stopped and pointed a finger at her. "Gilbert thinks of the plan first."

"I'm sure you did. Can we make for the shore, anyway? This isn't much fun walking in the river with our clothes on."

Once on the shore, he led the way along the sandy bank, occasionally diverting around rocks and plants. They both kept a lookout for any more creatures watching them. Gilbert was content to walk in his wet clothes as the water dripped off. Marisa wasn't quite as fond of her wet clothes, taking off her blouse and draping it over her backpack. She decided to leave her skirt on largely due to Gilbert's reaction to her the last time she took off her clothes to dry. With the danger of the gargoyles about she didn't want Gilbert to be distracted.

Several hours later, Gilbert and Marisa had made their way down the riverbank. Marisa was pleased her blouse had dried under the warm sun though her skirt was still damp. She watched Gilbert as he plodded his way by the river, quickly looking around in search of danger. So far there hadn't been any animals appearing to be dangerous, just a few odd-looking creatures that turned out to be plant eaters.

"Gilbert?"

"What?" He answered without turning around.

"What's the point of us following this riverbank? Sooner or later we're going to have to cross the river so why don't we do it now? It was a lot easier to travel than sneaking around here."

He was silent for a few seconds. "I's was just thinkin' the sames thing."

Marisa withheld her first thought. "So is this just as good a place as any?"

He stopped and looked across the river. "Suppose so."

"Good, I'm going to put my clothes in my backpack again. I'd appreciate it if you don't stare at me this time."

"You suddenly shy?"

"No, I just don't like it when men stare at me too long. Okay?"

"Okay. I start to swim."

She watched him wade out into the river as she rolled up her clothes and stuffed them into her backpack.

Gilbert's paranoia became evident again as he took out one of his knives in his backpack and tied it with the leather strap over his shoulder so it hung down his back. He did a final check on the closure of the backpack and tied a rope from it to his waist. He gave a wave before falling into the river and began to swim with his usual amount of excessive water displacement.

Marisa wasn't far behind. Like before she elected to wear her backpack. Gilbert was carrying the heavier items in his, though it was a bit buoyant from the trapped air inside. She quickly caught up to him, slowed to pace him for a moment, and resumed her own rate. She slipped under the surface for a few seconds and rose above the water to take a gulp of air before resuming her swimming under the water.

She was reminding herself how much she enjoyed swimming when something wrapped around her right leg, followed by a paw at her left shoulder. She twisted in the water and for a moment her head broke the surface of the water, giving her chance to scream before being pulled down again.

Whatever was attacking her tugged at her backpack as wrapping itself around her limbs. She continued to try to twist from her adversary and found herself on her back just below the surface of the water. She lunged forward and was rewarded with a gulp of air. Marisa guessed the only reason she was still able to fight was the creature was using its effort to rip at her backpack. Her arms were scratched from claws and her legs pinned by the creature's lower limbs wrapped around her thighs. Marisa began to try to slip off her backpack, hoping the beast would lose interest in her if it got that prize.

The creature suddenly convulsed once and then twice. It released her legs and one paw slipped off her right shoulder, giving her a chance to twist around as she slipped out of her backpack. She got her first look at the creature, almost as long as herself with a peculiar greyish body with long legs ending in fins. Its short arms ended with short, six finger claws. The body itself was short and round with the large head armed with sharp teeth and dozens of spiked whiskers around its mouth. The jaws locked around her backpack as it swam backward, away from its attacker. Gilbert was waving his arms and legs frantically as he brandished his knife at it, the tip of the knife releasing blood into the water. The creature had what it wanted and suddenly turned and swam away with blood still flowing out of the wounds in its neck.

Marisa swam over to Gilbert and pushed him to the surface of the water where he gasped for air and then coughed. He steadied himself and pointed to the shore. This time she paced him all the way to the shore where he fell down exhausted.

"Gilbert, you saved my life."

"I's knows. Yous okay?"

"I'm…" She looked at the scratches on her arms and marks on her legs. "…I'm fine."

"Goods." He sat up and looked at her. "You bleeding a bit."

"I'm okay, they're just scratches. What was that thing?"

"Don'ts really knows much abouts them, but sailors call thems water demons. Theys not really fishes but like water dragons that can breathe under water."

"So they're some sort of creature adapting to living in the water?"

"I's guesses so, but never heard of one coming out of water like water dragons."

"That had to be the ugliest creature I ever seen."

He nodded. "We have a problem. You lost yours backpack and I's had to drop mine to get to yous faster." He held up his knife. "This our only weapon."

"So what do we do?"

He shrugged. "Keep goings me guesses. Maybe we gets lucky and cans find a way to the gateway without gnants stopping us."

They began to walk a few minutes later, both wanting to get away from the river.

Marisa was glad the sun was strong; her close escape was giving her shivers still. "Gilbert, do you suppose you could give me your shirt?"

"It wet too, won't make yous any warmer."

"I know but I'm naked. I would like to wear something."

"Me shirt too small for you."

"But it would be better than nothing."

He looked at her body. "I thinks you looks fine naked."

She crossed her arms. "Thank you. But I'd feel better with something on."

Gilbert was quiet for several seconds. He stopped and slowly began to unbutton his shirt. "Okays, you cans have me shirt on one condition."

"Sure, what is it?"

"You tells nobody what you sees on me back. They's special tattoos me keeps quiet about. Okay?"

"Okay."

"Promises?"

"Promise."

Gilbert removed his shirt and held it out reluctantly to Marisa.

"Thank you." She began to put on the wet shirt. Her arms were far too long but fortunately, the sleeves were wide enough for her. The body of the shirt reached her hips, but she found she could only do the one button at the waist. She took off the shirt and tied the sleeves together at her right hip, making the shirt into a short wrap.

"Doesn't hide much of you."

She sighed. "No, it doesn't, but it's better than nothing."

"Maybe." He grinned at her. "We best get walking agains."

Less than two hours later, gnants noticed their presence and again seemed content just to watch, although this time they came in greater numbers.

Gilbert was nervous, as he rapidly looked left to right. Marisa was less concerned about the gnants. Two other things pressed on her mind, three if she considered she wore Gilbert's undersized shirt. One, her bare feet were getting sore from the small rocks she stepped on. Gilbert had also lost his sandals, but the ground didn't seem to bother him. And two, she was trying to discern what all the tattoos on his back meant. The symbols, obviously magical in nature, had words in Latin meant to ward off less friendly spirits. The symbols contained a swirl of colours she had seen before in books at Lord Troy's castle library. What they meant she wasn't sure except some symbols were meant to represent certain spirits and creatures. However, the tattoo of a naked woman sitting on her legs at the top of his left shoulder didn't appear to represent any type of magic she was familiar with.

PART THREE

Anything is possible if you don't know what you are talking about.

EIGHTEEN

Lord Perry continued to float toward where the others had disappeared, allowing the gentle tug to pull him. He relaxed, giving up any control on his destination or the speed he was traveling at. There was a prevalent greyness around him and as he looked around it became denser, obliterating his vision to the distant travelers initially and then even to the closer ones. Lord Perry moved forward in his grey tunnel, approaching the end destination with greater speed. In a flash of light, he entered a gateway and arrived in a white, translucent room.

He sensed a presence nearby, hesitated, and called out. "Where am I?"

The silence lingered for several seconds. "The next place." The voice was male, quiet and reserved.

"Are you implying I have died and gone on to this place?"

"You are here without your body. Death has no meaning here."

"Is this heaven?"

"If you want it to be. This place can be whatever you want."

"Like my library?" As he spoke, a library began to form in the void, similar to his own extensive one on Domum. At one of the tables sat a man, white hair, medium build and dressed in a style reminiscent of Domum royalty.

"If you like."

"Who are you?"

The old man smiled. "At one time I had a title of a king, but now I just go by the name of Ethelwulf."

"King Ethelwulf?" Lord Perry dropped to one knee. "Your deeds are of legend."

"Please, I no longer claim to be king; there are others of far greater power and influence. I am humbled by their wisdom."

Lord Perry remained on his knee. "Yet you are kind enough to welcome me to this place. Is this place heaven?"

"I have learned kindness and much more from others here. Is this heaven? It is if you want it to be. This place can also be hell for those who die with a guilty conscience for misdeeds in life. How you lived your life is how you will be treated here."

Lord Perry rose. "And the others who perished the same time as myself on the ship?"

"They are here. Patience, please. You will have an opportunity to meet them and others."

"If I may ask, has all of Domum been lost forever?"

Ethelwulf hesitated a moment before replying. "There is still a small pocket of the old Domum. A few individuals are left from that era and are attempting to restore the old order."

"Is there anything I can do to help them?"

Ethelwulf smiled. "I am not surprised by your question. But they have to make their own journey in life. While we can return to the other dimensions, we are discouraged from trying to influence it. This you will learn in time. Would you care for a glass of wine while we talk some more?"

"Gladly. I have many questions."

Ethelwulf laughed. "We knew you would."

———

"Gilbert?"

"What now?"

"There are some gnants pacing us."

"I's knows, Marisa, I's knows."

"Well, then, it wouldn't make much difference if we took a break, would it?"

Gilbert slowed down and nodded. "Suppose not. Just a wee one, mind ya."

Marisa rubbed her feet, wishing she could have a pair of sandals again. Gilbert sat on the ground and gazed around while looking rather grumpy. He held his knife tightly in his hand.

"Gilbert, if the gnants attack us do you really think one knife will save us?"

"I gives me best try."

"I know you would. You've saved my life back in the river and I want you to know how much I'm thankful." She took a deep breath. "But we're not going to get to the gateway by fighting the gnants all the way. They're watching us, they're curious about us, but they don't hate us yet. They might get the wrong impression of us if you continue to hold the knife like that."

Gilbert listened to her, squinting his eyes as she spoke. Then he surprised her. "Maybe you's right. Maybe this here knife ain't going to help. But I's not sure what to how to…" He waved his free hand at her, palm down. "Gilbert is not meant to be the one to save the world."

"You're still my hero. Together we can do this."

Gilbert slowly lowered his knife until it rested on his lap. "I's hopes you's right."

They continued their journey and finally reached sight of the gnants' temple holding the gateway to Gordon Miller's castle. They stood staring at the strange distant green and brown building. Gilbert still insisted on standing slightly in front of Marisa and turned around when he heard her speak, obviously not to him.

"Hello, little fellow. Are you lost or just curious?"

A small gnant, perhaps half the size of an adult, squatted on all fours and stared at Marisa. Its arms quivered in excitement as it tried to make up its mind what to do. Marisa slowly dropped down to her knees and spread out her arms.

"Come on. Don't be afraid."

Gilbert watched, not sure why she would want a gnant to approach her. Young creatures of species were often cute but not gnants. Young or old, they still appeared to resemble the cross between a small human and a demon. Gilbert supposed she had to have her own reasons and resisted the temptation of grabbing his knife hanging from a loop of leather at his waist.

The small gnant slowly stepped forward, one hesitant step at a time. Marisa continued to whisper encouragement to it until it moved within a yard of her. Slowly, it rose to two legs and took another step as its red forked tongue flicking out toward her. Marisa slowly held out her hand.

———

Angela peeled a potato and dropped it into a pot of water. She looked at Liz, "I was bored before but that might have been better than kitchen duty."

Liz smiled as she cut off the top of carrots. "I don't disagree. But someone has to make dinner and I guess we were elected."

"I suppose so. Madoc and Jon are pretty busy trying to figure out what happened, and I doubt Gordon does much cooking. I'm just surprised how much Tom and Tuck eat. They must have been starving before they flew over here."

Liz laughed. "I think they'll eat as long as they're not paying for the food. Last time they were here they ate a lot too."

"They're the experts on this problem, I take it?" Angela wiped her hands on her apron and sat at one of the kitchen chairs.

"They study physics at the university, so at least they know the theories. But right now, they're trying to find a better way to view Domum, to see if they learn something on what happened."

"Well, I hope they find something soon. Either that or we start bringing in large quantities of pizza so we don't have to do all the cooking."

———

"I do believe that should help us to see a larger portion of the countryside." Gordon stood with hands on his hips as he stared at the addition to the laboratory apparatus.

Tom and Tuck had devised and put together the mechanism allowing them to expand the field of view. Gordon had them fly it to Ballymiller at his expense.

They soon took over the laboratory and began devising a method to allow a better view of Domum. They spent another half a day to attach and calibrate the new apparatus.

"Tom, would you learn how to stabilize that circuit before Domum changes again? The sine wave is jumping all over the place."

Tom looked up. "It's not my fault. it was the idiot who couldn't design a proper negative feedback circuit. Wait, that idiot was you."

"At least my circuit didn't turn into smoke, Mr. Arcs and Sparks."

"That was because you put too much current into the module."

"Too much current? Is it possible you could design a module to withstand power surges?"

"Anything is possible if you don't know what you are talking about."

Liz interrupted their bantering. "Hey, you two, food is ready if you're hungry. That is, if you guys stop fighting."

Tuck shook his head. "I was just trying to give Tom a few valuable pointers. But we can hold off the lessons until after dinner."

Liz laughed as she followed them out the door. "Tom, are you going to be able to get this new circuit to work?"

"Oh, yeah, no problem. We're just joking about the stuff going wrong. We'll get it to work."

Angela sat in the main hall as the men ate and was soon joined by Liz.

"You would think they hadn't eaten for a week."

Liz laughed. "With Tuck and Tom that might be true. Starving students and all that."

"More like starving pigs. Do Tuck and Tom have girlfriends?"

"No, I don't believe so. They're nice guys and okay looking, especially Tom, but they're not exactly the type to set a girl's heart on fire."

"Yeah, a bit too much into the books." Angela shrugged. "Still, I thought they'd have some social life. Tom has a devil-may-care appearance at times."

"I guess he does. He can put on the charm when he has to. Right now, I hope Tuck and he can put on the charm to that apparatus they're working on."

———

Tom announced the circuits now worked fine after another three hours in the laboratory. "I gave Jon instructions on how to use it, so whenever you want to try it out you can. It's a little unstable but should do the trick."

Liz ventured forth and peered at the attachment. "What does it do?" she asked Gordon.

"It is, my dear, an electronic equivalent of a telescope and a fish-eyed lens. In the centre of our monitor we will see distant objects much better but at the same time will be able to capture the extreme edges of the landscape. The image will be distorted, of course, but should enable us to see a much broader area while bringing the centre in greater detail."

Jon stood back, munching on an apple. "So," he stopped to swallow "when do you want to fire this thing up?"

"Whenever we wish to, I suppose. Although it would be prudent to first check up on our other guests, to see if they're ready to do another visual of Domum."

"I'll go check on them." Liz turned to go out the laboratory door and headed down the two flights of stairs to the main floor. The staircases spiralled downward in small increments of long steps. When she first saw them in the castle a year ago, she saw them as an added elegance, but after going up and down to the third floor a dozen times she found them annoying. The steps slowed her down compared to the normal straight staircase, but she skipped down as fast as she could. Liz was worried about Domum, concerned the world she lived in for a short time no longer existed. By extension, she was even more worried about the people she'd met there, in particular Sir Anthony Graham, or Tony as she knew him. She was glad Jon had never pressed her exactly how good a friend he was to her, which also meant she didn't ask for all the details of his relationship with Nicole.

Angela had curled up on the loveseat by the fireplace with Madoc, her head on his shoulder. Madoc appeared to rest but his eyes opened as she approached them.

"You have news?"

"They've calibrated that device with the equipment. I guess they can fire it up anytime you like."

"Excellent." He tried to extract his arm from around Angela, but she stirred and sat up, yawning.

"Excuse me." She yawned again. "Are we going to try to use that thing again to see Domum?"

Liz nodded. "Whenever you two are ready."

———

Gordon flipped the switches on the control panel, causing amber lights to blink off and on and a steady humming noise to emanate from a power supply. As a faint smell of ozone filled the air the lights gradually changed to green, and he flipped a final switch. The humming noise dropped in level momentarily and rose back to its normal level while the monitor changed from a white speckled screen to an image of Domum.

Jon sat in one of two chairs in the room and used a joystick from an electronic game to manoeuvre the image around. The image jerked around until he mastered the technique.

Tom looked at the image jumping around and commented to Tuck, "Told you it needed more compensation on the horizontal image scanning."

"Yeah, but it would have affected the focal length."

"Not if we used…"

"Would you two be quiet?" Liz glared at them and turned her attention to where an image of Domum appeared. It wasn't the Domum she was familiar with, but they now could see more details of the new world.

Groups of gnants clustered around in the closest vantage point, moving around in quick bursts of energy when they weren't sitting. Their mud huts stood a few feet apart from each other and gave the appearance of a type of village. The individuals milled about but only occasionally could be seen close enough to each other to carry a conversation.

From Jon's experience on Domum he believed two main groups of gnants existed. The first group were not sociable, not to each other and even less so to humans. Females of the same family could be tolerant of each other and formed a loose association to help care for the young. Females cared for the young for the first few years of their lives but by the age of eight they had to be able fend for themselves for the most part. By their tenth birthday, they were expected to leave the security of their first home and strike out on their own.

Males were more territorial with each other, especially if females were close by. Males stayed with females only until they gave birth to their young, usually in sets of triplets. Afterward they would depart, looking for another female to impregnate.

A second group of gnants emerged after the arrival of humans. Called Tyreel Followers, after a gnant named Tyreel, they preached about a new way of life and adopted a new social order. Far more companionable than the first group, these gnants also cared for their young by both parents and stressed the importance of teaching their young. From a few eccentric individuals, the Tyreel Followers had grown to encompass almost half the population.

The gnants Jon watched seemed to lie between the two types of gnants with whom he was familiar. They camped together in a large group but maintained a minimum distance between themselves and their mud and plant huts. Occasionally he noticed a short quarrel between two gnants, more posturing than actual fighting as they snarled at each other on all four limbs. Some males and females paired off to the seclusion of a mud hut or behind the tree-sized plants.

Jon continued to scan the countryside, moving away from the largest concentration of the gnants. Liz rested a hand on his shoulder as the view raced toward a series of hills.

"There's a group of gnants on that hill. Let's see what they're up to." Gordon pointed at the monitor's top corner.

Jon nodded. Everyone was standing behind him, watching the scene unravel before them. As Jon guided the joystick, the motion gave a sense of flying over the landscape and the telescopic view magnified the apparent speed.

"What's that? They looked human." Angela pointed at an image disappearing off to the side of the monitor.

Jon moved back to where she pointed.

"They are human! And she's naked. Almost anyway. Who's the short guy next to her?"

"Gilbert," Jon whispered.

"Gilbert," spoke Liz louder.

"Gilbert." Madoc just held back shouting his name as he

clenched his fist. "I'll bet a dozen dragon eggs he had something to do with this disaster!"

———

Tom and Tuck talked to Gordon for a few minutes concerning possible causes for the way Domum now appeared.

"I dunno, it seems to come back to it might have been magic what caused this, especially since we see Gilbert and that woman in the viewer," Tuck said in a tired voice.

Tom yawned. "I just want to know who that woman is. She looked gorgeous."

Gordon nodded. "She is beautiful, and I wonder what she is doing with Gilbert. We will find out that answer, eventually. Now, I suggest you two lads head off to the hotel rooms I booked for you so you can get some shut eye. You worked long hours and need some rest."

Angela looked at Madoc. "You'll be okay by yourself? I can go with you."

"I assure you, Angela, I will be but a few minutes and will not be in any danger whatsoever." Madoc, after a brief conversation with Jon and Gordon, decided to go to the new Domum and ensure Gilbert and his companion arrived on Earth.

"Okay but be careful with that naked woman. Who knows what she's after?"

Madoc adjusted his cape around his neck and strode out of the castle. Angela walked with him, hurrying to keep up.

"How far do you have to go?"

"Not far. I just want to make sure I'm not going to be too close to the castle's equivalent on Domum when I arrive there. It is possible the gnants would not react favourably to my appearance in their shrine or whatever they call it."

Madoc continued to walk past the gate of the castle and crossed the street.

"I believe this will be sufficient." He stopped and looked back at the castle. "Best you step back when I transport myself to Domum."

Angela ignored him and wrapped her arms around his neck. "You better come back to me." She kissed him on his lips, refusing to let go for several seconds.

"I assure you I will return."

"To me."

"To you."

"Hurry back." She stepped away, watching him mumble a few phases and was gone in a small flash of blue light. She shivered as a wave of cold air descended on her.

She walked back to the castle, turning around to glance at the spot where he had disappeared.

———

Liz looked up as Angela walked into the living room. Her face looked flushed as she sat down in the easy chair in front of the fireplace. Liz glanced at Jon who was reading a magazine while munching on an apple, seemingly unaware Angela had returned without Madoc. She sighed.

"You okay?"

Angela nodded.

"Council Madoc will be fine. Believe me, he's in no danger. He knows how to use magic to get out of problems."

"I know. But all those little hairy things." She frowned.

"Gnants."

"Gnants, then. There's so many of them and if they all attack…"

"They won't. They're not like that, really. Besides, all he has to do is say a few magic phrases, and he's back here."

"I guess you're right."

"Come on. Let's make some tea. In another hour we can use the monitor again to see what's happening."

———

Liz stared at the kettle where it sat on the burner. "So how did you meet Council Madoc?"

"Literally, I bumped into him in a hallway at some amateur stage show. I invited him to go with me for a bite to eat and, well we became friends. Later, I became his assistant in his stage show."

"His magic show?" Liz grinned.

"Yeah, except it turned out to be a real magic show. Anyway, I found his book on magic spells and found out he was a warlock. Kind of threw me for a loop but here I am. I fall for the strangest guys but this really takes the cake."

"You could do worse. Council Madoc is known for being honourable at least." She picked up the kettle and poured water into the teapot.

"Hmm, honourable is good but I wish he would just show he really cares about me too."

"I know what you mean. Jon…"

Jon poked his head into the kitchen. "Tuck and Tom just came back. Is there anything for them to eat in here?"

Liz crossed her arms. "For them or yourself as well?"

"Well, if they're going to eat, I guess I could join them." He turned around and shouted out an answer. "It's okay, we got food here."

Angela looked at Liz and gave a smile. "I guess we both have our situations."

Liz sighed. "And mine has a large appetite."

NINETEEN

Gilbert watched Marisa talk soothing sounds to the young gnant. Slowly, the gnant approached and was now standing less than two feet away from her as she knelt down on both knees. The gnant took two more small steps and hesitantly extended a hand to her face. Gradually it touched her cheek with its fingers and short black claws.

Gilbert regarded she was being very brave or, more likely, extremely foolish. He watched as she wrapped her arms around the gnant and carefully picked it up. The gnant looked around as it was being picked up but didn't struggle. It now seemed interested in her hair, lifting her long strands and watching it fall down again.

They began to walk toward where the large mud shrine was located; a place they hoped contained the gateway to Gordon Miller's castle on Earth. Gilbert watched apprehensively as Marisa carried the gnant along the path. The gnant was curious about her; besides her hair, it also looked at her ears and lips, gently poking with its claws and fingertips.

He looked ahead. Their path was clear enough, a twisted path among the tree-like plants with gnants scurrying about, but many of them lined up to watch as if they were royalty. He supposed Marisa might be right, being friends with one of their young might reduce the chance of attack.

"Now stop that. Those you can't examine."

Gilbert turned to see what kind of problem Marisa was having. Marisa pulled the gnants hands from her breasts much to its disappointment as it whimpered out loud. She gave Gilbert a stare telling him his interest in her problem wasn't appreciated.

Undeterred, Gilbert continued to watch. "Watch his claws."

"She is being careful not to scratch."

"She?"

"She. Haven't you seen enough of my boobs? Turn around and watch where you're going."

"Gilbert will know when he's seen enough."

"Then maybe Gilbert will also know he's starting to irritate me."

"Okays, I's can takes the hint." He reluctantly turned around and led the way down the path, mumbling to himself.

Gnants continued to add to their numbers, some of them scurrying up to Marisa and touching her leg before running away again. Gilbert also received attention but none of them ventured close enough to touch him. The gnant Marisa was carrying continued to play with her hair, occasionally touching her ears and face. She also seemed to enjoy being carried, looking around over Marisa's shoulder and chattering away at the other gnants.

"We's getting closer to the gateway. Hope them gnants don't try to stop us from goin' in."

"I'll watch this little talker to see how she reacts as we get closer. If she doesn't get upset, then we'll probably be okay."

Gilbert looked back at Marisa once more, studying the gnant for few seconds. "You be careful. Gnants be tricky." He turned around and resumed walking, only to freeze in his steps.

"Coun…Council Madoc!" Gilbert fell down on one knee and lowered his head.

Marisa looked on at Madoc with his hands on his hips, looking none too pleased. She carefully lowered the young gnant she was carrying to the ground. "Council Madoc. How, what are you doing here?"

He glowered at the trembling Gilbert. "To find out what the devil has happened here. I suspect he," Madoc pointed at Gilbert, "has some explaining to do."

Gilbert shook his head. "Oh, no, Council Madoc. Gilbert do

nothin' wrong. I just sells Lord Troy a small artefact. I not have nothin' to do with this."

Madoc frowned. "Yet we find you in the middle of this disaster. Forgive me if I view your protests with scepticism."

Gilbert looked up and said nothing.

"Council Madoc, we truly do not know what happened. Gilbert did sell Lord Troy a crystal and Lord Troy did try some spells on it, but how this came about from that we don't understand."

Madoc peered at Marisa. "Very well, I accept your explanation for the time being. But be warned, Gilbert, if I find your greed had a part of this disaster then there will be dire consequences." He let the comment sink in for a moment. "In the meantime, I am to take you two to Earth where we can hopefully resolve this problem and restore Domum to its previous condition."

———

For Marisa it was a most bewildering experience. She had heard of Earth before, more commonly referred to as the Other-side. Still, she had never jumped between two worlds before and initially found her herself disorientated. She was glad Council Madoc had to touch both Gilbert and her to transfer them to Earth using his magic and reached out to his shoulder to steady herself.

She soon regained her balance and looked around. The sky was almost dark, and it appeared to be late evening, or she supposed, predawn. She also noticed it was cooler by a considerable margin than Domum and she wrapped her arms around herself to ward off the chill.

A streetlamp on the corner of the block cast a yellow light on the concrete sidewalk they stood on. In front of her, instead of cobble streets or a dirt path, stretched out a street of a dark grey material. Across the road, stood one- or two-storey dwellings, each of them sporting lighted windows.

"Come this way," Council Madoc commanded.

Marisa looked around once more at the strange surroundings and followed him, with Gilbert staying well back from both of them. She walked along the hard surface, turning around once when she heard an odd noise and saw a pair of red lights. They were attached to a dark rectangular object disappearing down the street. The dwellings had to be at the edge of town, she guessed, because there was now an open field containing a few sad looking trees. Beyond the field stood a castle and the dark grey structure looked familiar to her.

"That looks like Lord Bennett's castle."

"The counter part here to Lord Bennett's castle does have many similarities but there are differences. I assure you this is not any part of Domum, and this is not Lord Bennett's castle." Madoc did not stop as he spoke, continuing his quick pace.

"Is it always so cold here?"

"On this region of Earth, it is. Please, there will be time to answer questions in the castle. It is best we make haste before anyone sees us which could cause us difficulties."

Gilbert had kept well back of the others on the journey to the castle but once the door opened, he ran forward to greet Liz and Jon.

"Sir Jon, Sir Jon! Tis so good to see me very good friend again. And Lady Liz! Me eyes can hardly believe how lucky they are to set upon you again."

Marisa watched Gilbert make a fuss over Jon and Liz and she stepped around Madoc to see the inside of the castle. She had never been inside the great hall of Lord Bennett's castle but imagined it looked the same. She suddenly noticed everyone was staring at her. She immediately put her hands in front of herself, suddenly aware she was almost naked. She stepped back behind Madoc.

Liz reacted first, grabbing a blanket off the loveseat by the fireplace and walked over to Marisa. "Here, wrap yourself in this until we can get you some clothes."

Marisa quickly covered herself. "Thank you. I—I forgot I wasn't wearing my clothes."

"Believe me, the men hadn't."

"Sorry." She looked at the unsympathetic face of Liz.

Liz's expression softened. "That's okay. I'm sure you didn't intend to lose your clothes. Come inside and sit down while I find something for you to wear. Do you want anything to eat or drink?"

Marisa declined her offer and sat in one of the large chairs close to the fire, curling up her legs under her and wrapping the blanket up to her neck.

Gilbert walked over to where she sat. "Perhaps yous no need of me shirt now."

"And perhaps I do. This blanket doesn't offer perfect coverage and I need all I can get against the chill in this air."

"Still, it's me shirt."

"Are you seriously going to try to wrestle me for it here?"

Gilbert slowly shook his head. "Buts yous supposed to listen to me."

"That was on Domum. This is the Other-Side. I'm a free woman here." She leaned her head against the back of the chair and closed her eyes. "Free woman. It has a very nice sound to it."

Gilbert walked away, muttering. "Trouble. Gilbert sees trouble comin'."

———

Tuck Richards brushed the breadcrumbs from the front of his grey shirt and glanced over at Tom Markus. Tuck was medium height but heavyset with sandy coloured hair and liked to tease his friend. He reached over and lightly punched Tom on his shoulder. "No matter how hard you stare that blanket isn't going to fall down," he whispered as they sat with Jon on the other side of the coffee table where Marisa sat with her eyes closed. The two friends and co-workers knew each other well and Tuck recognized Tom's interest in Marisa immediately.

Tom shook his head. "She's gorgeous even with the blanket up to her neck." Tom reached up and pushed his dark, curly hair from his forehead. Lightly built, he had a tendency to slouch when sitting.

"She's a looker, all right. What did Gilbert say? She was a sort of sex slave."

Jon grabbed another sandwich after checking there was still plenty for everyone. "Gilbert says a lot of things, some of them even true. I wouldn't read too much into it. Domum is a different place, a different culture. You can't just transpose a situation there over to Earth and understand it completely. Everything has to be taken in context."

Tom shrugged. "I don't really care what Gilbert said. She just looks good in either world."

The men suddenly became aware of Liz standing just behind one of the armchairs.

"I'm going off to bed. I assume you're going to stay here with your friends?" Liz spoke to Jon in a tired voice.

"Uh, no. I'm ready to hit the hay, too." Jon quickly got up, stuffing the remainder of the sandwich in his mouth.

After the two had left the room, Tuck leaned over toward Tom and whispered, "Did I detect a slight irritation in her voice?"

Tom considered his response for a moment. "Well, as Jon said, don't try to take things we hear out of context. Having said that, Jon himself appeared to be a tad anxious there."

———

Lord Perry leaned back in his chair. "So what you're saying is there are multiple universes and multiple dimensions? How the devil do you keep track what's going on out there?"

"Careful, we don't like to use that name here." Ethelwulf gave a smile to indicate there was no offence. "I don't keep track, no need to except for my own curiosity. But the Almighty can and does. He sees everything and understands all of it."

"I wish I could learn how it does work."

"Use your library. Somewhere there will be a book which will explain it. Everything can be explained; we just may not understand it."

Lord Perry looked at his library that surrounded them. "I didn't have such a book before."

"True. But the library will change itself to meet your needs."

"Remarkable." Lord Perry took another drink of his wine. "Tell me is any of this real?"

"I asked myself that same question. I guess the short answer is it's real, but in a different way. Back on Domum we would regard a brick wall as solid. But those bricks and mortar were just made up of bits of particles and energy. It was shown to me that if took all the space out of a brick, you would end up with something the size of a dust particle. So what are we really made up of? I guess on Domum there was just a bit of substance to us and mostly energy that helped keep our form. Here I suspect that it's all energy that prevails."

"In essence, we are ghosts or spirits then."

"True. Being a ghost has its advantages. Come with me. There's a ship's captain that you asked about that is now ready to speak to others. He had a difficult time on the transition."

TWENTY

In the morning Gilbert, who now was wearing his shirt, sat with Jon and Liz around the kitchen table eating. Tom and Tuck still slept while Gordon and Madoc sat in the living room drinking tea.

"I's says to yous thee dragon screams in pain when me knife hits 'im." Gilbert embellished his exploits of scaring off the dragon, though Liz and Jon automatically adjusted the tale downward and got an approximation of what really happened.

"Hi. Any coffee?" Angela came into the kitchen yawning.

"I can make you some instant if you like." Liz got up from the table.

"Oh, no. I see you have tea. That'll be fine." She reached over the cupboard to retrieve a cup. "I can manage."

Angela sat on the last chair around the small table. "I was thinking if we have time, we should go shopping. That new girl needs some clothes, definitely needs clothes, and I could use some new ones as well." She looked up at Liz as she spoke.

Liz nodded. "Shopping can be arranged. You're right about Marisa. We can't have her walking around with only a blanket on." She took a sip of her tea and nodded toward the kitchen doorway. "And here she is. The blanket would be better."

Marisa came into the kitchen hesitantly. "I'm sorry to disturb you but could I get something to eat?" Marisa gave a hopeful smile. She was wearing one of Gordon's dress shirts as a dress, giving her a vulnerable look with its oversize sleeves and body. The white material wasn't completely opaque and light from the window accented her figure.

"Of course." Liz stood and walked over to the stove. "Eggs okay?"

"I can make them myself if you show me where you keep them."

"That's all right. Sit down where I was sitting." Liz decided they didn't need to watch her cook wearing only the dress shirt. The girl was just too good looking. "Jon, could you go and let your uncle and Council Madoc know Angela and I are going to do some shopping?"

Reluctantly, Jon got up and left the kitchen, leaving Gilbert alone with the three women. He immediately began to tell jokes and continue with his tales of Domum.

———

"So what size do you think she is?" Angela picked a dark blue top. "Fourteen? Sixteen?"

Liz laughed. "I wish. God, no matter what she wears she looks good. A blanket, a man's shirt, it doesn't seem to matter."

They shopped in the few stores in Ballymiller, picking at the assortment of clothes. They finally purchased a few items and stopped in at the Demister Pub for a bite to eat and a drink.

"This is the place where I first met Jon." She pointed toward the middle of the room. "I was sitting right over there with some friends playing darts."

"That was over a year ago?"

"About that. Seems like a long time ago now."

"Especially after your adventure on Domum."

"Yeah."

The silence lingered for a few seconds.

"So are you and Jon going to tie the knot?"

"I don't know. I thought he was going to propose last year when we made it back from Domum. Then during the year, he would suggest something and I thought for sure when he came back to Ballymiller. So far nothing."

"Maybe he's just waiting for the right moment."

"This is Ballymiller. Not many moments are different here." She gave a weak laugh.

"Look, he traveled all the way from America to be with you again. He must love you. I would guess he's just nervous about asking you."

"Hmm. I guess you're right. I've been short with him lately. I could be scaring him off." She took a drink of her beer. "And you and Council Madoc? How serious?"

"I don't know, I honestly don't. I got a crush on him the first minute we met. There's something about him that…"

"Like he's a warlock?" She giggled. "A lot of women fall for him. His voice, mannerism, strength and looks. And here on Earth it seems to just increase his appeal. But I did notice one thing different about him this time in Ballymiller."

"What's that?"

"The way he looks at you. He really likes you. How much I can't say."

Angela looked flushed for a moment. "Say, speaking of looks did you see the way Tom looked at Marisa?"

"Yeah, the look of lust."

———

Madoc had announced his intention of returning to Domum to try to undo the spells that caused the problem, indicating Gilbert and Marisa should return with him.

Marisa sat quietly, listening to him.

"We will leave late tonight when it would be morning on Domum. I was told by Gilbert you made a circular route to get here but we will travel in a straight line to Lord Troy's castle. We can arrive at the castle within a few hours. The travel will also give me an opportunity to study this new Domum and gather possible new information."

After he finished speaking, Marisa sought him out by the fireplace. She wore the new clothes Liz and Angela purchased for her, consisting of a long yellow skirt and a blue pattern blouse. She found the underwear uncomfortable, but knew women wore them on Earth and didn't want to offend anyone. She was also given a shorter skirt and a short top but was more at ease in the long skirt.

"Council Madoc, please forgive me, but do I have to go back to Domum?"

Madoc frowned. "Why do you wish to stay here? This is not your home. How would you survive here? Besides, Lord Troy would have to give you permission to do so."

"I don't know how I would live here, sir. But here am I not a free woman? I mean, does Lord Troy's authority extend this far?"

Madoc rubbed his forehead. "That is a difficult answer to ascertain. But I will say this to you. It has been my experience if one attempts personal gain by deceit or trickery, then bad karma will follow one such it will nullify any gain. I advise you to return to Domum and speak to Lord Troy and ask for his permission to return to Earth. I will present your case for you, if you should desire, and will facilitate your return here."

"Lord Troy will never agree to let me go."

"That may be but is not for certain. Lord Troy does have a compassionate side. I will not force you to return but I believe for you to stay on Earth will cause you great misery."

Marisa nodded slowly. "You're right, Council Madoc. I guess getting to Earth and being free was too good to be true."

———

Jon faced the small mirror in the bathroom, frowning as he did so. "Damn, what's wrong with you? You have the ring. She's here and still you do nothing. All you've done so far is eat and piss her off." He clinched his fists and leaned on the small sink. "Sir Jon, the dragon slayer. What a joke." Jon stood up straight. "It's time to get my mojo back."

Jon walked out of the bathroom and headed to the living room. He spotted Madoc speaking with Marisa. Marisa looked upset while Madoc looked concerned.

"Council Madoc, can I have a word with you."

Madoc looked up. "Of course, Sir Jon."

"When you leave for Domum, I would like to go with you."

Madoc looked surprised. "If you wish to accompany us, I don't have any objections. May I ask why?"

"Something I need to do. I'm here in Ballymiller for a reason. Perhaps it's helping you fix Domum."

"Very well then. Marisa, Gilbert and I will be leaving in approximately three hours."

Jon looked at Marisa. "Why is she going?"

"She resides there and should return to Lord Troy Sussex."

"Okay, but she's hardly dressed for trekking back to where Lord Troy lives. If you can't undo the spell, if it was a spell, then don't we have to evacuate all those living in the castle anyway to Earth? And if we can change Domum back to the way it was, then she could return at a later date when there would be roads again to travel on."

Madoc looked away at a distant point and turned his attention back to Marisa and Jon.

"You make a good argument. Very well then. Marisa may stay here until our return."

———

"This is very nice of ye to show me around Ballymiller." Marisa gave Tom a warm smile.

"Oh, no, I don't mind at all. I wanted check it out myself." Tom hurried his words as he stared at her, ignoring the surrounding streets.

"Ye don't mind if I hold your arm, do yer? I'm not use to shoes this upper heel has on them."

"Those are just normal women shoes here, Marisa. No, you can hold my arm as much as you want."

"Thanks, Sir Tom."

"Just Tom. There aren't too many Sirs around here."

They walked along the road until they reached an asphalt sidewalk and followed it into Ballymiller business district. Marisa continually looked around, asking questions. The homes made of brick and wood fascinated her, causing her to wonder what they looked like inside. On Domum individual dwellings were small except for the castles lords and nobles inhabited.

"I'm living in a hotel right now, but Liz stays with her parents here in Domum during the summer. She could show the inside of that one."

"Do ye think she would? I get the impression she doesn't care for me."

"Na, she likes you. She's just is going through a tough time with Jon right now."

"Aren't she and Jon going to get married? That's what Gilbert said."

"I dunno. I suppose they will, but you never know. I guess there are some issues to be resolved."

"How about you, Tom? Are you seeing someone special?"

His pulse quickened. "No, no one right now."

She reached over with her free hand and patted the arm she was using for support. "I'm sure you'll make a fine catch for some damsel in the future."

"Thanks. But for now, I'm concentrating on my studies."

"And what might they be?"

"Physics, quantum mechanics. It's a little hard to describe."

"But it's got something to do with how to travel between Domum and Earth?"

"Yeah, though more like how it happened rather than figure out a way to do it." He pointed. "There's a woman's clothing store over there. Want to look inside?"

"Sure, if ye don't mind."

Marisa looked around inside, feeling the fabrics and holding the garments up to herself. The young saleswoman was content to read her magazine as they browsed, after giving a smile and a hello when they entered the shop. Marisa was also intrigued by the costume jewellery, trying several pieces on before putting them away. She turned down Tom's offer to buy her something.

"It would be a waste of money when I return to Domum. Lord Troy decides what I'm allowed to wear. I doubt very much if he would allow these garments."

They continued on to other stores, even stopping in a hardware store for a few minutes.

"We don't see many tools like these on Domum."

"No? They're pretty basic. Hammer, screwdrivers, saw, pliers."

"I don't know about being basic, but they're all made of metal.

On Domum very little metal is used. Some silver, copper and gold but anything with iron is avoided if possible."

"Why's that?"

"Most metals, but iron and steel in particular, disrupt magic. The spells don't work as well and can even twist them to cause them to do odd things."

"Can you do magic?"

"Very little. Even less here with all the metal and noise in the aether."

"The what? Aether?"

"It's what carries the magic spell. You can't feel it or see it but it carries the magic spells. It's everywhere, though it thins out high above the mountains."

Tom looked sceptical but kept silent.

"You don't believe me?"

"It's not that. I never heard of it before. But if you say it's there, then I'll take your word for it."

"That's okay. You don't have to believe it. It's what I've been told, and I assumed it was true." She watched as another car drove by. "What makes them work?"

"If you open up the front of them, you'll see a motor that burns petrol to make it run." He frowned. "Sorry, that must have been as clear as mud. Hey, are you hungry?"

She appeared to consider the possibility of food for a moment before speaking. "I guess a little."

"There's a pub over there. Let's sit down and get something to eat."

She looked across the street at the Devon Pub. "Women go to pubs here?"

"Definitely. I don't know about the pubs in Domum, but ladies are welcome here."

"Okay, I'm curious if these are the same as the ones back home inside."

She looked around in the interior of the pub and took a deep breath. "Clean, much cleaner than the ones on Domum. And it doesn't smell of old ale and stale food." Marisa looked at the tables and chairs as they walked to a table by a window.

Tom let her sit and asked her what she wanted to drink. "I'll find out what's on the lunch menu when I go up there."

"I don't know. Any ale would be fine. Surprise me."

Tom returned with two pints of beer. "I ordered two bowls of soup and sandwiches for us. I hope that's all right with you."

"'Tis fine with me. Thanks, Tom." She took a sip of the beer. "Oh, this is good. Much better than the ale back home. Like, it's not bitter at all."

"I'm glad you like it. So can you do any magic spells?"

"A couple of small ones. I'm not sure if even they would work here."

Tom almost spoke of the magic spell she must have put on him but took a sip of his beer instead. "What type of spell?"

"Hmm. Ask the serving wench…"

"Waitress, or she'll have our heads."

Marisa grinned. "Okay, I better remember that. Ask the waitress if we can have two glasses of water."

———

"You're going back to Domum? Why?"

"Something I have to do."

Liz looked up at Jon. She opened her mouth to give a retort to him but there was something intangible about his demeanour that froze her reply. He was determined, confident and looked not just big but powerful. It reminded her of the way he looked last time they were on Domum. "Okay, if you you must."

He didn't give a reply, and she immediately understood why. He wasn't asking for her opinion or her approval. He was telling her of his decision. "Please be careful."

"I will. When I get back, I think we best have a talk about us. I have something to say when I return."

Liz wondered what the missing words were, and her heart jumped at the possibility.

"Do you want me to make you something to eat before you leave?"

"No thanks, I'm not hungry."

Liz blinked. She couldn't remember the last time Jon turned down food. He was definitely acting differently. It was a nice change.

———

"Okay, both glasses of water are at the same temperature, right?"

Tom reached out and grasped each glass. "Yeah, they came out of the same tap. Stands to reason."

Marisa leaned forward. "Okay, now be quiet while I concentrate." She began to move her lips to silent words and focus her attention on the glasses.

A minute passed and several more. Her brow creased as she concentrated.

Tom looked between her and the glasses, not noticing anything until a drop of water ran down the outside of one of the glasses. Then another as the condensation began to cover the glass with small water droplets. The surface of the glass began to look uneven. Suddenly Marisa stopped her concentration.

"Now feel the glasses."

He reached out to the two glasses. One was definitely warmer than before. The other glass was cold, cold enough to have small particles of ice floating on top.

"Wow! You transferred energy from one glass of water to the other. That's really cool." He looked excited. "I wonder how much energy is lost in transfer process. We should measure the temperatures before and after…"

She waved her hands at him. "It's just a simple piece of magic. I don't want others to know about it here on the Other-side. Best they don't know how it's done."

"You're right. I just get excited about stuff like this. Physics training and reproducing results under controlled environments and all that stuff. That's a great trick. You could use it to keep soup hot."

She laughed. "It always comes down to food to you men."

"There are other things too."

"Yeah, I forgot. Sex, drink and food keeps men happy." She grinned at him. "Believe me. I know what men are all about."

"I can't argue with you there." He paused for a moment. "So do you really have to go back to Domum, eventually?"

"I guess so. I talked to Council Madoc about it and he said if I stayed here, I would be miserable from bad karma. He's right. Lord Troy owns me until I pay off my debt to him."

"How much is that? Maybe I could help you there."

She looked at him carefully. "Tom, you're a sweet man. But Lord Troy has no need of money. He's not a bad man but I don't see him giving me up. Besides…" She stopped and collected her thoughts. "I see how you look at me and I'm flattered you like me. But I've been with many, many men. I've done things a lady shouldn't do. You see me as a desirable woman, but you don't know my past. I'm afraid I'd be a disappointment to ye, even if I was free to stay."

"You're wrong. I won't judge you by your past. I see you as you are now, and I like you very much."

"Thank you. But let's not go any further. In a few days, I'll be going back to Domum. So let's enjoy the present and not plan any future together, okay?"

Tom reluctantly nodded but didn't speak.

TWENTY-ONE

Council Madoc led the way, with Gilbert hurrying behind him. Jon brought up the rear, glancing at the gnants as they dashed along their sides. It seemed every gnant in the area wanted to have a look at them. As before, the gnants seemed only curious about the humans walking among them and didn't act aggressive. Madoc was prepared to use a spell to keep them away, but so far found it was unnecessary.

Gilbert occasionally grumbled how fast Madoc was leading them as he puffed along. He wasn't looking forward to when they reached Lord Troy's castle and when Madoc would find out more about Gilbert's involvement. Madoc considered using a spell to transport them to the castle after walking an hour on the muddy ground but decided a bit of discomfort was worth it to examine more of the countryside.

For Jon, there was almost a sense of relief as he walked on Domum again. He suddenly felt in control as his confidence returned. He carried a sword borrowed from his uncle's castle, out of Liz's concern about danger, but regarded there was little need for it.

The gnants were curious, but he ignored them as he looked around. He tried to figure out the layout of the land and where the town of Horstruff would have fit in, guessing where the Cobbler

Inn stood. It was a journey to a strange land, but he felt at home. A climb to the top of a hill gave him an opportunity to scan the countryside. He recalled the smaller curvature of the sky signifying Domum was much smaller than Earth. Against the far horizon, he made out a group of dragons as they flew together. He stared at them a moment and called out to Gilbert.

"Gilbert, are those lupus dragons?" He pointed at the far sky.

"Aye, that be lupus. Have no fear, Sir Jon, ol' Gilbert scared them off last time and he cans do it agains."

Jon almost laughed but held back. "Thanks, Gilbert." In truth, lupus dragons didn't normally attack more than two of anything, not wanting to have to fight too much for a meal. In addition, Madoc would be able to use a spell to repel any attack, so the likelihood of Gilbert saving the group from a dragon attack was remote. Still, Jon admired Gilbert's ability to give himself credit whenever a chance existed.

Jon watched a small gnant running next to Gilbert for the past half an hour, gradually drawing closer to him. Now it would scamper up to him and grab at his pant leg, chattering away at him. Gilbert didn't want the attention of the gnant, telling it, "Leaves me alones."

"Gilbert, that gnant seems to like you."

"Sir Jon, tis Marisa's fault. She makes friends with it and nows the demon likes peoples."

"Now, that isn't a bad thing, is it?"

"Maybe yes, maybe no. I's not like gnants."

"Ah, well, they're better friends than enemies."

Gilbert brushed the creature away with his hand. "Maybe."

———

Lord Troy paced about the corridors of his castle, occasionally looking out through one of the balconies.

"I'm sure they're all right, Lord Troy."

He nodded and turned to face Patricia. "But I can't help but worry, for several reasons. Have we sent Gilbert and Marisa to a date with death? As horrible as that would be, it also means there's no help for us. You and the others are my property and I feel a heavy responsibility to ensure your well being."

"Thank you, Lord Troy. But I'm sure Gilbert and Marisa will be fine. After all, Freeman Gilbert is a world traveler even if half his stories are true. I'm sure he can defend himself and Marisa." She touched his arm. "And so far, we are all doing fine. Come to the garden and I'll bring you a drink."

He smiled. "Thank you, Patricia. You make me feel better no matter what the situation."

Lord Troy followed her, his smile disappearing. They still had plenty of food and supplies in storage. But when that ran out, he knew they would have to choose between producing food with magic or obtaining it from the outside world. Food produced by magic looked and tasted the same but didn't carry sufficient nourishment for the body. Eating only magical food meant slow starvation while having a full stomach. Lord Troy himself couldn't venture past his castle's property. If he did, he would die of old age within minutes. It left the alternative of sending the women to go out and collect food. That would be dangerous to those unused to hunting. Not all life native to Domum was edible for human consumption, and they would have to be careful what they chose to eat.

The cause for his greatest concern was the knowledge he had caused the end of Domum, and he cursed himself for his selfishness when he invoked the spells on the Dacron gem.

The garden looked the same as before with flowers filling the air with fragrance. There had not been any more problems with various Domum life forms trying to invade the castle grounds after Lord Troy used a spell to keep them away. Patricia handed him a pint of ale and sat down on a small chair with a table separating them.

"You still look worried, m'lord."

He frowned and took a long drink of the ale. "You're always perceptive to my needs and moods, Patricia. Yes, you are quite right. I've put us all in a situation, not to mention the destruction of the whole of Domum. I have a heavy conscience for what I've done. From there is no escape."

"I fear for your well being, Lord Troy. We need you to be strong now or none of us will survive."

"You are correct. I owe it to you and the others to carry on and find a solution for this dilemma. You must all hate me now."

"Oh, no! All of us care about you very much."

He hung his head, staring at the pint of ale. "How very kind of you to say so."

She sat on the chair next to him. "Lord Troy, my obligation ended with you almost two years ago. Yet I've stayed here. Do you know why?"

He shook his head. "The reasons are not clear to me other than I offer you a comfortable place to live."

She closed her eyes for a moment and leaned forward and reached for his hand. "Lord Troy, when you first purchased me, I resisted your control over me and several times in the first weeks you sent me to spend the night in one of the cells in the lower levels. Each time you offered to send me back if I wished back to the labour house and each time I declined, promising to behave in the future."

"True."

"I swore at the time I would leave as soon as my four years were up, but I'm here still. The reason is I love you, Lord Troy, and want you to be my master. I won't leave you no matter how difficult things are. I trust you to care for me and the others."

Lord Troy's face lost his colour for a moment before turning red. "I had no idea."

"Now you know. So, no matter what our fate, I will be at your side."

He closed his eyes, wetness showing at the corners. "This changes everything." He stood up. "It's time I stopped being concerned about what I did wrong and did something for our future. Come, there's much work to do."

———

Jon followed Madoc, wondering how the older man managed to keep up the pace he did. Gilbert was half walking and half running to stay up with them, puffing as he did so. The gnants continued to follow them, although there seemed to be different ones showing up as they traveled. One gnant continued to stay close to Gilbert, trailing him by a few steps. Gilbert was too tired to chase her away, and the gnant took that as a sign she could continue to stay with him.

"Your friend again, Gilbert?" Jon gave Gilbert a grin.

"I's not her friend. I's told ye that before."

"You did." Jon dropped to one knee and extended a hand to the small gnant.

Slowly, the gnant approached him, her eyes fixed on Jon's.

"Come on, little fella. I won't hurt you."

"Marisa, she said it be a female."

"Okay, come on, little lady."

The gnant stopped within a foot of him, extended her hand to Jon's knee and lightly touched it. Jon slowly moved his hand and touched the gnant's arm. The gnant wiggled a dark red forked tongue at him and gingerly climbed onto his lap. Jon slowly stood up as the gnant clung to his shirt and arm.

Gilbert shook his head. "Gnant's tricky, pretends to like ya."

"Oh, come on, Gilbert. Just how is a gnant supposed to trick me? What could it want from me?"

Gilbert narrowed his eyes as he looked at the gnant. "Don'ts knows. But ye can't trust 'em."

Jon shook his head and began to try to catch up with Madoc.

Madoc eyed the landscape carefully, looking for any clues, anything giving him an insight into what might have happened. He noted Jon was carrying a young gnant and approved of his decision. He wondered if there was any difference between these gnants and the ones on the old Domum and would examine the gnant closer later on. He glanced back at the puffing Gilbert and wondered how much he was to blame for what happened and what portion was at the hands of Lord Troy.

———

"Now, steady, steady. Slowly squeeze the trigger and keep your shoulder firm."

First Patricia, then Gwyneth and finally Lena fired the crossbows.

"Ow, my shoulder." Lena dropped the crossbow and rubbed her shoulder.

Gwyneth giggled. "I think my arrow went the farthest."

Lord Troy rolled his eyes. "Please, ladies, please. You must concentrate harder on the task."

"It's harder than it looks, Lord Troy." Patricia gave him a pout. "We need to practice, that's all."

"Very well. Reload the crossbows."

Lena handed him her crossbow. "Can you reload mine? My arm still hurts."

Lord Troy sighed. "What are you going to do if you are attacked by a dragon and need to reload?"

"Run?"

Lord Troy closed his eyes for a moment. "Let's go through the proper stance again. And let's try to approach the target with an arrow this time."

"Would anyone care for a drink?" Alicia carried drinks on a silver tray, stopping on the edge of the patio. The others turned to her from the grass where they practiced.

Lord Troy nodded. "I really could use one." He sighed again. "Make that two drinks."

———

Madoc continued to make rapid progress under the warm sun. Jon didn't find it difficult to keep up, despite carrying the small gnant. He even tried to talk to the gnant and was pleased when she tried to repeat his phrases.

Gilbert trailed behind, cursing at the gnants following them. It didn't escape Gilbert's attention when they reached Lord Troy's castle Madoc would hear a slightly different version of the events leading to end of Domum. He tried to recall exactly what he said to Madoc and how he could bend any new facts away from pointing at him.

His thoughts were broken by Madoc calling out, "I see Lord Troy's castle."

Gilbert stopped in his tracks. "Trouble. Gilbert sees trouble."

———

Patricia fired the crossbow, the arrow piercing the paper target. She jumped up and down. "I did it! I did it!"

Lord Troy clapped his hands. "Very good, Patricia, very good, indeed. I knew you could do it with a bit of practice."

She stood there beaming at him.

Lord Troy was preparing to give her a kiss of congratulations when Alicia came running onto the patio.

"Alicia, is there a problem?"

"Lord Troy…" She stopped to catch her breath. "…Gilbert has returned! And he has two others with him!"

———

As Madoc stood in front of the entrance of Lord Troy's castle, the door swung open, exposing an excited Alicia.

"Gilbert! You made it! And you've brought back help." She grinned at all three men.

Jon was taken back by the sight of her, forgetting what the ladies of Lord Troy's castle usually wore. In this case, it was just a long yellow skirt hanging around her hips. Only her long hair gave a minor degree of modesty at her top.

Madoc didn't act unduly surprised by her state of dress. "Please inform Lord Troy we wish to see him."

"Oh, please sirs, do follow me. Lord Troy is waiting for you in the main room."

Alicia led the way into the castle and to the main room where Madoc strode in front of the rest.

"You!" He bellowed at Lord Troy as he pointed a finger at him.

Lord Troy stood with hands on his hips and glared back at him.

"Council Madoc! What the devil are you doing here?"

TWENTY-TWO

L ord Perry sat at the long table facing the grinning man across from him.

"So, Captain, you have found a home here as well."

"Lord Perry, this is a truly remarkable place this old sea dog has found. My joints don't ache no more and the oceans here have no storms."

"Oceans?"

"Aye, Lord Perry, aye. You seem to have been given libraries, and I've been given a vast sea to sail upon. I can sail as far as I wish, but if I tire for land, it is always only an hour away. It's magic, I know, but I enjoy it all the same."

"Good on ye, Captain." Lord Perry paused, working out the next words he had to say. "Would you return to the old Domum if you could? I ask you in all seriousness. I have been privileged to observe the new Domum and have discovered there remains a pocket of our old world. There appears to be an attempt to resurrect the original Domum. If it came to be Domum was available for you again, would you return?"

Captain Wright sat in silence.

"Come, Captain, surely you have an opinion on this."

"I don't know what to say. I'm not sure which I should choose.

I'm not even sure if I'm allowed to decide." He shook his head and looked down.

"Don't be concerned about deciding. As you point out, such decision may not be ours to make. But while I for one enjoy this paradise, I wonder if I'm depriving myself of the challenges of life."

The Captain looked up. "Are you saying we have to go through a lifetime of struggles first to have this?"

Lord Perry frowned. "My libraries here are full of the answers I seek. Yet I miss the joy of discovering the truth by piecing together the small clues from many sources."

"Perhaps heaven has come too soon for us, Lord Perry. But what will come of us if we cannot stay here?"

———

Tom sat on the loveseat, staring at the fireplace. He took another sip from his beer and watched a flame lick at a log but failed to ignite the surface.

"Hi."

He looked up at where the voice came from.

"Hi, Angela."

"It's none of my business and I'll understand if you tell me to get lost, but you seem lonely and depressed and I thought I should come over and…"

"Angela, could you please come to the point?"

"The point. Oh, okay. Uh, well, it's like I said, you look so sad."

Tom let out a small sigh.

"Sorry. We—I noticed you like Marisa, but you're not doing anything about it. She's lonely and bored and in a new country, well, a whole new world actually. She really likes you…"

"Angela, I tried to get to know her better but she…she really likes me?"

"Uh, yeah. Like, it's pretty obvious. Maybe she turned you down once before, but I think you can try again?"

"Where…"

"She's sitting upstairs in the lab, staring at a blank monitor."

"Thanks." He put down his beer and headed upstairs.

———

"Marisa." He spoke quietly at the edge of the doorway.

She turned and looked at him for several seconds before responding, "Hi, Tom." She stood up from her chair.

"Mind if I come in?"

She gave him a smile. "Sure, come on in."

He walked in and stood by her. "Look, I know what you said before about just enjoying some time together. But it's been a few days and while we've enjoyed each other's company, I want more."

"Tom, you know…"

"I know." He leaned forward and put his arm around her waist. When she didn't resist, he kissed her.

At first, she hesitated, but put her arms around his neck and kissed him back before pulling away.

She grinned at him. "You sure are determined. Let's go for a walk. Talk a bit."

———

Tom had been on a couple of other walks with Marisa, noticing she really enjoyed looking around the town of Ballymiller. She asked a lot of questions and apparently was trying to figure out the culture and social behaviour of Earth. This time when they stopped in a small clothing store, she let Tom buy her a T-shirt.

"Thanks, Tom. I don't have much to wear and this shirt will give me one more change of clothes. It's really pretty, isn't it?" She held up the pink shirt in front of her.

"On you it will look gorgeous."

"Oh, Tom, you're such a charmer." She grinned at him and stuffed the shirt back into the bag. The first time Tom had offered to buy her something she had turned him down. But he had been persistent in offering, and Liz and Angela had indicated it wasn't considered taboo to accept a gift from a man. They did mention making sure he didn't feel he was also buying something else.

"So, Tom, I be thinking about your, your proposition. If Domum cannot be changed back, then it's be possible I would be sent to Earth with my freedom. If that's the way things turn out, then perhaps we could become friends. I wouldn't have much to offer, being from Domum though."

"You have yourself. That's good enough for me."

She reached over and squeezed his hand as they walked down the street.

"Tom, you make me feel special. I wish Lord Troy, as nice an owner as he is, didn't control me life."

"Maybe I can talk to him."

"That's wishful thinking. There's that pub you took me to before. Fancy buying a lady a pint?"

He grinned at her. "It would be a privilege."

The waitress, Eileen, seemed to recognize them from their last visit and greeted them warmly. Marisa narrowed her eyes when Eileen left her hand on Tom's shoulder a bit too long as she took their order. After she left, Marisa checked to see if Tom watched her walk away.

He kept his eyes on Marisa, getting a smile from her in the process.

"So, tell me, Tom, you said you're finishing yer schooling next year. Then what will ye be doing?"

He shrugged. "I haven't really decided yet. I could do teaching, or more likely do research. There are several university positions open and there are various firms requiring help in physics."

"Sounds like ye will be doing important work."

"I guess so. It's what I'm interested."

"Now if I was going to live here, on Earth, what would I be doing?"

"I haven't thought about that. What do you like to do?"

"I like children a lot."

"Well, you could look after kids then, preschool children, that sort of thing."

"I'd like that." She pulled the fingers from her left hand through her hair. "But if I was to stay on Earth, I would need help to be able to survive."

"I'd help you, make sure you'd be okay. You know that."

"I do, Tom. I know you're willing to take care of me. But that wouldn't be much different from what I have on Domum, dependent on someone else. I know what you're going to say, I wouldn't be a slave here. But it amounts to the same thing, doesn't it?"

"I don't think it does. You could leave me anytime you wanted to."

She frowned. "But I still wouldn't have any place to go to."

"You missed my point. Whether you had a place to go to or not, that is your responsibility. Your decision is how to prepare yourself. On Domum you didn't have that responsibility. Here you do and you have to take advantage of it."

Marisa was quiet and took a sip of her ale. "You're right. I was looking for an excuse not to stay here. Earth, you, seem too good to be true."

He reached across the table. "Marisa, I want to do what I can for you, that's all. I won't try to keep you if you want to leave."

She took his hand. "In the meantime, we should have another pint."

———

Angela sat with Liz by the fireplace. The afternoon was warm and while there wasn't any need for the fire it was still a comfortable place to sit with the large chairs.

"Fancy some more tea, Angela?"

"Sure, though I could use something stronger."

Liz grinned. "Me as well."

Liz got up, walked over to an old wood cabinet and looked inside the door. "Gin or whisky?"

"My man, Jon, now he can eat. An' drink." Liz burst into a giggle. "Sometimes more than my man can 'andle."

"He seems nice." Angela grinned at Liz. The alcohol hit, and Liz's accent had become stronger along with her manner of speaking changed.

"Aye, he be that." Liz took another drink of her gin. "What is happening between you and Council Madoc?"

"Things are going okay. I was having a rough time just before I met him. Mom and Dad were giving me the gears about working in a bar and pursuing a singing career, which was going nowhere. Then my love life was zippo. I had just dumped my idiot boyfriend and thinking about going into teaching. I have my degree..." Angela paused to take another drink. "Hell, I was feeling just lost.

You know what I mean? Like absolutely nothing is going right in your life?"

"Aye, I do." Liz nodded remembering she was last year stuck in Domum.

"Then I collided with Madoc, and right at that very second I could sense the power in him. He was a rock, something strong, someone to whom I could cling. I wasn't thinking of romance or anything like that, just he could be someone who would… I dunno what I was thinking. Just he was strong, and I needed someone like that in my life."

"I know what you mean. Like when Jon, was in Domum an' was known as Sir Jon, the dragon slayer. I felt so safe in his arms when I found him again."

"But I fell for Madoc and now I'm worried he will disappear from my life. What if he stays in Domum and doesn't come back? What will I do?"

"He'll be back soon enough. But eventually he's heading back to Domum if it can be saved. That be his home, where he's held in high regard as Council Madoc, the voice to the king and lords. On Earth, he doesn't have that power. Here, he must feel like he's in shackles."

"So to stay with him I'd have to go to Domum?"

"Aye." She looked at Angela's blank expression. "'Tis not a bad place to be if you be with Council Madoc. Live in a castle. Servants. And as a bonus, a warlock who can keep you looking young."

Angela studied her drink. "Hmm, that doesn't sound so bad when you put it that way."

———

"You're such a fool. An egotistical fool." Council Madoc sat on one chair with a glass of red wine in his hand. Across from him in an identical green leather chair sat Lord Troy Sussex. On the other chairs placed in a large oval sat Jon, Gilbert, and Patricia n the main room.

"Ha! You're a fine one to talk about an ego."

"Your ill thought out spells have made you a prisoner in your own castle. It serves you right."

"And you managed to get yourself exiled from Domum itself thanks to your thirst for power. Justice, there, I would say."

"Justice? What justice is there for Domum when a madman casts magic spells on it?"

"What do you know of magic spells other than your cheap parlour tricks you do on the Other-side?"

"Bah!"

"Dragon's breath!"

Jon, Gilbert, and Patricia listened to the exchange without speaking. Behind them at the room's entrance, stood the other ladies of the castle, also quiet as they listened to the insults going on for almost a quarter of an hour. At first, Jon thought they might come to blows and cast spells at each other. But they remained content to using speech to inflict points on each other.

Council Madoc took another drink of the wine and studied it a moment in the crystal goblet. "Remarkable quality for Domum."

"Thank you. The wine requires a special process I perfected over the years. Magic spells alone cannot accomplish the layers of flavour."

Jon was puzzled by the sudden change of conversation and looked at Gilbert. But Gilbert was intent on his own beverage and not paying much attention.

"Well, perhaps it's best we study this problem we have."

"Of course. Please follow me to the upstairs library where I keep the rare books."

Jon followed them out of the room and caught up with Patricia.

"What the hell was all that about?" he whispered.

"Lord Troy and Council Madoc do this every time they meet. You should hear them during a chess game. I think they do it to relieve the stress of being polite to everyone else."

"They had me worried. I thought they were going to start casting spells at each other."

"Not to worry, Sir Jon. They're both too powerful in magic for that to happen. "'Tis easier to defend against magic than to create it."

———

Council Madoc studied the open spell book on the table. "Then you added this spell?"

"Yes. The previous spells didn't appear to have any effect on the gem so I decided this one would have a better chance."

Council Madoc frowned and shook his head. "I regret to inform you this is more complicated than I first anticipated. At first, I thought I could just use undo spells to reverse what was done, but that does not appear to be the case now."

Jon looked at the large leather-bound book and at Madoc. "Why not? Not that I understand spells."

"Well, for a way of an explanation suppose you mix flour, water and egg together. I can use a spell to withdraw the water or the egg or the flour and return them to their original forms. But if you take the same mixture and bake it, I can no longer use a simple spell to pull out the flour. It is no longer just flour but has changed to something else. The same is true for the spells Lord Troy has invoked. The spells have combined in such a way it will take a great deal of work to return Domum back to normal, if in fact it can be done at all."

———

Jon sat with Gilbert in the rose garden eating lunch, listening to Gilbert as he rattled on about his innocence between gulps of his ale.

"I's says to ye, Sir Jon, how was a poor freeman supposed to knows what evils them gem possessed? I's not knows what Lord Troy plans."

Jon held a piece of meat on his fork, stopping it in the middle of its journey to his mouth. "Gilbert, I don't know what happened back then, but there's no way in hell I'm going to believe you didn't know what that gem was or if Lord Troy was going to try to use it."

"Truly me says to yous, Sir Jon…"

"Hold it there, Gilbert. I'm thinking if I catch you telling one more lie I should cut out your tongue. Now, what were you saying?"

Gilbert took another drink of his ale as he studied Jon's face. "I's sorry if I misleads yous, Sir Jon. But I's swears on a dragon's egg me meant no harms."

"That I might believe. But Council Madoc may be the one you

should be concerned about. He wasn't happy when I last saw him going over those spells."

Gilbert's eyes opened wider. "Sir Jon, yous stick up for yer ol' friend Gilbert, won'ts ya?"

"Only if you tell the truth and stop pretending you're innocent of this whole mess."

Gilbert held up his mug. "Aye, Sir Jon, aye. Gilbert tells the truth from nows on." Then he quickly took another drink as he peered at Jon.

———

"I can't solve this dilemma. If I remove the second spell by using these two spells, then the first one affects the third spell differently that won't be any better than the situation we have now."

Lord Troy shook his head. "You're the expert on using multiple spells. I thought perhaps we could work backward from the third spell…"

Council Madoc shook his head. "That won't work. It's too ingrained with the second spell. The second spell is the key, I'm sure of it. If we can remove the second spell, then the third spell becomes more potent, but we can then remove it. Unfortunately, the first spell is bound to both the second and third spells and we have to find a way to separate the spells into separate entities."

"What do you suggest?"

"I'm not sure anymore. What does that book have to say on interlocking spells?" He pointed at a green and black spell book.

"Very little, I'm afraid." He slid over the book resting on the table. "It does have some excellent complex spells but doesn't describe any counter acting spells which may be useful."

Council Madoc opened the book and began to flip through the pages. He stopped at a page and briefly ran his finger down the lines before shaking his head and going to the next page.

"These may be complex spells, but they are not very well put together. This one actually has two extra lines in it to accomplish the same thing." Madoc examined several other spells. "Dragon's breath. This youth spell is actually written wrong. They used too many lines, and they put one of the spells in the wrong place. Do you know what would happen if someone used this spell?" Madoc looked up at the frozen face of Lord Troy, his eyes wide open.

Council Madoc looked at the youth spell once more and back at Lord Troy who remained standing still, staring at the book.

"What do you mean the spell was written wrong?"

TWENTY-THREE

"Just it was written wrong. Whoever used…" Council Madoc blinked. "You used this spell?"

Lord Troy nodded.

"No wonder you're trapped in your own castle."

"So I didn't read the spell wrong. It was written wrong." Lord Troy leaned on the table with his hands, his head bowed down. "All those years."

Council Madoc frowned. "You should know better than to read off spells from an old, unknown textbook. The reason some of these books became rare is the spells in them weren't very good and the copies then thrown away."

Lord Troy looked up. "I suppose you're right. Here, I thought I was fortunate to find this rare old book."

"In a way, it was a blessing. You ended having a preservation spell on the castle property instead of just a youth spell on yourself. Because of that, you and the others are still alive to send for help to Earth."

Lord Troy considered what he said. "I suppose that's true. Although if I hadn't put a spell on the gem in the first place, we wouldn't be talking about the need of any blessing."

"Fate has a way of setting up circumstances to give us a chance to survive. We have been given a chance to save Domum. The how is what eludes us right now."

———

Patricia approached Jon as he sat on the patio, sipping a pint of ale. He looked bored as he stared at the top of the table until he saw Patricia wearing only a long blue silk skirt. Jon had never entirely gotten use to the manner of dress of the ladies at Lord Troy's castle, and the sight of her almost caused him to spill his drink.

"Sir Jon, I hope I'm not disturbing you." She smiled as she stood by his table.

"Not at all, not at all." Jon began to rise from his chair.

She sat down on the chair opposite of him. "It truly is nice to see you again, Sir Jon. When I heard you went back to the Other-side I never expected to see you again, or at least so soon. But I'm glad you decided to help save Domum like the last time you were here."

"Thanks, but I'm not sure what I can do to help yet."

Patricia played with her hair with her fingers. "Well, Sir Jon, there is one thing you can do if you're willing."

"Sure. What would that be?"

"We need to have some fresh meat and was wondering if you would be able to do some hunting." She bit her lower lip.

"Sure, I guess I could do that."

She gave a quick smile and leaned toward him. "We, us ladies, want to go with you on the hunt. Perhaps you could give us some instructions."

Jon frowned, wondering how he was supposed to hunt with a group of women hanging around him. Any chance of silently approaching an animal would be impossible. "I tell you what, how about I just take you? It will be easier to teach you by yourself and I can take the others another time?"

"All right. I'm sure they'll understand when you explain that to them."

He stood. "We might as well do this now. Where do you keep the weapons?"

"I'll show you, Sir Jon." She smiled happily at him.

———

Patricia, Gwyneth, and Lena chatted away as they followed Jon past the property of the castle. Jon thought he would have more success hunting by himself, but the three women acted so happy when it was hinted they might be going outside he didn't have the heart to leave them behind. The fact they wore just a skirt hardly influenced his decision at all. They did put on suitable clothing for going outside such as leather vests, sandals and a heavier skirt, and carried their own crossbows as if they knew how to use them.

Gnants had ventured onto the property but scattered on their approach save for one small gnant that ran to Jon when she saw him.

He picked her up. "Okay, okay. Nice to see you too. But I'm going to do some hunting so I'll have to let you down soon."

The gnant chattered back at him, clicking out sounds at him and then one word, "You."

Jon looked at the gnant. "You're learning to speak."

"To."

Jon put down the gnant. "We'll talk later."

"Talk later."

Jon gave Patricia a smile. "Quick learner."

"That she is."

They walked among the odd tree-like plants looking for any possible game. The gnants continued to keep a safe distance from them as they followed along except for the one small gnant running around their legs.

It was Lena who spotted the first deer-size creature lurking among the trees. The head was oversized for the body as it attacked the plants with a large mouth. The coat consisted of hair of a mixture of yellow, brown and black with the body supported by heavy legs with a thin tail swishing back and forth. Near the creature, they saw several more of its kind, each one munching on the tough plants.

Jon spotted the largest member of the group. It had a set of two small horns on its head and he decided it was the male to provide protection for the rest. It stood a short distance away on a small rise, its head swaying back and forth.

"Okay, let's see if we can get one of them straying away from the others." Before he could select one, the gnants made an attack of their own.

The gnants had followed their hunting party and after some high-pitched chatter decided to take advantage of the available prey. Three of the gnants attacked the lone male to distract it, darting in and around as it tried in vain to catch one of them. Meanwhile, a half dozen other gnants attacked a small female on the opposite side of the herd, jumping on its back and digging their claws and teeth into it. Another gnant bit and hung onto the throat of the frightened creature as it desperately tried to shake off the gnants.

The rest of the creatures scattered, running in a zigzag pattern. Jon pointed at one of them coming in their direction, lowered his crossbow and fired at it. The women fired as well, but only Patricia managed to sink an arrow, landing in its hind quarters. Jon's shot penetrated the chest causing it to freeze in one spot. Jon loaded another arrow and was prepared to shoot again when the beast dropped to its forelegs and fell to its side.

Jon immediately headed toward it. The gnants had taken down the other creature and had begun to feast on it. The three gnants left the male alone to join in the feast. The male was panting from its exertions and choose not to interfere with the gnants as they worked on the body of the female.

The gnants not participating in the hunt waited nearby until the other gnants had their fill of the beast. A few of the others headed toward the fallen creature Jon had shot.

Jon immediately recognized a problem was occurring. He aimed his crossbow and shot another arrow into the dead beast, causing the gnants to turn their attention to him.

"Hey, leave it alone!" Jon hooked the crossbow to a strap on his back and pulled out his sword. He continued to advance rapidly as he swung the sword around. He paused to slice the two-inch trunk of one of the pseudo trees at his waist height causing it to tumble to the ground.

The gnants shrieked at him one more time and ran off.

"Sir Jon, you scared them off. You're so brave." Patricia looked up at him with admiration.

He blushed. "It's nothing, really. I've had to deal with gnants before."

Jon, with the help of the women, pulled the beast with a length of rope back toward Lord Troy's castle. Jon noted the creature had three claws on each foot looking suitable for digging into the ground. The mouth was full of large flat teeth looking like it was capable of taking a large amount of plants at one time.

The small gnant had stayed with them, occasionally riding on the creature. This time she entered the castle, chattering as Patricia carried her.

Lord Troy was pleasantly surprised how fast they had managed to accomplish their task and heaped praise on both Jon and the ladies. The women immediately filled Lord Troy in on the details of the hunt and in particular, how "Sir Jon had boldly charged forward and scared the gnants away while whipping his sword in the air."

"We must commission a painting of such bravery," Lord Troy stated as he focused on a blank area of the wall.

They decided this was also a cause of a celebration and a round of drinks was consumed.

Council Madoc joined them, curious what the creature looked like before it was taken to the butcher shop located just behind the kitchen.

"And what of this?" He pointed at the gnant sitting on Patricia's lap, "Is there a particular reason you brought her inside?"

"Oh, Council Madoc, she just likes to stay with us. She's not causing us any problems and is learning how to speak," Patricia turned her attention to the gnant. "Don't you, you little talker?"

"Very good. If you can teach her how to talk, it may prove to be beneficial later."

"How is the problem of removing the spells going?" Jon asked.

Council Madoc sighed. "It has been difficult. There are three different spells interlocked with each other. I cannot simply invoke a spell to remove one of them because it is no longer the same spell. I may have to write out a spell that does the same as those three together and then design a counter spell."

"Is that hard to do?"

"It can be. I have to study very carefully the effects of the present conditions."

"Well, I guess we have time to work it out."

"Not necessarily. A spell like the one we are fighting to remove is very powerful and is eroding away at the spell used to preserve the castle from destruction."

"The spell is eroding the castle?"

"I will explain. All spells fade with time. How fast will happen depends on the strength of the original spell and the power of the person evoking it. Some spells can last a thousand years. Others can fade in a few hours. For example, I can turn water into ice and after a while the ice will return to water. You might assume the air around the ice is causing it to melt, but that isn't true. The spell itself is slowly eroding. I can make the ice remain frozen easily for a day or a week if I wanted to."

"So how long do we have before the preservation spell disappears?"

"Well, it doesn't just vanish immediately but just continually gets weaker. If one studied the edge of the castle property, you would notice signs of the preservation spell fading in due course. As far as your question on how long it will take is hard to ascertain. Certainly a few more weeks but less than a few months."

"So we don't have long to solve the problem of returning Domum to its previous state."

"Time is not on our side, Sir Jon."

———

Lord Perry wandered the halls of what seemed to him the largest castle ever created. Occasionally, he would enter a room, look about the contents and be amazed at what he saw. Rich paintings, furniture, decorations and ornaments gave him pause to reflect on the beauty he saw around him. He wasn't alone during his journey as scores of people walked around him, many of them engaged in conversation.

He had learned this new place had miracles within it. No matter how far he walked if he thought about his library, he would be within a short distance away. Strangers, no matter what language they spoke, could easily be understood when they conversed with him.

So far, the new world had been much like Domum as he remembered but his guide, the former King Ethelwulf, told him if he wanted, he could show him the people that came from the Other-side and their habitat.

"Would they be spirits as well?" he inquired.

"If that is the name you wish to use for our state then the answer is yes."

"I would like to take you up on the offer someday soon. However, I was curious where I might locate a Lady Beatrice? I never had much time for romance and now I wonder if I spent too much time in books and not enough for other pleasures."

King Ethelwulf smiled. "I'll see what I can do to assist you there. Come with me."

They walked down the marble halls, passing rooms large and small. Lord Perry talked about the many wonders the castle showed, yet they had seen only a portion of it.

"The castle doesn't hide any secrets, Lord Perry. Everything can be learned here. The trick is to ask the right question and know where to look. Then it becomes a matter of accepting the truth and what it means." He smiled. "The truth sometimes can startle you with its simplicity. We look for a deep meaning to what we ask and find out the answer is as simple as turning over a coin. The question and the answer are tied to each other like two sides of a coin. If you have a question, you have to understand the answer is within your grasp too. What is astonishing is once you work out the answer to your question, no matter what it is, you realize you always did know the answer. You simply forgot it for a little while."

"Then I've forgotten a lot, King Ethelwulf."

"You do keep forgetting I'm no longer a king."

"My apologies, Ethelwulf. It seems awkward to me."

"We all need time to adjust here. I do believe this is where you can find Beatrice." He paused at an open doorway. Inside, a dozen people moved about a flowered garden. Some read while others simply strolled about.

"A garden inside the castle?"

"Why not? If people wish to have a garden here, then they shall have a garden. It can be as big as you like. Picture the garden twice this size and it will happen. All things are possible in the castle."

"Which one is Beatrice?"

"Go inside. You will find her easily enough."

Lord Perry walked inside, smiling back at those who acknowledged him.

"Lord Perry." A soft voice came from behind him.

He took in a deep breath and turned around.

"Beatrice."

"Lord Perry." She inclined her head.

"Please, it is now Perry. I came here looking for you."

"Really? How odd. I came here to find you. My guide said you would be coming here."

Lord Perry broke into a laugh. "Then perhaps it is not such a coincidence after all."

They strolled about the garden exchanging stories of their experiences. She had been in the castle several days before him and was adjusting to the strangeness of it.

"It is truly remarkable, Perry, Whatever you wish for happens. Except you. I was looking for you the past two days, but I was told you hadn't arrived yet. I was suspicious as almost everyone I knew was here except you."

"I had avoided the end of Domum by going out to sea. Alas, the curtain of change encircled us. But you were looking for me?"

"I've dropped many hints at you over the years of my interest in you but you never seemed to notice. I decided if I missed one lifetime of opportunity, I wasn't going to miss out on this one too."

He shook his head. "Really? How could I be so blind? I just could never sum up enough courage to invite you for dinner."

She stopped and took one of his hands in hers. "What we did or didn't do then doesn't matter now." She smiled at him. "Come and let me show you more of the garden."

He smiled broadly. "That sounds wonderful. That is a beautiful dress you have on." He looked at the yellow gown with small blue flowers embroidered along the edges.

"I'm glad you like it. It is the dress, or rather a copy of it, I was going to wear if you ever invited me to attend a formal function."

PART FOUR

Life without uncertainty is a predictable life of monotony.

TWENTY-FOUR

Marisa held hands with Tom as they walked next to Liz. Tom had asked Liz if she would mind showing Marisa the inside of her parents' home. Liz had readily agreed and the next day the three strolled to where the O'Douls lived. Now, she squeezed his hand tighter as they used the front steps.

Marisa was taken aback by the size and the layout of the home. The bathroom was located inside the home to her pleasant surprise. The use of hallways was not something she saw in the modest homes on Domum, where one often had to go through a bedroom to go from the drawing room to the dining room. She saw electrical devices everywhere, and the television was something baffling. Liz's parents were good hosts and didn't react to Marisa's wide-eyed excitement of their home. She sipped her tea as she stared at a photograph hanging on the wall.

"Tom, what kind of painting be that?" she whispered.

"It's not a painting. It's a photo, uh, a chemical process, converts light to, well, it's not a painting. It's a real image."

"Oh. It looks so real." She didn't appear to understand his explanation.

"Well, that's how a camera works. It captures a moment in time. So it's supposed to be real."

"I don't know if I could ever get use to all the strange things here. It may be best I go back to Domum."

Tom was silent for a few seconds then he spoke in a whisper. "Don't say that. Don't look for an excuse to leave here."

She took another sip of her tea and placed it on the saucer resting on the kitchen table. Slowly she reached across and squeezed his hand.

"Have some more biscuits, dear." Mrs. O'Doul pushed the plate toward her. "More tea?" She picked up the teapot and moved it toward Marisa's cup.

Liz watched Marisa struggle to keep her composure. She saw how Marisa found everything mysterious, causing her to look around wide-eyed at common objects. Then Tom had whispered something to her, and she suddenly looked like she was on the verge of tears. Her mother had caught it as well and quickly pushed the biscuits and an offer of more tea as a cover up.

"Come with me, Marisa. I want to show you the garden out back."

Marisa nodded, quickly got up from the table and followed Liz. Tom began to rise but Liz fixed him with a stare and he quickly got the hint and sat again.

"It be a nice garden."

"Are you okay? You looked upset back there."

"Tom, he's so kind to me. Really wants me to stay here. But I can't and he doesn't understand that, won't accept it. He said, 'Don't look for an excuse to leave here.' I'm not. I don't have a choice. I belong to Lord Troy and that's all there is to it."

Liz touched her arm with her hand. "I'm sure Tom understands that. He just doesn't want you to leave." She gave her a smile. "It's nice to be wanted, though, isn't it?"

Marisa nodded. "You're right. I guess I've been on a dragon's tail ride these past few days."

"That you have. I guess if you can survive a journey with Gilbert, you can survive anything."

"True words you speak. Thanks for your concern. I'll be all right now."

They walked slowly back to the Miller Castle with Marisa and Tom saying little but holding hands. When they walked inside, Tuck

THE CURSE OF THE DACRON GEM

and Gordon Miller were sharing a drink of sherry, discussing quantum time effects.

"Where's Angela?"

"She was here for a bit but kept yawning and then went to bed." Gordon Miller held up the bottle of sherry. "Care to join us?"

Liz laughed. "You must be joking. Poor Angela, you two must have bored her to tears."

Tuck looked surprised. "She didn't say anything."

"Because she was being polite. Me, I'd start singing until you two switched subjects."

Marisa also immediately turned down their offer to join them. Tom declined as well after a small hesitation and followed Marisa after she bid them goodnight. Liz trailed the couple as she went to her own room and wasn't surprised when Tom disappeared behind Marisa's bedroom door.

———

Jon carried the crossbow slung around his back with Patricia strolling next to him. He had managed to shoot two rabbit-sized creatures, though that was where the similarities ended. Their heads had small ears with large eyes and snouts with the body covered with long black hair and a long thin tail. Jon decided to hunt again after they found the creature, they killed earlier had musky tasting meat.

"I hope these will be better."

Jon hefted the two creatures in his arms. "Well, I hope so. Lot of them running about, but they're on the small side."

As they approached Lord Troy's castle, Patricia pointed at a part of the hedge making up the maze used to protect the castle. "Look, it seems like part of the hedge is missing."

Jon studied the area where she pointed. "Oh, that's not good. Not good at all."

Council Madoc came out with Jon and Patricia to study the hedge. "You are quite correct, Sir Jon. The hedge is now eroding away. It would appear Lord Troy Sussex's preservation is now weakening."

"Any clue on how long we have before the castle itself is attacked?"

"Of course such an assessment is hard to make but once the preservation spell starts to fail, the rate accelerates. I would estimate less than a week, perhaps four or five days."

Patricia stood silently, biting her lip.

Madoc turned to walk back into the castle, wondering what he could do to solve the spell before time ran out. A hand tugged at his sleeve and he stopped, surprised anyone would do such a thing. As a powerful warlock few people dared to impose themselves on him or to interfere with him in any way. Madoc looked at the red-eyed Patricia, her mouth trying to speak as she stumbled out whispered words.

"Patricia, what is wrong?"

She clutched at his sleeve. "Council Madoc. Please, please. You must save him."

"I assure you, Patricia, I'm doing the best I can to save Domum." He looked down at her hand gripping his sleeve.

"I don't care about Domum. Find a way to save him. Please, I will give you anything I have. Anything you desire."

Madoc took a deep breath and gently removed her hand. "I assure you while your offer is genuine it is not necessary. I will endeavour to save Domum which is also the best way to save Lord Troy."

"But if you can't save Domum, maybe you can change the youth spell on him."

Madoc shook his head. "I understand what you are saying. But Lord Troy would agree with me, the priority is to save Domum. Saving Domum means saving countless lives. Lord Troy is but one man who already has had a long and prosperous life."

Patricia burst into tears and fell to her knees. "Then you're condemning him to death."

"I must do what I must do. This is not easy for me to do but I must devote all my efforts toward saving Domum."

"I hate you," she whispered.

Madoc clenched his jaw and walked back to the castle.

———

Angela took another bite of her toast and watched Marisa and Tom giggle as he poured her tea at the kitchen counter. He was wearing his jeans, and it seemed nothing else. She was wearing his shirt, and it was definitely the only thing she had on, with his T-shirt exposing the bottom of her cheeks. So far, they had ignored Angela and Liz sitting at the table other than laughing a good morning to them.

Marisa and Tom carried their mugs out of the kitchen with Marisa at the last moment tugging down the front of her shirt between her legs.

"Well they seem to be getting along rather well."

"Hmm. It was bound to happen with the way Tom drooled every time she came within range and her being lonely." Liz raised her eyebrows.

"I'm glad she found someone she can spend time with, but I hope she doesn't make a habit of walking around undressed like that. With her high beams on there sure wasn't much hiding what she had under that shirt, including the part escaping from under the shirt."

"She was used to showing off her body back in Domum, so I guess we should be thankful if she has at least learned total nudity isn't acceptable here."

"Either she learns to wear more than a shirt too small for her or we'll have to start walking around in our underwear to compete." Angela laughed.

"Excuse me, boys, but does this thong make my ass look fat?" Liz laughed out loud.

"Come on, let's clean up here and head downtown and have a look around. There's a danger the men will get up and start discussing quantum mechanics again."

"Oh, God forbid. I couldn't believe how they kept talking about string this and gravity that even after I tried to change the subject."

Liz and Angela cleaned up the kitchen and left the castle with a note they had gone for a walk. Marisa and Tom had not returned from the bedroom after taking their tea there.

Liz liked Angela's attitude. She seemed to be able to adjust to different situations quickly and wasn't averse to pushing the envelope to have some fun. They went through the clothes in the small shop and, as Liz indicated, they were on the conservative side. Angela did pick in the girl's section a flared skirt. The skirt was meant for a girl with a large waist and Angela felt she could fit into it. "Gives me an innocent school girl look, don't you think?"

"School girl look, all right, but not the innocent part." Liz laughed.

"What about you? Find anything?"

"No, maybe I have something at home."

"Come on. Let's look over there." She pointed over to a rack of discounted items.

After shopping, they stopped at a pub for lunch and a drink.

"Are you worried about Jon?"

"No, he can take care of himself. I do miss him of course but I'm anxious to see what he's going to be like when he comes back."

"What do you mean?"

"He has two personalities. In one, he is passive and unsure of himself. He also eats too much—way too much. Then there's a Jon that is confident, determined and makes me want to fall into his arms. So when he returns again from Domum, which Jon will he be?"

"I guess you will find out when he gets back." Angela took a drink from her pint. "If he proposes, will you say yes?"

Liz blushed. "I dunno. I have to think about that one."

"Let me guess, if it's the confident Jon you will say yes."

"I would if he would stay that way."

"Maybe all he needs is a woman, such as yourself, to help him be confident. Sounds like he needs you to give him that strength."

"I don't know 'bout that. Fancy another pint?"

Liz laughed as Angela told a story of a time she had to share a dressing room with three other women when she was trying to make a career as a singer.

"Seriously, there we were all cramped in this small dressing room, and the two men each had their own rooms by the way, banging elbows and bumping bums as we tried to get ready. Then this girl, a sophisticated looking redhead, is watching me as I'm trying to pull the top of my dress on. I smiled at her because my boobs were hanging out when she propositions me!"

Liz grinned. "What did you say?"

"I stood there with my mouth open and finally shook my head no. I had this image what lesbians looked like or acted. Not her. She looked like the wife of a successful businessman."

"I know what you mean. I have a girlfriend at university, an acquaintance really, who has a boyfriend but also has the odd fling with a girl. She doesn't hide her feelings either, claims she'll pick sides when the time is right."

"Marisa was telling me at times she would share a bed with two, three, four other females with one man. I couldn't even imagine what that would be like."

"Well, she certainly is experienced then. Poor Tom, does he know what he's getting into?"

"Well, he did go willingly back into the lioness' den this morning." Angela laughed as she took another drink. "She has certainly attracted his attention since she arrived. Arriving almost naked will do that, I suppose."

"Can I ask you something about Madoc concerning that?"

Liz nodded.

"Well, I'm a bit confused about when I wear different clothes. When we did a show, I would wear different costumes, and one of them was essentially a thong bikini. It wasn't something I thought was too risqué, especially for a stage show. But I had a feeling he was uncomfortable with me wearing it even though he denied it later. Now, I find out from Marisa, she and other women wore next to nothing in this Lord Troy's castle. So what's the deal there?"

"Oh, Council Madoc isn't judgmental about what you wear here. It's just he doesn't know what is acceptable here. On Domum women are expected to be covered up for the most part when in public and can be arrested for too much exposure. But that law only applies being out in public. In bars, the waitresses—Gilbert called them serving wenches—had slits on their skirts to their hips and their tops would be left half open. As long as they covered up when outside they could dress or be undressed as they pleased. Lord Troy is one of those lords who liked his ladies long on exposure, and it's considered scandalous what goes on in his castle. Kind of like the Playboy Mansion, I suppose. Anyway, he does throw parties at the castle and I guess no one turns down an invitation. When Council Madoc sees you in a bikini, he's trying to relate it to Domum."

"He doesn't think bad of me, does he, like I was a serving wench?"

"Oh, no. I suspect he likes you quite fine. He was just a bit a shocked to see what Earth women wear. I remember I was going horseback riding with Tony and I was wearing a long skirt. I pulled up my skirt and exposed a bit of my leg above ankle. You should have seen his eyes bug out at that! It was as if I had flashed my boobs at him." Liz giggled at the memory.

Angela laughed with her. "If only it was that easy to attract guys here."

"I'm not so sure we want the kind of men that live on Domum. They can be rather chauvinistic."

"Tell me more about Domum. If I want to figure out Madoc, I guess I better know what kind of world he came from."

Liz and Angela laughed as they walked and stumbled back to the Miller Castle.

"They're going to wonder what happened to us."

"More like wondering who's going to cook dinner," Liz retorted.

"Uncle Gordon, he does make a good tea." Liz laughed as she opened the gate to the castle front yard.

"Maybe Marisa knows how to make the Domum delicacy of cooked dragon."

"Angela, look!" Liz whispered as she tugged at her sleeve.

Angela looked across the yard near the castle and saw a small figure. At first, she thought it might be a garden gnome until it moved. She held back a gasp by covering her mouth, but the small creature turned and looked at both of them. The creature appeared to be a small man, about three feet high and wore a dark brown coat over grey pants. It began to reach inside its coat as it backed away from them.

"Wait! I have something for you." Liz dug into her purse and pulled out a few coins. "Look, these are for you. I just want to ask you something."

Laquil peered at the shiny coins in her hand. They did attract his attention like most shiny or sparkling items did and she didn't react to his presence with screams or other hysteria. He had seen her before as well, both on Earth and on Domum. Still, being cautious was how he managed to survive on the different worlds and was prepared to use his crystals to disappear if they made any move to capture him. "Wha' ye want?"

"Just want you to answer a few questions."

"Wha' questions?"

Liz slowly put the coins on the ground and took a step back. "You know Domum has changed."

"Ya, no good to visit now."

"You mean because only gnants live there now?"

"They would eat Laquil but I leave quick like."

Liz pondered the thought of the gnants with their sharp teeth and claws trying to catch Laquil and have him for food. "Do you know why Domum changed? What caused it?"

"Ya, enchanted crystal causes it."

"Council Madoc is going to try to use magic to reverse its spell. Do you know how he's doing? If he succeeded or not?"

"Laquil not know how Council Madoc do. Crystal cannot be stopped by magic alone. This Laquil know."

"Magic can't stop it? Isn't there anything that can be done to stop this crystal?"

"Laquil know how to stop crystal."

"How?"

Laquil looked at the coins. "Want more coins. Shiny metal. Then tell."

TWENTY-FIVE

Lord Perry strolled with Beatrice, wondering if he dared to touch her hand. "I am amazed how big this castle is, but I guess it has to accommodate a lot different people from different eras. The rooms seem to go on forever yet one can never get lost."

"Perry, you do know you are babbling, don't you?"

"Yes, I suppose I am."

"Are you really nervous being around me?"

"I admit I am."

"I'm nervous being around you too, Perry." She took his hand into hers. "Perhaps we need to first accept we both like each other and then we will be a little more relaxed." His big hand felt damp in hers as she waited for his reaction.

"Then I like you very much, Beatrice." He turned toward her with a big smile.

"Look, there is Ethelwulf."

Ethelwulf walked casually toward them and gave them a warm hello as he approached.

"Discussing many things, may I presume?"

"Yes, we are. Well, actually Beatrice told me to stop babbling about the size of the castle and to relax." He chuckled.

"The castle is a marvellous structure, but you may be surprised not everyone sees this as a castle."

"No?"

"Father lets us see what is most comfortable with us. For people from Earth, they see a large house. Gnants see a large mud hut."

"Gnants have a place here too?"

"I can take you where they reside sometime. They will see themselves in a mud hut with many rooms while you will see it as part of the castle. Father has a place for all his creatures who want to be with him."

"Even the very small?"

"If they are capable of love and understanding when they are alive then Father has room for them."

"This is truly amazing."

"Every day I learn something new about this wonderful home." He paused and looked first at Beatrice and then at Perry. "I thought I should tell you the end of your old Domum is near now, perhaps another day or two before it will be too late for Council Madoc and his friends to reverse what has happened. The last people from Domum will be joining us then, including your uncle, Lord Troy Sussex. I was wondering if you would be so kind as to be his guide when he arrives here and help through the transition."

Perry was silent for a moment. "The end you say?" He nodded. "I would be honoured to help Lord Troy."

"Excellent. No doubt he will have guilty feelings as he was the one who caused the demise of Domum. I trust you do not harbour any ill towards him?"

"None. What is done is done. I am at peace here and I have Beatrice here to walk and converse with now."

———

Council Madoc stumbled into the dining room for dinner. His eyes red as he looked around the table at the others.

Lord Troy waited until he sat before speaking, "Council Madoc, perhaps you should have a rest after dinner."

He shook his head. "No, I will use a simple spell to keep me alert. Time is of the essence here. I do have a bit of good news. I have managed to unlock the third spell from the first two."

"Bravo, Council Madoc, bravo!"

"Thank you, but I have much work to do to unlock the first two. Still, I now know it can be done." He began to eat the food on the plate set in front of him by Gwyneth.

The rest of the table stayed silent as Council Madoc ate, not wanting to disturb him as he hunched over his plate. After he cleaned off his plate and downed a goblet of wine, Patricia walked over to where he sat and kneeled by his side.

"Please forgive me for what I said earlier. I spoke from fear of losing Lord Troy. I mean you no ill at all and am thankful for what you are doing to save Domum and him."

Council Madoc nodded and touched her cheek with his hand. "I understand." He stood. "I must get back to work now."

———

Lord Troy ventured into the library where Council Madoc was working, writing out lines for a spell. He waited at the doorway until Madoc paused at his work.

"Council Madoc, I shall inform you the last part of the hedge has been affected. That gives us two days at most."

Council Madoc nodded. "I suspected that was happening. One can almost feel the difference in the air, though perhaps that is my imagination."

"The air is kept fresh by the preservation spell so perhaps it's not your imagination."

"I have a bit of good news. I have unlocked the first and second spell as well, but for some reason the effects of the spell have not been repealed. There is something very mysterious about that crystal."

"I am optimistic you will find the answer, Council Madoc. But, if by chance you do not find it soon enough, may I ask for one final favour from you?"

"Of course, Lord Troy."

"My death will not be a pleasant one, as you know. My body will age rapidly, and my mind will surely suffer first. I do not wish Patricia to see me that way and I ask you to prevent her from entering the library where I'll be staying during my final minutes. I want her to remember me as I am now and not as a withered old man."

"Of course, I understand perfectly."

"Also, in my final statement that I have written, I have left you in charge of all my possessions. I also beg of you one additional favour. As far as Patricia and the other ladies are concerned, grant them their freedom if they desire or allow them to live under your protection until they are able to survive by themselves."

"I will do as you request."

"My humble thanks, Council Madoc."

"Now, I best get back to work." Council Madoc turned back to the paper he was working on. "Time is not on our side. Once the castle itself has fallen to this crystal's power then no one will be able to reverse what has happened, for the crystal itself will have fallen to its own curse and ceased to exist."

———

"Now let me get this straight—this gnome named Laquil said magic alone cannot remove the damage done by this crystal?" Gordon Miller looked at Liz and then Angela.

Liz held back a sigh. It was the second time she had to explain the conversation with Laquil. First, it was to Tom and Tuck, and now again when Gordon Miller had sat down at the dinner table. The dinner itself was also on her mind. Marisa had cooked it by herself, and she had to admit the roast with potatoes, gravy, salad and fresh baked bread was something far beyond what she could make and was making her mouth water.

She also was trying not to allow her resentment toward Marisa show as she watched her place butter on the table. She was wearing a pair of jeans showing too much of her flat stomach, and her loose T-shirt not only showed she wasn't wearing a bra, but she was one of the women who didn't require one.

Liz wasn't sure if it was fair to be annoyed at someone who had lost their whole world but still managed to be cheerful and do her share of work.

"No, magic isn't enough. Once the crystal has been activated, it can't be shut down by magic. You have to remove spells around it apparently, but the crystal has to be made harmless as well."

"How does one go about doing that?"

"It's rather simple actually, something that was told to me before when I was on Domum. Iron stops magic, it's used as a defence to hold off spells. So once the spells have been removed from the crystal then you have to put it in an iron box."

"That is fascinating information. But how do we get that knowledge to Council Madoc?"

Liz listened to the chatter around the table as she scooped food on to her plate. It tasted as good as it smelled and as she shovelled a fork full of potato in her mouth, she saw Marisa cutting a small piece of meat before putting in her mouth slowly. Liz immediately slowed down her eating and hoped no one was watching her.

Gordon Miller directed his words to everyone at the table. "It seems the only way for us to get the message to Council Madoc is for one of us to go there. My apparatus can transport one of us to Domum, so now we must decide on who should go. I should stress this is strictly voluntary, as this will be a very dangerous mission."

"I will go."

Everyone turned their attention to Tom.

"Are you sure, Tom? As I said, this will be dangerous..."

"I'm sure. I want to go." Tom hadn't touched his knife and fork, his attention riveted to Gordon Miller.

"Tom, I don't want you to do this." Marisa rested a hand on his arm as she sat next to him. "I should go. I know where Lord Troy's castle is and about gnants that live there as well as the dragons. Tom, as much as it is brave for you to volunteer, I should be the one going there."

"You can tell me where the castle is. Time is important here, and I can run for miles without getting tired. I belonged to a running club before and I was pretty fast."

"You can't outrun a dragon. I'm in good condition and I can get there fast enough."

He sighed. "Marisa, I want to do this. Please don't argue with me."

She looked at him. "It's because you think Lord Troy will owe you a favour then and will try to get my freedom from him." Her voice raised in volume as she spoke.

He looked down at his plate.

"Maybe I want to get me own freedom." She crossed her arms.

"He would thank you for doing your duty, but would he give you your freedom?" He finally turned back to her his voice quiet.

She opened her mouth to speak and closed it.

"I'm right. Let me go. If you can find the way to his castle, then so can I."

"I don't want you to come to any harm on my account, Tom."

"I want to do this for you, for us."

Marisa rested her forehead on his shoulder for a moment and straightened up again. "Damnit, Tom, you better not get yourself hurt."

Liz and Angela washed the dishes after noticing Tom and Marisa had gone off to the living room talking to each other in whispers and Tuck had vanished faster than his second helping.

"She sure can cook."

"Looks gorgeous in jeans and a T-shirt too." Angela dried off and a plate and put it in the cupboard. "What's even more annoying is she is so nice you can't even hate her."

Liz washed the last of the silverware and leaned on the counter as she watched Angela dry them and put them away. "I hope she truly appreciates what Tom is doing."

"I think she does." Angela suddenly spun her towel into a rope and snapped it at Liz's hip.

"Hey!" Liz jumped out of the way and laughed.

Angela snapped the towel at Liz again and folded it. "Come on, let's check on the others.

Angela and Liz found Tuck, Tom and Marisa sitting in the living room.

Tuck sat in an armchair across from Tom with Marisa sitting on his lap. A small fire Tuck had started crackled and smoked in the fireplace.

"Tell me, Tom, when did you belong to this running club? It wasn't in university, was it?"

"No, a bit before then."

"Would it be fair to say a long time ago?" Tuck had a big grin on his face.

"When I was about twelve, actually."

Marisa hit him on his chest. "You lied to me!"

"No, it was the truth. Just a misunderstanding about when it occurred."

Liz laughed, "Yeah, male truth. No wonder me Mom said not to trust any man as far as you can throw him."

Angela joined her. "How come men always end their lies with it must have been a misunderstanding?"

Tom rolled his eyes. "Fine, pick on me. I'm leaving in an hour and this is how you treat me?"

Marisa kissed him. "We only pick on ye because we like you."

Liz looked surprised. "An hour?"

"Yeah, Gordon said it will take that long to set up his apparatus. Marisa here has been telling me about Domum and what to watch out for. She also made me a small map to find the castle. If I leave here in the evening, it will be near morning on Domum, so it makes sense to leave now."

Liz nodded. "I guess that's true. I better make up some food for you to take along and find a container for water."

Angela turned to Tuck. "How come you're sitting there? Shouldn't you be helping Gordon set this apparatus up? The other night you bored me to tears talking science with him so I assume you know the work he has to do."

"I offered, but he said he could do it by himself."

"So you would rather sit there and poke fun at Tom's running ability than to do something useful? If that's the case, then perhaps you can come to the kitchen with me because there's still a lot of cleaning up to do in the kitchen after that fine meal Marisa cooked."

"Okay, okay. I'm going to help out Gordon. Man, I can't even sit down for a few minutes." Tuck stood and strode out of the room.

Liz grinned at her, "You managed to spur him into action."

"Some people say I talk too much, but sometimes it comes in handy when you need to motivate someone. I would've kept talking until he moved."

"Come on, let's give Marisa and Tom some time to themselves and make up a food hamper for him."

Tom slung the backpack over his shoulder and looked at the plywood board standing in front of him with the array of crystals set in an oval. A year ago, he had seen Liz step through the same board and disappear for months. Now he watched as Gordon adjusted each crystal that gradually made the centre of the board vanish.

"You sure you want to still do this?"

Tom grinned at Marisa. "You better believe it. The chance to go to another world? I don't want to pass that up."

"You're not fooling me. You're nervous about going to Domum. That makes you a very brave man."

He gave her a kiss and turned to Gordon to accept a crystal hanging on a chain.

"Put it around your neck. As you approach the crystal array, you will see Domum. Simply step through but once you go through it will take at least another half hour for the crystals to regenerate enough power so you can return here. I hope you remembered to remove any metal as that causes some problems."

"I got rid of what I could." Tom turned to shake hands with Tuck and receive hugs from Liz and Angela. He turned to Marisa and received a long kiss, her arms wrapped around his neck as if she never intended to let go.

"Promise me you'll be careful and return soon."

"I will."

Tom stepped through the array, grimacing at the sparks from his jeans' metal fly and he was through to another world.

TWENTY-SIX

Lord Troy Sussex sat on a loveseat in one of the castle's lounges, holding Patricia's hand. "Please don't cry. I simply want you to remember me this way. There is little point in you being with me as my mind and body go. It will be painful for both of us."

"I don't want to let go of you."

"I know, but that is not for us to decide. I made a foolish mistake and now must face the consequences. I wish it was different, but we cannot change what is done. I have asked Council Madoc to grant freedom to those who wish it and to protect those who need it. Despite our differences, he is an honourable man. I suspect you will be able to fend for yourself quite well."

"On this world? Survive, yes, but I will be merely existing."

"Perhaps he can arrange for you and the others to live on Earth."

"But I want to live here with you," she sobbed.

He hugged her close. "You will get over this calamity, trust me on this."

"I trust you, but I will never get over this. I saw a ghost in the hallways yesterday."

"You did?"

"Yes. It, he looked liked the painting we have in the main room over the fireplace."

"King Ethelwulf?"

"That's the one. He just stood in the hallway and smiled at me. It was a friendly face, but it was as if he was trying to bring comfort to a terrible ordeal that is about to occur. I got scared and ran off. I haven't told anyone, save you."

"That may be a good sign, that there is indeed a place after this one for me. Fear not, Patricia, I am glad of this journey and look forward to the next."

She buried her head into his shoulder and cried.

———

Tom was prepared for several sights when he stepped through the array, ready to face dragons, gnants and the strange plants on Domum. What he came to instead was a warm, humid air, mud and rain. Lots of rain.

He looked down at his boots, sinking into mud as water poured off his head. *Today's weather forecast, a chance of rain.*

He began to plod in the direction he memorized from Marisa's instruction and soon saw the large mud hut the gnants seem to revere as a temple. The temple wasn't entirely made of mud; there were leafy plants growing on its sides that dominated the other plants. The plants were a pale-yellow green standing out from the darker green and red plants surrounding the area and looked like they'd been placed there rather than naturally growing there by themselves. He trudged unhappily in the cool rain making his clothes wet in a hurry. To his right, he saw the strange tree-sized plants constituting the edge of a forest. A shadowy movement behind the plants made him pause and try to see what was causing it.

He resumed his journey but kept glancing back at the forest, increasing his pace as he became certain whatever it might be was big and was stalking him. He was approaching the mud temple when the creature stepped out of the forest. Tom gulped and started to run on the muddy, slippery grass. From what Marisa told him, it was a dragon, a flightless one judging by the small set of wings on its back, and it was big. It resembled a forty-foot crocodile standing on four long limbs, and it was heading toward him with its mouth open.

Tom raced to the mud temple, hoping he would find a place to hide when he saw a second dragon coming toward him from his front. He increased his speed, focusing his eyes on the mud temple as his heart pounded in his chest. One dragon let out a roar as he reached the temple and ran along the perimeter. He looked and saw a mist of yellow and red erupt from one dragon's mouth. Marisa and Liz and told him it was dragon fire, a type of acid that dissolved flesh to make it easier to digest. Fortunately, the mist didn't penetrate far into the rain and Tom scrambled toward the front of the temple. He had hoped to avoid the temple and the hoard of gnants camping near the front of it, but preservation of his life had rapidly changed his plans.

Tom skidded to the front of the temple, wishing he actually still belonged to a running club, and collided with a hairy humanoid. The gnant chattered excitedly as it tumbled to the ground and quickly jumped to its feet, pointing a clawed hand at Tom.

Tom wasn't going to let the gnant stop his flight from the dragons. He quickly got to his feet and continued to run, sliding on the mud. He came across the entrance to the mud temple, a large oval hole at the front. He looked inside where a soft blue-green light emanated. The dragons had disappeared.

He glanced around, first at the chattering gnant nearby and to where a multitude of gnants slowly advanced. Tom suddenly realized why the dragons had gone; they didn't want to take on the hundreds of gnants that found him interesting. He took one more look at the gnants slowly drawing closer and stepped inside the temple.

The blue-green glow intensified as he walked inside enabling him to see the interior of the temple. On his left, a spiral walkway made of mud and stones wound its way up the side of the temple. At intervals, it opened up to rooms where even more blue-green light glowed showing off a group of gnants huddled together. Tom didn't pay much attention to them; there were enough gnants focusing on him on the main floor of the temple. They slowly advanced toward him, and Tom began to move to his right.

His eyes had adjusted to the strange light and he could make out more details of the temple, realizing there could be a hundred gnants inside the large structure. The blue-green light he was able to determine came from roots of plants hanging in clusters. The odd plants, he reasoned, growing on top of the mud temple provided a light source for the gnants below.

So far, the gnats seemed more curious about him than wanting to attack. Tom tried to calm himself down and slow down his breathing as he looked around the room when he spotted what looked to be statues of people along one of the walls. He slowly made his way there and looked closer at the statues. Two of the statues had been completed and two more partially completed. It appeared the statues were made out of the same building material of the temple, mud. One of the completed statues was of Gilbert and the other was of Marisa, completed naked.

Tom was impressed with the details of the mud statues, though he thought there was too much detail of Marisa.

The gnants around him made obvious reference between him and the statues and he tried to indicate it was true he was also human by nodding and saying "yes" several times. Tom was getting the impression he was in a gnants version of a library or learning centre. He pointed at the unfinished works of Council Madoc and Jon and pointed at the temple entrance.

But the gnants showed they wanted him to stay by blocking the way and excitedly pointing at another wall. Reluctantly, he walked over and followed a spiral ramp up. The ramp led to an alcove containing a series of drawings and after a bit of study he understood it told a story.

That was what the gnants wanted to show him, it seemed, for then he was allowed to walk back down. He slowly began to make his way back to the entrance, hoping the gnants wouldn't try to stop him again. The hairy gnants looked like small demons and he didn't want to test those claws and teeth.

He just made it back to the entrance when a gnant ran past him and stopped a few feet ahead of him. It turned to face him and, as it chattered at him, made various hand gestures. Tom stared at him and pointed at himself and at the gnant. He guessed the gnant was trying to indicate he was to follow him and soon he was hurrying after the gnant as it scampered sometimes on four legs and sometimes lurching on two.

They traveled past the smaller mud huts and soon made their

way across the way past the strange plants. The rain had stopped, and though the ground was muddy in places, the day began to warm up to a point where he had to wave down the gnant to catch his breath and take a drink of water.

The gnant watched him, curious as he extracted the canteen from his backpack. Tom offered him the canteen, but the gnant merely looked at the spout and gave it back to him.

"Well, Hairy, I guess we better get moving again. Lead on."

"Ead on."

Two hours later, they stopped again with Tom pulling out a sandwich from his backpack. The gnant went searching around the plants and a few minutes later came back with a dead rabbit-sized creature. Blood dripped from the neck of a limp, brown furred body as the gnant squatted down and began to tear into the still warm flesh.

Tom took a final bite of his sandwich and put the rest away, rapidly losing his appetite. He watched the gnant consume what was left of the creature, even snapping the small bones to get at the marrow.

Several gnants followed them as they made their way, but lost interest, only to be replaced by another set of curious gnants. Each time there was a chatter among themselves and especially with Hairy. The day became hot and muggy, prompting Tom to remove his shirt and just wear the backpack. That received more attention from the entourage of gnants, and Tom had to put up with the odd clawed finger touch.

Tom and Hairy stopped again in the late afternoon with Tom rediscovering his appetite. He ate the remainder of his sandwiches from lunch and started on the ones for supper, finishing off an apple as well. The gnants were interested in his food, though his offer to share was met with limited success. They tried the small sample he placed in front of him, but didn't care much for the bread, leaving it and only eating the ham in between the slices.

"Fussy eaters. This is a good sandwich." He took another big bite.

"Fusssssy eatersss."

"Good grief, you guys can learn to talk fast."

"Goo greef."

Tom shook his head and stood, stretching his arms. Hairy jumped up and led the way.

Tom occasionally saw dragons flying overhead, but the big creatures, while definitely observing them, ignored them. It was a nice change from when he first arrived on Domum and a flightless version of the dragons found him appetizing. He began to suspect the dragons attacked solitary prey and the large group of gnants around him kept them at a distance.

Evening came and Hairy began to chatter and gesture toward the horizon. Tom looked and saw the stone walls of a castle standing a few miles away.

"You found it for me. I'm not sure I could've done it without you."

Tom began to pick up his pace with Hairy still leading the way.

———

Patricia ran into the library where Lord Sussex and Council Madoc worked over a dark wood table. A dozen books lay open on the large surface plus several sheets of paper had been scribbled on. "Council Madoc! Lord Troy! Sir Tom has made a journey here from Earth with news how to tame the crystal!" She gasped as she stopped at the edge of the table.

Council Madoc recovered first to her news. "Where is he now?"

"Downstairs in the main room."

Council Madoc stalked out of the room with Patricia and Lord Troy in tow. He bounded downstairs two steps at a time. As soon as he reached the main floor, he called out for Tom.

Tom quickly began to repeat the short message he was given. "The crystal keeps repeating the original spell. It's kind of locked in. To stop the spell, you have to put the crystal in a box made of iron. I guess iron stops…"

"Of course! Lord Troy, perchance do you have a container made of iron?"

"No, I don't. Iron isn't a common material to make containers out of."

"Then we will have to fashion one out of iron pieces. It will be difficult but at least we know what to do."

"Yes, I have tools and weapons made of iron. We can forge them into a box by using magic and fire."

"Let's get them quickly. Time is running out."

"Won't these work?" Patricia stood there holding two iron pots. "We can put one over the other."

Council Madoc and Lord Troy exchanged looks.

Council Madoc took the pots from Patricia. "My dear, you are a genius." He ran upstairs with them with the others hurrying behind him.

Once he reached the library, he put the Dacron gem into the first pot and held the second pot above.

"Before you do that, can I ask a question?"

Everyone turned to look at Tom.

"I guess it's a little late for this but I should say it. Once you close the second pot on the gem this Domum will cease to exist and a previous one will return?"

"Yes, it's not immediate of course. Likely will take three, four days."

"Okay. It's just that this gnant named Hairy and others helped me find the castle. I'm repaying their help by extinguishing their lives and their world." He shrugged. "It just seems so, so wrong. I guess we don't have a choice in this but I wanted to say it. To do this without acknowledging them, well, I just wanted to say it."

Council Madoc nodded. "I understand your dilemma. But this world should not and would not have existed if we hadn't interfered in the first place. We are correcting a wrong."

"Wha' correct?"

Council Madoc turned and saw Talker, the adopted gnant standing next to Patricia.

"Yes, Talker. A mistake was made before and now we must fix it." He set his jaw and lowered the second iron pot on top of the first. "I will use a magic spell to seal the two pots together."

Patricia hugged Lord Troy and looked down at Talker. She picked her up. "Come, let me make you something nice to eat."

"Talker like to eat."

"I know, sweetheart, I know."

Lord Troy looked at the two iron pots. "How long before we know if it's working?"

"It's working now. I can sense it."

"That is a relief."

"Indeed. The spell will start to reverse its influence, starting where it ended and then retreat until it reaches here. In the meantime, I have some work to do here but I must leave for Earth soon for I am still in exile."

"I will lend my support to having that decision overturned and will no longer oppose you being promoted to being a lord."

"Thank you, Lord Troy."

"It is the least I can do. I am in your debt."

Lord Troy sat on the patio with Patricia, sipping on his wine, when Tom came to join them.

"Well, Sir Tom. You have done this world and me a great service. How can we ever thank you?"

Tom sat across from them, his gaze tracing the half-undressed form of Patricia. "Well, there is one favour I wish to ask."

"Just name it, I will grant it if it is within my power to do so."

"I am in love with Marisa. I'm asking you if you will either grant or sell me her freedom."

Lord Troy looked stunned. "You, you want to have Marisa?"

"He said so, Lord Troy. Grant him this." Patricia looked from Tom to Lord Troy, smiling.

"Yes, of course. Marisa is a wonderful girl."

"Thank you."

Patricia looked at Tom. "Now, may I ask you for a favour?"

Two days later Council Madoc, Jon, Gilbert and Tom prepared to set off back to Earth. Tom was burdened with his backpack and a small gnant. Council Madoc was of the opinion anyone who was in the castle when Domum changed the first time was safe during the next change. For himself and others it was best to be on Earth during the next change.

Lord Madoc shook his head. "We are to take this gnant with us so she will survive the change on Domum? I suppose I should take solace in the fact you didn't make friends with every one of them."

Tom looked around for Hairy as they walked but besides the fact all the gnants looked the same to him, he also didn't find any gnant coming up to him. He assumed Hairy had gone back to the mud temple where he had met him.

After a half day of travel Council Madoc stopped. "I wanted to see this Domum one last time. I'm not sure when or if I'll be allowed to return here but I'm optimistic the exile will be over-turned, eventually. But now it is time for us to depart to Earth. Each of you must make physical contact with me and I will then transport us to Sir Jon's home."

Tom looked around one last time as they joined hands. He listened to Council Madoc's whispered chant, and he saw a gnant moving on all four legs toward him.

"Hairy!"

Then the vision blurred and faded, replaced with the dark image of Ballymiller.

TWENTY-SEVEN

Tom stood staring at an empty spot on the street. "Hairy," he whispered.

Council Madoc looked at him. "Are you all right?"

Tom nodded. "Just that I saw Hairy just before we left."

"There's nothing we can do about that now. Let's go to the castle before we are seen by any townsfolk."

Marisa watched Council Madoc lead the way through the front doors with the others spilling in behind him. She worked her way past the others to grab and hug Tom.

"I missed you and was worried you might be eaten by a dragon."

"I was quite safe. The gnants helped me out there."

"Really now? You make friends fast."

"Come with me to the kitchen, I have something to tell you."

Tom led her by the hand to the kitchen to be alone.

"Now, what is it you have to tell me?"

"I talked to Lord Troy and he has granted you your freedom. You can stay here on Earth if you like."

Marisa stood quietly staring at him with tears filling her eyes. She wrapped her arms around his neck, whispering, "Thank you."

Talker was excited by her new surroundings, trying to see everything at once. Inside the Miller Castle she ran around, examining everything she could touch. Gilbert chased her from the dinner table, trying to protect the snack food placed on it. Angela was intrigued by the small gnant and tried to talk to her. Talker listened to her for a few minutes before running off to find more rooms to explore.

Council Madoc watched the small gnant explore the castle as he sipped a glass of wine when Tuck came by, munching on an apple.

"So is it okay to have this gnant running around here? I mean what happens when Domum reverts back to its original self? Does this gnant have to stay here or can it go back to Domum?"

"Good question. As far as I know, the gnant can go back to Domum. There is a concern about upsetting the balance of cosmos by transporting a body from one universe to another. I don't have an answer to that."

Tuck spoke around a mouthful of apple, "Like, now this universe has a sudden increase in mass due to the weight of her body?"

"That is one possible problem. But I was thinking more along the lines the cosmos may not like the fact we have saved the small gnant's life, which interfered with the total life energy of the cosmos."

"So the cosmos gets pissed off if someone does a good deed like saving a life?"

"It's more of a case of balance. There may be only so much life energy available and if the gnant uses some of that, there may be less for someone else. I, or anyone else, can go between Domum and Earth without a problem normally. But what we have here is not just going between two universes but from one that won't exist anymore."

"But you managed to survive on Earth after the old Domum disappeared without a problem."

"True. I sometimes wonder if I caused a problem in some small fashion because of it."

Tuck stared at his apple core and back at Madoc. "Well, everything we do has an influence. People jumping up and down cause the Earth to move a fractional amount. I think you just have to do what you think is the right thing to do at the time."

"You have an excellent point there. Perhaps I should stop trying to determine all the consequences of a particular action when I don't have sufficient information."

"Well, I guess that is one way of putting it. All I meant is fate sometimes puts you in the crossroads. Don't get hung up that you should have done this or that later on."

Madoc looked at Talker as she ran up a bookshelf and pulled out a book and scurried back down. She ran to a table and began to look through the pages.

"That gnant seems both remarkably curious and intelligent. Maybe she has something to offer." He stood and walked to where the gnant sat on the table leafing through the pages. "Do you understand anything within that book, Talker?"

"Paper."

"Yes, there is paper." He placed his finger on the black text. "These are words printed out."

"Wordsss."

Madoc nodded. "Yes, words." He touched the paper again. "This says '… giving a glimpse of the polaron's internal dynamics.' See each group of these symbols make a word."

Talker looked quickly from him back to the book and where his finger rested at the end of the sentence. "Glimpssse of the polar."

"That is very good. You mimic very well, either that or you can read."

"Mimic."

Angela spoke from behind Madoc. "We should get her one of those kid's books and teach her how to read." She put her arm around his waist.

"We could do that."

"And we could do something else instead of watching Talker."

Madoc looked at her.

"You've ignored me since you got back."

"I'm sorry, there's just a lot on my mind." He took her hand.

"I don't like being forgotten or ignored."

"Trust me, you're very hard to ignore."

"You were away for a long time and the first thing you reach for is a glass of wine."

Tuck walked away. "Man, some women are touchy."

Angela shouted after him, "Touchy? You think I'm touchy? No

wonder you don't have a girlfriend. All of us females are too touchy for you."

Tuck continued to walk away, waving his hand above his head.

"Come, Angela, let's retire to the bedroom."

"Boy, he has some nerve. Touchy. I'll show him touchy next time he pretends to understand what's going on."

Madoc sighed as he led her by the hand to the bedroom.

———

Beatrice's smile faded as she listened to Lord Perry.

"Ethelwulf has indicated there is now a chance the world of Domum may be reverting back to its old self. We may be returning to Domum after all but without any memories of this glorious palace."

"Perry, I'm willing to lose this memory of here but to lose my memory of our time together..." She stopped and composed herself. "I don't want to lose you now that we have found each other."

Perry twisted on the park bench and gave her a hug. "Let us trust Father will do the right thing for us, for everyone." He pulled back and kissed her.

Beatrice held back a sob. "You are right, Perry. I must accept what will happen and trust in the Father. Did Ethelwulf say how long we might have?"

Perry nodded. "He said approximately two days by our old reckoning." He paused, "Beatrice, he did say to me, 'Do not worry. Do not despair over what you may leave behind, for there are treasures still to be found and loves are never lost.'"

"Perhaps there is hope for us after all, Perry."

"Regardless of what will happen, let us make use of the time we have now."

———

Liz sipped her tea as she waited for Jon to finish showering and change into clean clothes. When he returned from his visit to Domum, she hugged and kissed him. The memories of when she was living on Domum before came back to her immediately. Jon's unshaven face scratched her cheek and her nose registered he hadn't properly washed for some time.

It wasn't necessarily a strong or bad smell. Unlike many of the usual residents of Domum, there wasn't a significant body odour coming from him. It was more of the masculine smell of a man who had been working. Still, she was glad he was getting a bath if she was going to be spending the night with him.

If his smell didn't remind her of the time they spent in Domum, his attitude certainly did. He looked and acted like a warrior, a man who knew his business. He seemed to have lost some of his waist, but likely due to a better posture than when he left. Liz felt her heart beat in her chest as he gazed at her and took her in his arms. She knew positively she was in love with him and any uncertainness she might have had about him melted away the instant he walked back through the front doors.

The usual noise of the castle had dropped considerably in the past half hour. Madoc and Angela had disappeared into a bedroom and likewise for Tom and Marisa. Tuck had retreated to the kitchen while Gordon Miller had fallen asleep in a chair by the fireplace. Only Talker playing with a deck of cards on the floor made any sound. Liz heard the water being drained from the bathtub down the hall and put down her tea. She got up and walked down the hall where the lone bathroom with a bathtub was located and opened the door.

"Hey! Oh, it's you." Jon had quickly placed a towel in front of himself.

"I was wondering if you needed any help drying yourself."

"I can reach my back with the towel."

"I wasn't thinking about your back."

She walked up to him and gave him a kiss as she wrapped her arms around his neck.

Much later, Jon led Liz out of the bathroom door by the hand as she giggled.

"What's so funny?" he asked.

"Oh, I was just thinking how many people have made love in the bathroom of a castle. Something to brag about to my girlfriends at university."

He stopped in the main room where Gordon Miller still slept in the big easy chair. Talker was organizing the cards into thirteen piles, with each pile containing the same card denomination.

Liz watched him give the slightest shake of his head and then continue to walk out the front door. She looked around as they reached the front gate of the Miller castle, not sure what he was looking for but was hoping for one question from him. If he was going to propose, she expected him to at least act nervous. Jon wasn't behaving nervous or worried at all but instead confident and self-assured.

"I wasn't sure where to ask this. Then it occurred to me this is where the journey began, when we first went to the Miller castle. Once we stepped through these gates, our lives changed forever and it was like fate was putting us on this path of no return." Jon smiled. "But during that journey, I found I didn't want to be or go anywhere without you."

He dropped to one knee. "Liz, I love you and always will. Will you marry me?" He reached into his pocket and held out a velvet box. With trembling fingers, he opened it and pulled out the sparkling ring. "I guess I should have taken it out of the box earlier." He quickly tore off the small white tag attached to the ring. "That was smooth," he muttered.

Liz stared at the ring, at him and back at the ring. She took the ring from him and slipped it on her finger as she turned her attention back at him. "Jon, I love you. Yes!" She squeezed her arms around his neck and leaned in to kiss him, causing both of them to fall over. She laughed. "I'd fall for you anywhere."

TWENTY-EIGHT

Tom sat alone in the main room by himself drinking a scotch. The room was dark, lighted only by a table lamp. He looked at his watch for the third time since he entered the room, noting an hour passed since he first sat down at two-thirty a.m.

Marisa wandered in, holding a bed sheet against her chest.

"Tom, I woke up, and you were gone. Is something wrong?"

"No, nothing to do with you or anything here. But I'm thinking about Domum and feel I've abandoned this gnant I named Hairy. He's going to perish when Domum changes back, and he helped me for it to happen. Now, he's going to just disappear without a trace and I feel guilty about it. Hence the scotch and sitting here by myself."

"You did what you had to do, Tom. You shouldn't feel guilty about that."

"I know. But I still feel bad."

"What would make it right so you would feel better?" Marisa released her sheet and sat on his lap. "Is there anything I can do?" She put an arm around his shoulder and leaned forward, kissing him gently on his lips.

Tom returned her kiss. "You're already doing it." He gave her a quick smile. "But I want to talk to Madoc about going back to Domum."

She sat up. "Now?"

"No, in the morning." His hand cupped her breast. "I've something else to do until then."

———

Tom watched Madoc's face as he explained he wanted to go back to Domum. There was a small glimpse of emotion as Madoc pursed his lips and leaned back his head.

"Are you certain that is wise?"

"No, I'm not. In fact, if you said I was crazy to do this, I'd agree with you. But it's something if I don't attempt, I'll be kicking myself for a long time."

Marisa sat next to Tom on the loveseat. "Sometimes it's better to do something not wise than to live with the consequences."

Madoc stared at her, as if trying to interpret exactly what she just said. "But to do something unwise…"

"Council Madoc, if you were a woman who lived as I had, you would understand exactly what I mean. You know it's wrong, even dangerous, but you know if you don't you will suffer."

"Oh, I see."

"No, you don't entirely. Unless you bedded a man you disliked." She took a deep breath. "Tom needs to do this. Understand, I don't want him to. But if he doesn't, he has to live with something awful for a long time."

Madoc nodded. "I understand." He rubbed his cheek. "Very well, I will facilitate Tom's return to Domum. But I warn you we don't have much time."

———

Jon insisted on going to Domum with Tom and Council Madoc, just in case of a dragon attack. Council Madoc resisted informing him he alone could handle any danger, deciding Jon wanted to return to Domum once more for his own reasons.

They waited until evening and Council Madoc transported them to Domum.

Tom immediately looked around, searching the landscape as a few gnants began to appear nearby.

"Are you certain you would recognize this Hairy if you saw him? I must say while I distinguish between some gnants the differences seem to be very slight."

"I think so. Anyway, I'm counting on him finding me instead." Tom shrugged. "Either that or I resort to calling out his name."

Council Madoc pointed to the gnant's large mud hut serving as a temple. "Shall we proceed in that direction? I suggest that might be the most logical place to find him."

The three walked toward the mud hut as more gnants began to circle around them. Jon lagged behind, gazing past the scurrying gnants as he carried a small plastic pail.

At first only more gnants appeared, coming closer as they became braver. Within minutes, gnants had surrounded them with more approaching. Then one gnant broke through the rest, forcing his way to the front, and came up to Tom.

"Hairy!" Tom bent down and reached out to the gnant, who chattered excitedly at him.

Tom tried to use words and sign language he wanted Hairy to come with him. The gnant listened carefully, tilting its head as it tried to comprehend. After watching Tom gesture, Hairy began to show signs he understood.

"I think he understands!" Tom reached out with his hand to grasp Hairy's hand.

But instead of letting Tom pull him closer he tugged on Tom's hand, trying to pull Tom toward the temple.

Tom allowed himself to be pulled along and entered the temple with Council Madoc trailing behind. The rest of the gnants followed them up to the temple but did not enter.

It took Tom a few seconds for his eyes to adjust to the eerie glow from plant roots above. But as his eyes adjusted to the low light, he recognized part of the inside of the temple. The gnants had added to the mud statues he had seen previously. Tom now stood next to Marisa and Gilbert. The detail was excellent, as far as the soft material would allow. Hairy let him look at the statues and tugged on his hand to lead him up a spiral ramp. Council Madoc followed, not commenting on the statues.

They entered an enclave, cut out by the spiral path near the top of the temple. Hairy pointed at the wall inside.

Tom looked at the drawings and symbols stretched along the wall. "These are like they're telling a story." He followed the drawings etched into the wall. "Isn't that a drawing of Gilbert and Marisa?"

Council Madoc stepped closer and looked at the rest of the drawings. He studied the symbols and drawings as he moved down the wall. "It is indeed. This is not just a story." He pointed at the end of the drawings. "See, Lord Troy's castle is symbolized in different parts of the story line. Right at the beginning and notice there are waves radiating from it. Then over here, we see the castle again and that small figure there is you going to the castle."

Tom looked again at where Council Madoc pointed. "You're right. Do you think this is a story recounting what happened?"

Council Madoc shook his head. "I believe it is more than that. Take a look at the drawings, all of them are much older than when the spell first changed Domum."

"You mean this is a prophesy?"

"I believe so. These are not recent drawings. One can see mould in the crevices and the wearing of the surfaces. What is interesting if one looks at the end here, it shows the castle once more with waves radiating from it." He touched the final drawing. "And then nothing."

Tom looked. "They know. That is why all these gnants are camping around this temple. They know their world is coming to an end."

"It would appear they understand what is happening."

"They even helped me find the castle. Perhaps they believed in fate."

"It would appear so. I'm not sure what those symbols at the end represent, but I would speculate it means something to do with the afterlife."

Tom and Council Madoc returned to the outside, once again meeting with a hoard of gnants waiting for their return. Hairy stepped in front of them and chattered excitedly at the other gnants. Gradually, they made way for them, chirping and gesturing, as a path was formed. Beyond them, Tom saw Jon, standing with his bucket and watching them as they reappeared at the temple's entrance.

Tom turned to Council Madoc. "Why did Jon come along with us?"

"Sir Jon mentioned something about providing protection."

"How, with an ice cream bucket?"

"I admit I was dubious of his answer at the time."

Tom grabbed Hairy's hand. "Let's go to where he's standing and return home. Maybe we can learn more from Hairy what those writings mean and if they truly know their world is coming to an end."

Hairy was content to follow Tom and Council Madoc to where Jon stood waiting.

Tom looked at the pail Jon was holding. "What exactly did you put in there? Dirt?"

Jon looked a little sheepish. "It is. I feel so much more confident on Domum than on Earth so I thought I'd take some of Domum back with me."

Council Madoc rubbed his chin. "Well, I guess Domum won't miss it. However, it is time we depart. Does Hairy understand he is leaving with us?"

Tom shrugged. "I'm not sure. I tried to show him, but it was hard to explain."

"Very well. I suggest we stand as close to the temple as possible so we will be within the castle's property."

They stood next to side of the temple and Council Madoc silently mouthed the chant to send them back to Earth.

Tom held Hairy's hand as Domum vanished and the backyard of the Miller Castle appeared. Hairy looked around, chattered high-pitched sounds and ran off.

"Hairy!" Tom ran after him, cornering him near the dock. The gnant didn't want to get any closer to the river and crouched on all fours looking at Tom.

"Come on, Hairy. We won't harm you." Tom bent down on one knee and spread out his hands.

Hairy suddenly bolted toward Tom and scampered around him, heading straight to the door to the castle. The door was locked, and the gnant clawed at the door.

Jon looked at the gnant and turned to the exasperated Tom.

"He hears the other gnant inside the castle. Gnants have very good hearing and they can produce sounds we can't hear."

"Let's just open the door before anyone in the town hears or sees him."

Council Madoc walked over and opened the door. Hairy ran inside, chattering away.

———

Lord Perry held Lady Beatrice's hand. They sat on a bench in the garden and spoke quietly to each other. They spoke words of little substance but revealed everything about their feelings.

Ethelwulf came by and interrupted their intimate conversation. "I have come to inform both of you your time here nears to an end. Domum is reverting back to its original self and as that happens it will call upon your souls to return."

Lord Perry blinked as he took in the information. "Will Father allow us to remain here instead?"

"He could, but your life's journey is not complete yet. You shall return to Domum. Fear not, your home here will be ready for when you do return."

"Then how long do we have, Ethelwulf?"

"The transition of Domum has started already and will complete in a few days time. You will move back to Domum a few hours before the change occurred to the new Domum, without a memory past that event."

"But what about us? Will Perry and I have no memory of each other?"

Ethelwulf smiled. "It is complicated to explain. Your memory will disappear of this place and of each other, at least until you return here. But I will leave you with this thought, love is more than a memory."

Perry sighed. "When I think of all those years I wasted on Domum for my own self-indulgence of knowledge, not knowing how much I missed of the pleasures of the world around me. I was such a fool to think to understand the world of science is to understand life. I studied for years and learned so little."

Beatrice patted his arm. "That is so untrue, Perry. You helped so many people with your fair and just rule. You furthered our knowledge of the world that will benefit others. You did so unselfishly, sacrificing your own wants and needs."

Ethelwulf smiled. "Perry is thinking he was selfish, that while striving to increase his own needs he just happened to help others."

Perry looked surprised. "But that is true. My help to others was a result of trying to fulfill my own wants."

Ethelwulf shook his head slowly. "You have a choice like everyone does. We all have needs and wants. We all try to find a way to obtain them. It is how we achieve those goals that define us." Ethelwulf placed a hand on Perry's shoulder. "You could have obtained your knowledge and ruled Horstruff by being truly selfish and arrogant. But you sought knowledge graciously and ruled fairly. You are a good soul, Perry. You acted with compassion in whatever you did." He removed his hand and stood smiling. "Now, I shall leave you two to spend time together."

TWENTY-NINE

L ord Troy watched the morning sunrise from his bedroom balcony. He stared at the landscape as the shadows receded and a slow smile creased his face. Details were still hard to make out but there was no doubt old Domum had returned.

Lord Troy returned to his bedroom, moving quietly so he didn't wake Patricia, and opened the door to the hallway. He walked with stealth down the hallway and down the staircase, his hand tightly gripping the handrail.

Carefully, he opened the main doors of his castle and proceeded through the maze. Lord Troy followed the twists and turns of the maze and arrived at the front gates. His fingers clutched iron bars, and he stared past them to the road beyond. Thrusting his right arm in front of him he took a hesitant step forward and then another.

When he had gone ten feet past the front gate, Troy fell to knees and crumpled to the ground.

———

Patricia swung her arm across the bed and felt the empty space. She opened her eyes and lifted her head. "Troy?"

She slipped from the silk sheets to the floor and, yawning, walked to the French doors that opened to the balcony. Patricia stepped outside and looked around her. "Domum's back. The trees and plants have returned." She grinned and then laughed. "It worked, it really worked. The spell is broken." She hurried back into the room and grabbed a robe as she made her way to the hallway outside the bedroom. "Troy! Where are you?"

She hurried downstairs, noticing the front doors stood open.

"Troy?" She walked barefoot through the maze, stepping carefully as she followed the memorized path. She reached the front gate and saw a figure slumped on the ground.

Patricia ran. "Troy!"

He slowly turned toward her.

"What are you doing outside here?" She looked at his face, distorted by tears.

"I am free."

She dropped to her knees and held him. "You're free?"

"Council Madoc. He removed the part of the youth spell holding me prisoner."

Patricia began to cry as they held each other.

———

"Talker, you're doing really well." Angela looked over to Council Madoc who was sitting across from her in one of the armchairs. "She's reading these primers without hardly any problem."

"That is remarkable how quickly she learned. She still has trouble speaking, I noticed."

"Oh, her enunciation is hampered by the shape of her mouth and her forked tongue. But she is getting better and makes most sounds close enough."

"How about Hairy? Has he settled down some?"

Hairy had either smelled or heard Talker when he was in the backyard of the castle and frantically tried to get inside. When the door opened, he quickly found Talker, and they chattered excitedly. Eventually, he settled down but remained nervous in his new surroundings. Tom was able to get him to eat and drink later but Hairy clearly wasn't sure what happened to him.

"He has calmed down today. I was thinking about showing him the viewer on the third floor, but I'm not sure of what his reaction would be. He might get upset seeing the change of

Domum. Then again, it might help him prepare for the change he's going to."

"I should think he has seen enough change for the time being. We will take him back to Domum in a few days and hope he will be able to adjust to the new surroundings. Meanwhile, it's good you are able to teach Talker how to read and speak."

"Did you hear that, Talker? I'm going to continue to teach you how to read and talk." Angela gave Talker a smile as she sat on her lap.

"Well, if she's going to learn how to talk, she might as well learn from the expert." Tuck came walking in, a can of pop in his hand.

"And if she learned from you, it would be a series of burps and grunts. Or perhaps how to talk with her mouth full."

"Ouch."

Angela looked up at Tuck. "Honestly, do you even think before you make a smart-ass comment?"

Tuck turned and walked away. "I surrender. My words are no match for yours."

"Hey, Tuck?"

"Yeah?"

"Would you be a sweetheart and get me a cola?"

Tuck stopped and slowly shook his head. "Unbelievable. First, she insults me and then asks me for a favour. She is so evil." He resumed his walk.

Council Madoc looked at her. "Do you really think he is going to get you something after how you spoke to him?"

"Sure. He knows I was just teasing him."

"Really?"

"Yup. Besides, he wants to get on my good side. Most men want to avoid having me pissed off at them." She gave him a smile.

"I see. So the result is you expect him to bring you a drink?"

"Well, I can't recall anytime a man passed up an opportunity to get me a drink."

Tuck returned to where she was sitting and passed her a cola. "There, now stop insulting me for five minutes."

"Thanks, Tuck."

Madoc looked at the departing Tuck and returned his attention to Angela. "We will soon have to return Talker and Hairy to Domum, even though it's not the same one they left."

"I'm sure they will be able to adapt."

"True, especially Talker. We need to return home. It seems the time for me to live on Domum has not yet arrived."

———

Lord Perry worked at his desk, feeling troubled he had overlooked an important task. After a few minutes of testing his memory, he gave up and pressed on to other work.

One of the servants carefully entered his study and after Lord Perry acknowledged him announced, "Freeman Gilbert is here to see you, Lord Perry."

He sighed. "Of course. Send him in."

"Lord Perry, I have the information you wants." Gilbert dropped to one knee in front of the huge dark wood desk behind which Lord Perry sat doing paper work.

He dropped his quill pen and frowned. "Very good. But where in hell have you been for the past two days?" Lord Perry pointed his finger at Gilbert. "I only hired you because of Sir Jon's request I give you a chance to redeem yourself. Are you trying to make a fool of both him and me?"

"Oh, no, Lord Perry. I's just ran into a spot of difficulty trying to get the right information for ye. Just tried to make sure I's not making a mistake. Ol' Gilbert very thankful for a job."

Lord Perry squinted at Gilbert and the silence lasted for several seconds. "Very well. This time I'll take your word for it. Now, just what did you find out about this dragon master, Sir Nolene?"

"Ah, Sir Nolene. Well, it seems he has the ability to train dragons…"

"Hence the name dragon master. Gilbert, I already know he was a dragon master and I do know what that means. Tell me something new."

"Yes, Lord Perry, of course. Sir Nolene comes from the town of Waleington, in the county of Larope. He's a man of means and has a large stable of mature patiri dragons, maybe eight or so. He sezs he wants newly hatched dragons to raise and teach, but there's more."

"Go on."

"Took me some time to finds this, but Sir Nolene also looks for men to join his army. Pay more than regular soldiers."

"How many men is he looking for?"

"Don'ts know, lots, I guess."

"That's interesting information, Gilbert."

"Thanks."

"But it took you three days to find that out?"

"Uh, well, these men are sworn to secrecy. Had to bribe a couple to learn truth."

"Where is this Sir Nolene now?"

"Gone to Homested."

"Well, we can't have mere Sirs raising their own private armies, especially one who is a dragon master. I shall have him summoned to come before me."

"Uh, Lord Perry, no disrespect, but he sez he bows to no man or king."

"We'll see about that." Lord Perry stood and eyed Gilbert. "I do have another task for you."

"Yes, Lord Perry?"

"One of my messengers informed me there was a disturbance of some sort in the air. Some townsfolk reported seeing bubbles in the air moving rapidly. Some thought they saw some strange creatures and plants just before the bubbles went past. It sounds like a magic spell of some sort. See if you can find out whom or what caused it."

Gilbert stared at Lord Perry.

"Is something wrong, Gilbert? You look like you have seen a ghost."

"Oh, I's fine Lord Perry. I's just remembered I's supposed to see Donna later. She be mad if I's is late."

"Very well. You best hurry along then. We wouldn't want you to get into any more trouble than you usually are in."

———

Donna swept the wood floor of the bits of wheat meal that had spilled from the cloth sacks. The store held a variety of goods piled haphazardly wherever it would fit. Like most businesses in Vegrandis, they did most of their commerce in trade, which meant they never knew what they would have to cram into the main floor of the former brick home. The tax collectors of Horstruff had long ago given up trying to collect monies from businesses that didn't deal in the king's coin and sometimes didn't exist a fortnight later.

Donna was tall for a female in Vegrandis, which meant she almost reached four and a half feet. Her blonde hair, in the tradition for women on Vegrandis, was kept long with the ends decorated with beads.

"Donna, this needs sweeping." Edward Garnet pointed at a spot behind him.

Donna sighed and looked at her father. Only an inch taller than her but with a great deal more weight, he placed his other hand on his hip. The appearance reminded her of a teapot.

She walked over and began to brush up the bits of tree bark. "I's not the only ones who can use a broom yous knows."

"Your mother be busy right now."

"I's not talking abouts her. What abouts yourself?"

Edward shook his finger at Donna. "Your sisters not ever talk to me likes that."

"That 'cause they be married and left longs ago. I wish I was lucky likes that." Donna was the youngest of three sisters and a brother. Each sibling passed the work down to the next youngest when they left to start their own family. Unfortunately for Donna, she was the youngest. Over the years, her parents became less capable of doing the hard work, resulting in Donna having less time for her own social needs.

"Shames on yous for speaking that way. Ever since Gilbert start comings around, your tongue get sharp like a knife. Fine way to talk to your old papa after all he dos for yous."

"Gilbert be a fine man. He be a traveller and sees the world, unlike me."

"Ha, fine man, is he? Where is he now? He not show up like he says he would."

"He be busy, that's all. He tells me all the difficult adventures he's in."

"Adventures you says? I say he has big mouth but has holes in his pockets."

Donna dropped the broom and covered her face with her hands.

"Papa!" Trudy slapped her hand on the wood table serving as a counter. She glared at her husband and began to advance toward him. "You not like any of Donna friends, scare away all her boyfriends."

"I just try to protect her from swindlers who are after her money."

"What money? She not have any. I say let Donna's heart decide who be best for her, not her Papa who has deep pockets but short arms."

"Fine thing. Picked on by the two women who I protect from the savages outside." Edward stomped away to a back room where he kept a flask of whisky.

Trudy put her arm around Donna. "All be well, child. Papa just trying to make sure his last daughter cared for."

Donna sniffled. "I knows, but if Gilbert not be my man, will I ever find another?"

Trudy knew what her daughter was thinking. She wasn't young anymore, and it was difficult to meet men when she worked every day and most nights. "You must let fate guide you and not force change. Gilbert, or someone else, will be there when the time is right. The Book says so."

Donna nodded. "I hopes so."

"You go home. I clean up and talks to Papa."

"Thanks, Mama."

Donna headed down the street. It was already dark, but she was used to making her way on the quiet streets. She was careful not to take a shortcut down the narrower streets but used the wider but more secure places.

She reached her home, a one-room affair that was once a business. She found it vacant and claimed it as her own, as was the rule on Vegrandis. A place not lived in was free for someone else to use. The only modification she had to do was to have an outhouse built in the backyard.

Donna was proud of her home and worked to repair the minor problems that came up. She closed the door and stared into the dark interior, wishing Gilbert had shown up yesterday like he had promised. She wondered if her father was right about him.

Gilbert hurried down the streets, turning into the smaller, less traveled areas. It wasn't the type of street he would use during the night, but he had to make haste. The shortcuts led him to the area called Vegrandis, where people of Gilbert's stature normally lived. He quickly went to one of the buildings, a former place of business converted to a dwelling and knocked on the door.

It swung open and a woman, slightly taller than Gilbert, stood staring at him without a smile.

"Hello, Donna."

"So you decided to show up, after all."

"I's sorry, Donna, but me work kept me aways."

"I'll bet. Did your work also includes gambling?"

"Oh, no, Donna, I's stays away from that."

"Hows about other women? Cans you tell me you haven't been with another woman since yous seen me last?"

Gilbert gulped. "I tries to be faithful, but …"

"I don'ts want to hear the details." She put her hands on her hips and gave a small smile. "Women finds you irresistible, I guess. Come on in."

"Thanks, Donna, I truly misses you."

"Enough to give up your drinking and carousing?"

"For yous, I try."

Donna gave him a kiss and sat on one of the three small armchairs in the living room. "So, tells me what was this business you were in keeping you away."

Gilbert leaned forward and lowered his voice. "'Tis a secret, mind you. Mustn't repeat this to anyones."

"Go on." Donna folded her hands on her lap, ready to listen to another of Gilbert's tales of bravery.

"Well, it starts with Lord Troy asking me if I could finds this gem he heards about. I was busy with Lord Perry's work, but I's didn't likes to turn down a friend."

Donna, unlike many others, believed most of what Gilbert told her. She saw him as a brave, debonair adventurer. She longed to see what the world was like outside of Vegrandis, and Gilbert became her eyes and ears.

"…so I sees what Lord Troy has dones and he begs me to help him."

"What did the spell do?"

"Oh, well, it be complicated. It, well, in a few days would starts causing big problems in all of Domum.

Donna nodded.

"I hads to travel to the Other-side and convince Council Madoc, to help Lord Troy. Council Madoc was reluctant to helps him, but he owes Gilbert a few favours. So I gets Council Madoc to remove the curse. Lord Troy was most grateful to Gilbert."

"Oh, my, Gilbert. How brave you are."

Gilbert got off his chair and bent down to one knee. "Donna, I knows I not always the best boyfriend, but would yous marry me?"

Donna covered her face with her hands. "Oh, Gilbert, I woulds like nothing better, but Papa forbids it. He thinks you be too poor to support me."

Gilbert was too stunned to speak, never expecting to be turned down.

THIRTY

Jon tried to stifle a yawn as he sat in the O'Douls' living room. Liz caught him and gave a stern look.

"Look, it's your wedding too. Don't you think it's important to make sure everything is right?"

"Liz, this is far beyond what I know anything about. I suggested we use my uncle's castle for the reception, but I don't know the difference between lemon-yellow and canary-yellow, other than one is a food group."

Tori giggled. "Then we can presume you like the lemon-yellow better."

Liz gave a quick glance at Tori and turned her attention back to Jon. "But you haven't said much else about anything." She crossed her arms.

Margaret O'Doul smiled. "You know, Lizzy, when I was about your age I was upset with your father too. He didn't want anything to do with the planning of the wedding. Jon at least sat with us so far. I think we would get more done without him and he would be happier too."

Liz frowned. "Probably you're right. I just think men get off the hook from all the work that's done to plan a wedding."

"But dear, at least if we are doing it, it will be done right. Do you really want to use help that may be colour blind?"

Liz smiled. "You have a point there. Jon, I think my dad is in the garage working. Why don't you go and see if he needs help?"

Jon got up quickly. "At least I may be of some help there."

———

"Hi Jon. Women chase you out?" Patrick O'Doul grinned at him after lifting his head out from under the hood of his car.

"I'm sure glad they did. Apparently, I don't know enough about the various shades of yellow. What are you working on?"

"It's nothing serious, just changing the oil. I'm just about done."

"Good timing on my part then."

Patrick chuckled. "That's real important in life. I'll clean up, then why don't we head down to the local for a pint?"

"Sounds good to me. I'll even buy the first round."

"So how are things at your uncle's castle?"

"Noisy. My uncle has the two gnants running around inside, and they like to chatter."

"Well, I'll take your word for it. I've never seen those creatures and don't plan on it, either. But you say they're smart and are learning how to talk?"

"Angela taught Talker how to speak and then how to read simple words. Hairy at first didn't want to do anything. He seemed to be in a state of shock. But he has started to adjust finally. In fact, he can say a few simple words and can read a bit too. Apparently, he was a student for the higher ups they call Adapts, so he was used to reading their language and had to be pretty smart."

"Was it nice to visit Domum again or are you glad to return here?"

Jon took a long drink of his beer. "Well, it's hard to explain. Here, it's safe and, well, maybe I take it for granted. But when I was on Domum, somehow, I felt I wasn't exactly at home, but I was meant to be there."

———

The messenger stood at the doorway until Lord Perry looked up and recognized his presence.

Lord Perry placed his pen down and signed. "Yes, what is the interruption this time?"

"I'm sorry, Lord Perry, but your uncle, Lord Troy Sussex, requests to meet with you."

Lord Perry closed his eyes momentarily. "When does he need to meet with me? I do need to finish this work."

"Lord Troy is here, Lord Perry, downstairs in the main drawing room."

Lord Perry stood. "What? Is this some kind of joke? He is unable to travel beyond the boundaries of his castle."

The messenger took a half step backward. "Lord Perry, I saw him with my own eyes. It is no joke."

Lord Perry hurried as fast as he could downstairs. Puffing, he entered the main drawing room, a room that dwarfed the furniture and the two figures standing inside looking at a painting.

The couple turned as he approached.

"Lord Perry." Lord Troy smiled and spread his arms out in a greeting.

"It's true! Heavens above, I never thought I would see the day." Lord Perry hesitated a moment and gave his uncle a hug.

Lord Troy returned the hug and turned his attention to his companion. "Lord Perry, this is Lady Patricia."

Patricia curtsied and extended her hand to Lord Perry, who bowed and kissed her hand. "It is wonderful to see you again." Lord Perry's memory of her was of a sullen slave who served him and others drinks wearing only a thin, lace skirt. It seemed to him a remarkable and curious change from a barefoot slave to being called Lady Patricia dressed in the finest clothes.

"The honour is mine, Lord Perry." She looked him in his eyes and suddenly blushed.

"Please, let us sit and have refreshments." Lord Perry led the way to the drawing room, followed by a group of servants.

Lord Perry sat with his guests in large chairs as servants presented drinks and food.

"So, tell me, Uncle Troy, how did you manage to free yourself from the curse that kept you confined to your castle?"

"It is a long and rather complicated story. But to simplify things, suffice to say in my attempt to remove the spell I inadvertently made it worse. In desperation, I contacted Council Madoc for advice. He was kind enough, without asking for any favour in return, to help me out of my predicament."

"I see. Council Madoc traveled to see you?"

"Actually, he never had to travel to our Domum to assist me. It was more of a case of Council Madoc sharing his considerable knowledge to help me."

Lord Perry nodded slowly. "As long as he didn't enter Domum to help you, I am grateful he helped you."

Troy smiled broadly. "As I said, he didn't want to or need to enter our world." He took a bite of one of the snacks provided. "There is an announcement I wish to make. Lady Patricia and I going to be wed next month, with the reception at my castle. I would consider it a great honour if you would not only attend, but to stand in as my best man."

Lord Perry stood. "I would be delighted to have that privilege." He lifted his glass to the smiling Troy and to Patricia, who seemed to be trying to hide in her chair.

Later, Lord Perry walked his guests to the front entrance. "Congratulations, Lord Troy, on removing the spell confining you and to your upcoming marriage to Lady Patricia."

Lord Perry waved at his guests as they entered the carriage, standing at the main entrance until the carriage disappeared from sight. "Life is full of surprises. Who would ever thought Lord Troy would ever get married?"

———

The carriage bumped along the road as they returned to their castle.

"Troy, he knew about me. He remembered me from before."

"Are you sure?"

"Oh, yes. I saw it in his eyes. He remembered when I was a half-naked slave."

"Lord Perry may be a strict disciplinarian when it comes to ruling Horstruff, but he does have a humanitarian side. He does not judge you."

"I wish I could be sure." She turned to him and smiled. "But as long as I have you, I can be happy."

He patted her hand. "I do hope Lord Perry believed what I said. I felt awkward deceiving him about Council Madoc."

"You told him the truth."

"Yes, but I implied something different about him not returning to Domum. I didn't tell him the truth, but I don't believe I had a choice. I wanted him to know Council Madoc helped me."

"You did what was right, Troy."

"Yes, you are right. I do dislike it when truth is a casualty."

"The truth is Council Madoc helped you and we are getting married. That is what you told him. If you told him what really happened, he probably would think of you as a liar." She gave him a smile.

He nodded. "I shall let the subject go then."

"Good, because we have to work on our wedding plans, such as the guest list and decorations."

"It shall be a well-attended wedding, I should think."

"We also need to obtain more help at the castle. Marisa is gone, and you have told me I should not be doing any of my former duties. So, we need at least two, perhaps three more servants. Do you want me to go to the labour house again?"

"Why don't we go together? I have never been there or many of the places in Horstruff for that matter."

"That would be fine. Are we staying to an all female staff?"

"I think so for inside the castle. But I believe I will establish a stable for horses. For the first time I have use of them and a carriage. Therefore, I will also have to find a couple of stable hands."

"So we require three women and two men from the labour house. Are you going to keep the men undressed like you do to the ladies?" She smiled at him, already knowing his answer.

"Men look better clothed, Patricia."

She laughed. "In your opinion. Just as long as none of those other women enter our bedchambers, I don't mind if they remained dressed according the Sussex Castle tradition."

Lord Troy smiled. "Some traditions must be kept."

———

Lord Perry tore the paper again and tossed the fragments in the garbage. He picked up another sheet of paper and rewrote the two lines again, forcing each word on the paper. He stared at the black ink, blew on the paper, and carefully folded it. After he secured the envelope with his wax seal, he called a messenger to deliver it.

"It is of the utmost importance Lady Beatrice receives this."

"Yes, Lord Perry."

"In her hand directly, even if you must wait there all day."

"I understand, Lord Perry."

"Good, now make haste." Lord Perry eased back in his chair and closed his eyes. *I wonder if she will wear her yellow dress with the blue trim,* he pondered. He opened his eyes. "Now why the devil did I think that?"

———

Council Madoc sat in his easy chair; a full glass of wine sat on the table next to him as he stared across his living room.

"Hey, don't you want the wine I poured for you?" Angela took a sip from her own glass.

"Hmm? Oh, yes, of course."

"You sound and look depressed."

He shook his head. "No, just thinking how nice it was to return to Domum, even though it wasn't like the one I remembered. I wish it was possible to return there now."

"Now, you really sound depressed. Madoc, you'll get back to Domum some day."

"Perhaps. But this hoping and waiting is starting to get tiresome."

"Focus on something else."

"Like what?"

"Me." She grinned. "I'm pretty interesting if I do say so myself."

He smiled slowly. "You are right, there." He took a drink of his wine. "You do make life here tolerable all by yourself."

"Now you're talking." She stood. "Let's say we finish the wine in the bedroom?"

The next morning, Madoc poured the hot water into the teapot, then turned toward the living room when he heard a strange noise.

"Angela, there is an unusual noise emanating from your purse," he called out to her in the bedroom.

Angela ran out wearing only her T-shirt. She turned her handbag on its side on the table and dug out her mobile.

"Hello?" A pause. "Hi Liz, how are you doing?" She walked over to a chair in the living room and sat down.

Madoc listened to Angela's side of the conversation for a few seconds and returned to the kitchen.

"Oh, that's wonderful news." She took the teacup from Madoc.

Madoc sat quietly in his favourite chair and waited until she finished her phone conversation.

"That was Liz and guess what?"

"I would not be able to guess specifically from the number of possibilities."

"Oh, wow, I never heard that answer before." She laughed. "It seems this Lord Troy Sussex is getting married, and we have been invited to the wedding. It's being held in his castle."

Madoc raised his eyebrows. "That is interesting news, but I'm not permitted to enter Domum, at least until Lord Perry changes his mind."

"Liz told me Lord Perry has consented to allow you to attend the wedding."

Madoc sat forward. "That is fantastic news. I get to return to Domum."

"I get to go with you too." She grinned. "It'll be so much fun."

"You may find it interesting, but fun is not a word I would use."

THIRTY-ONE

Marisa sat in the chair, watching the TV intently.

"It's just a soap opera located in some American city."

"Shh. I like it and it gives me a chance to learn about your culture."

"But people really don't act that…"

Marisa turned up the volume of the TV.

Tom sighed. "There was a game on the telly." He got up and went to the kitchen.

A minute later, he felt her arms around him as she stood behind him.

"I'm sorry, Tom. I didn't mean to ignore you over a silly show. How was your day? Did you discover anything interesting today?"

He twisted around so he faced her. "That's okay. Lab work was the same as usual. How was your day?"

"Kids are kids. But I like playing with them. I'm pretty happy to have the job and it was nice of Council Madoc to make me the necessary documents so I could work. All that information you have to provide just to work is amazing."

"I'm glad you're happy. Now, go back to your show. We'll talk later."

She kissed him. "Thanks Tom. You're so good to me."

Tom took a beer out of the fridge and returned to the living room, plopping down on a chair. His mobile picked that moment to ring, eliciting a curse from Tom.

"Hello."

Marisa listened to the conversation and as soon as he put down the phone, she turned to him. "Who was that?"

"Liz. It sounds like she's phoning everyone. Lord Troy is getting married to Patricia."

"I knew it!"

"I guess we're all invited to the wedding. She's thinks Madoc will be able to transfer all of us if we want to go."

"Oh, we want to go, all right. I wouldn't want to miss that."

"Great, more dragons to worry about."

Madoc reached for his tea as he sat by the fireplace in the Miller Castle just as Talker leaped on his lap and then bounded away. "There seems to be a definite lack of decorum here."

Liz laughed. "Don't be so serious. She's just having fun."

"Perhaps, but I have some problems to be concerned with."

"Such as?"

"Making sure you and the others are safe when we reach Domum, for one. You may be excited about going to another world but there are dangers."

"You told me about them. I'll stay close to you."

"There is also the matter of Talker and Hairy. When we send them to Domum, they will be most confused."

"We discussed that already. They can't stay here much longer. Gordon has been very accommodating in letting them live here."

"I don't disagree. I'm just trying to make sure I have anticipated all the possible situations."

Liz shook her head. "You can't have a plan for everything that might happen. It's impossible to plan for everything, and it's good to try to look ahead but you try to cover every detail. You're going back to Domum and that should make you happy. I know it's just for a visit so far but that is a good thing. Let's try to relax a little."

Tom entered the main room in the Miller Castle with Marisa, and saw Madoc brooding, with Angela trying to cheer him up.

"Hi, Angela, Madoc. Is everything okay?" He sat down on an opposite armchair and Marisa settled on his lap.

Angela looked at Marisa's short skirt, not surprised she had abandoned wearing the long skirts she used to wear. There was more leg showing than what she thought was necessary, but it was obvious Tom didn't mind at all as he rested his hand on her thigh. "Madoc is trying to make sure there aren't any unforeseen problems."

Tom frowned. "If he detects any problems, then they're not unforeseen."

Angela closed her eyes for a moment. "Tom, don't be such a smart-ass."

Tom grinned. "I saw Hairy and Talker earlier. I understand we're taking them back to Domum. I'm sure they'll be happier there."

Madoc spoke. "I am concerned they may have trouble adapting to a different Domum to which they are accustomed. They won't have the same language and behaviour as the other gnants."

"They're smart. I'm sure they'll acclimatize."

"I hope you're right. There is another problem. Hairy believes we deprived him of the chance to live forever.

Angela interjected. "That isn't entirely what he said, and we had to use Talker as an interpreter."

Tom whispered to Marisa, "Now we get the long-winded version of what Madoc said."

Angela continued, "Hairy, and the group of gnants he was with, believed in fate. They could foretell the future by using crystals and saw the arrival of humans as the predecessor to the end of their world. They didn't believe humans caused the end because they didn't have a choice. What Troy and Madoc did had been already decided for them.

"But Hairy was upset. At the end of the world they would go to a new world where they could live forever. When we took him here to save him, he feels he lost his chance to be with the others in the new world. Talker is too young to understand all of this so she is acting fairly normal."

"So Hairy feels deprived about not going to the afterlife? Or because he is spending this life with you?"

Marisa immediately gave him an elbow. "Behave yourself."

Angela frowned. "Are you trying to be funny, Tom? If you are, I can generate a lot of laughs at your expense. Would you like me to talk about how you reacted when you saw a mouse in the castle a few weeks ago? Or how about when you came out of the bathroom this morning without a stitch on? I could describe that in detail. Then there is…"

"Okay, okay, you made your point."

"Good, because I don't appreciate your bits of sarcasm at me."

"All right then. Can I ask how Hairy is feeling now about going to Domum?"

"Hairy is okay about going to Domum. I told him, it seems Liz and I are the only ones who really try to talk to him, that must be part of his destiny. He now believes fate has more for him to do before he is allowed to go to the afterlife."

"Oh, so he's not upset with me about taking him to Earth?"

"No, not after I explained to him you only did what you thought was right. You can thank me now."

"Thank you. I'll try to talk to Hairy more."

After Tom had gone to look for Hairy with Marisa, Angela looked at Madoc. "Maybe he should realize there's more to life than Marisa's pretty legs."

"I'm sure he understands that." He looked at her carefully. "You're not jealous, are you?"

"Of her? What is there to be jealous of a former sex slave? I really don't know what you are talking about unless you think I should be jealous of her."

Madoc took a deep breath. "No, I don't believe you should be jealous. But you are acting that way. Marisa is still learning how to act and dress in our world."

"Well, all right." She stood. "Time for me to get ready for our big trip."

"We're not leaving for Domum until after dinner."

"You have no idea what it takes for a woman to get ready when she's going to a fancy ball."

He sighed. "Just as well I don't know."

———

Angela looked over at Jon as he joked with Tom. The rented suit fit him fairly well. Since the last time she had seen him, he had lost weight around his middle and with the sword hanging from his side, he appeared to be quite an imposing figure. Tom's suit did fit him but was slightly on the worn side. Madoc wore what he usually wore, and she began to see his suit as a uniform he never took off.

Angela was hoping to wear something a little less drab for herself. Liz informed her she had to wear a long skirt and a blouse covering her arms to protect the decency of the citizens of Domum when she was in public. After a search at a discount store she found what was appropriate, a long brown skirt and a pale-yellow blouse. Liz had a dark blue skirt with a white blouse, and though they fit her, they didn't accent her looks any. Marisa meanwhile stood looking happy and somehow managed to make her borrowed black skirt and ivory coloured blouse fashionable.

Angela pushed her thoughts about the clothes away and noticed Madoc was speaking to her.

"Are you certain that container is necessary?"

Angela stared at him. "The suitcase has our dresses, shoes and make-up. Just what did you expect us to do? Wear a dress under these peasant clothes? We need to change before the gala event tonight, unless you want to conjure up new clothes for us when we get there."

"No, I couldn't envision something you would find appropriate and that fits you. But that is a rather large suitcase."

"I'm not about to squash my gown into a paper bag. We are taking the suitcase."

"This will take more energy to accomplish the transfer."

"But less energy than arguing with me and then losing that argument."

He sighed. "I yield to your logic."

"Thank you." She gave him a kiss. "I knew you would understand."

Upon their arrival in Domum, Angela looked around at the stone and brick buildings. She took a deep breath of the warm, humid air and wrinkled up her nose. "It doesn't smell very good here."

"It smells exactly the way it should. This is Domum. Some might think the air on Earth doesn't smell good." Madoc looked around. "This is my home and I think it smells wonderful." He smiled.

"For you it smells of home. To me it smells of horses and garbage. Something to get used to, I suppose." She gave Madoc's hand a squeeze. "So where is your castle from here?"

"It lies at the outside of town, a full day's travel by horseback. Most of the other castles are located at the perimeter of Horstruff. What you see in front of you is the centre of town. There is only one castle in this area and that is the duplicate castle of the Miller Castle. The castle here was owned by the deposed Lord Bennett and is used for administration."

"Horstruff? That's the name of this town? Not a very picturesque name."

"It is a historical name. I can give you the history of the name if you wish."

"Sure, some time when I'm having trouble falling asleep. How come this deposed Lord Bennett had the only castle in the centre of town?"

"The castle, like most of the buildings, is hundreds of years old. That castle at one time was the centre of Horstruff and where the king resided. As Horstruff grew both in size and influence, it obtained the attention of other kingdoms. The result was Horstruff lost its independence. The lords supporting the successful takeover were rewarded with part of the surrounding area and they built new castles."

"Oh, but those wars are a thing of the past now, right?"

"Not necessarily. There is an alliance among the various lords around Horstruff, but that could change if the present king loses support or dies. He is rather old."

"And you want to move back here with all that uncertainty?"

"Life without uncertainty is a predictable life of monotony."

"Well, you certainly have made my life unpredictable."

"I believe that is a positive. I shall return in a few minutes with the others. Sir Jon will look after Lady Elizabeth and you during my absence."

After Madoc disappeared, she turned to Liz. "Seems you not

only have been added the title of Lady, but your name grew by several letters."

Liz laughed. "Council Madoc likes to be rather formal and his return here has enhanced that nature. I can't remember the last time anyone called me Elizabeth."

THIRTY-TWO

Angela walked a few feet down the sidewalk, peering into the shop windows. "They all look like they sell used stuff."

Jon stopped behind her. "A lot of it is. Some new, some old. They sell what they can."

Angela turned to Liz. "I take it they don't have a shopping mall."

Liz laughed. "What you see is what you get. Of course, those with influence don't shop here. It's more of the case a shopkeeper or tailor will go to them. Personal service."

"Madoc has returned." She walked back to where Madoc stood with Marisa, Tom and the two gnants. Marisa was carrying Talker while Hairy, with his tongue darting out constantly, stood very close to Tom.

Madoc surveyed his surroundings and pointed down the street. "Shall we proceed to Lord Troy's castle?" Without waiting for a reply, he began to stride down the sidewalk.

Angela grabbed his arm. "Can you slow down a little? I want to look around as we walk and can't do that if we're in a race."

"Very well, but I doubt there will be much in this area of interest to you."

Jon added, "I don't care how fast or slow we go, as long as there aren't any detours. This suitcase is not light." He lifted the red suitcase up a few inches. "In fact, I suspect Liz may have put a couple of concrete blocks in here."

"Oh, hush up. When you see us ladies in the dresses, it will make your complaint seem rather small." Liz wrapped her arm around his waist and gave him a hug.

Angela walked with her hand on Madoc's arm, looking at everything she could. The people on the sidewalks stepped aside to allow them to pass, and she heard whispered comments among them.

"It's Council Madoc, he has returned!"

"Sir Jon, the dragon slayer, is back too. He's carrying a strange container with him."

Angela heard other comments as well but in every case the town folk stepped away from their path, some bowing their heads as they passed. Despite Madoc having told her he had been exiled from Domum, there was no doubt they were being treated with respect.

She turned around and watched the gnants look around in amazement. Talker clung to Marisa but Hairy was more adventurous, peering into the shop windows.

"Madoc, the people here act like you're royalty."

"I'm far from that, perhaps even the opposite. As a warlock I am not exactly welcome in some situations. I admit there is respect, but it comes from fearing what I could do."

"You're not evil. I know that."

"You may know that. But they are not sure and that makes my life easier."

"What about Jon? They respect him, too."

"They see him as a warrior, one that can kill a dragon. That is enough to earn respect."

"True enough. What about the gnants? The people here aren't reacting to them much."

"Gnants are seen as a nuance at best. The gnants native to this area have already been trying to communicate with them but unfortunately for them the language is different."

"How are they communicating with them? I don't hear anything."

"They can make and hear sounds beyond our hearing. Gnants are not trusted and certainly do not garner respect."

Angela was too warm in her long sleeve blouse and long skirt. She observed some women in Horstruff did wear less confining clothes, but Liz informed her that wasn't an option.

"The working poor are given more leeway as far as dress standards are concerned, but ladies of the court are expected to be carefully dressed while out in public. It would be scandalous for us to wear short sleeves. Now, inside the castle is entirely different, as you will see when we arrive at Lord Troy's home."

"So a mini-skirt and a tank top are out?" Angela grinned.

"That would get us arrested." Liz laughed.

"I also see why flat shoes are popular here. Imagine trying to walk with heels on this sidewalk."

"It gets worse. Later, the sidewalk disappears, and we walk on the road or on the ground."

"This castle better be worth it. I wish Madoc would transport us the rest of the way to the castle, but he said he was enjoying the walk through Horstruff after being away so long. I don't see what there is to be sentimental about so far."

"It's his home. It's where he wants to be."

Angela sighed. "I know. If he's allowed to return here to live, I will have a tough choice to make."

After walking some distance, they paused before an eight-foot high hedge. "A maze?" Angela asked. "We have to travel through a maze to reach his castle?"

Madoc nodded. "It was designed to keep intruders out. Fortunately, I know the way through, so it won't take long."

"Good, because I'm getting worn out wearing these clothes. It must be ninety and the humidity is over the top. It's ridiculous to wear this much."

"I would like to point out Sir Jon, Sir Tom and myself, are wearing clothes fully covering us. In fact, Sir Jon has been carrying that suitcase as well."

"Big deal. Men don't mind if they're sweating. And don't get me started about what the humidity has done to my hair."

"Angela, we have arrived at the front entrance."

Her gaze was drawn to a fountain made from white marble featuring a group of life-size nude women playing in the water. "We have to wear all these clothes and then there's fountain of naked women in too much detail. Isn't that a little hypocritical?"

Madoc pulled a cord at the large front doors. "Sir Troy is known for his eccentric behaviour. In fact, I must warn you inside the castle…"

The door opened, revealing a blonde woman wearing a white gown where the top of the left side of the gown hung from her shoulder but the right side of her torso was bare. "Marisa!"

Marisa ran past Madoc and Angela. "Juliana!"

The two women hugged each other, grinning away.

Angela whispered to Liz. "I'm definitely overdressed."

Angela took in the lavish furniture, draperies and art as they were escorted to the main room. She jumped when she saw the mounted head of a dragon, the open mouth looking ready to eat the intruders.

The main room had been decorated in vibrant colours and featured several large paintings.

Angela eased into one of the oversized chairs and took an offered goblet containing fruit juice from another servant, the woman also wearing only a light skirt.

Marisa disappeared with Juliana, leaving Tom and the others behind after telling them, "I got some catching up to do."

Lord Troy entered the room, his cane making a clicking noise. "Welcome, my friends, welcome." He fixed a gaze in turn at each person in the room. "It is fantastic to see Council Madoc, Sir Jon and Sir Tom again." Smiling, he walked over Liz. "Lady Elizabeth, I have heard so many wonderful things about you. It is a pleasure to finally meet you."

Liz stood up and extended her hand. Lord Troy took it, bowed and kissed the top of her hand. "I do hope your stay here is an enjoyable one."

Angela watched his approach and stood.

"Lady Angela, it is so good to make your acquaintance. I can now see why Council Madoc has been hiding on the Other-side. Your charms would keep any man there."

"Is Lord Perry handling the affairs of Horstruff without too much intrusion into his time?" Madoc sat relaxed, swirling red wine in his glass.

"I am afraid his want of studies have taken a back seat to all the difficulties of being the king's administrator. The alliance of the lords in this region and others seem to be changing. Now, needless to say, Lord Kevin Graham and his sons fully support Lord Perry, and he has considerable influence with the other lords and sirs. But there are a few lords giving only token support to the king and Lord Perry, waiting to see if there may be a new king arising."

"I saw this happening just before I left for Earth. Lord Perry has not promoted anyone to lord status. Lord Bennett's castle is still vacant?"

"True. Some sirs are pressing for promotion, but Lord Perry is reluctant to give that seat of power unless he is sure they will support him and the king in times of trouble."

"And how is King Charles doing?"

Lord Troy shook his head and lowered his voice. "I'm sorry to say I heard his condition, both physical and mental, has deterio-rated. His two sons are commanders of his army but have not shown signs of leadership. This has caused speculation the next king may not come from his family."

"That is unfortunate to hear. Tell me, has any lord openly chal-lenged the king?"

"No, that would be premature. But I heard there was a Sir Nolene raising his own army and acting rather arrogantly toward Lord Perry."

"Sir Nolene? Do you not know who he is?"

"No, he appears to have come from Larope and suddenly appeared around Horstruff, hiring men for his army."

Madoc pursed his lips and leaned forward. "This Sir Nolene is the illegitimate cousin of Lord Darius, and his sudden rise is not a coincidence. Lord Darius is ambitious and will use whatever means at his disposal to gain power."

Lord Troy looked shocked. "I was aware Lord Darius seeks power, but he has been reserved in his activities lately. But if he is using Sir Nolene to carry out his plans that would be bad news indeed. You know for certain Sir Nolene is his cousin?"

"I would not have said so if it wasn't true. If Lord Perry had not exiled me, I could have informed him of this situation. Now, we must be concerned with exactly what Lord Darius is planning."

Angela wished she could follow the conversation better, but she never was interested in politics. "Is there something else we can talk about? I don't want to be rude, but I don't have a clue what's going on."

Madoc sighed. "What would you like to talk about?"

"How about the wedding? The reason we all came down here."

"If you need information about the wedding, you'd better ask me. Lord Troy forgets to cover details like that. Hello, I'm Patricia."

At least she isn't half-naked. Angela looked at the blonde woman walking slowly into the room. Her dress was tight fitting in the middle like a bodice but did cover her from her bare feet to her shoulders. Angela also noticed the dress was thin enough to show off her best assets. "Hi, I'm Angela." She stood up, ready to shake Patricia's hand but the other woman hugged her instead.

"I consider any lady of Council Madoc's being a friend of mine." Smiling, she looked over at Liz. "You must be Liz."

Liz stood up with a smile. "I guess I must be."

Patricia gave Liz a hug. "I'm sorry I left you two ladies so long with these men who probably bored you with talks of great battles and politics. Please come with me and I'll show you around. We can get to know each other better."

Angela breathed in the fragrance of the roses around her. Beyond the brick patio, she saw footpaths weave around the flower beds. "This is amazing."

"It's my favourite spot to relax." She turned toward where several women sat around tables and chairs. "Here are the rest of the ladies and Marisa."

Marisa quickly walked over to Patricia and gave her a hug. "I was just telling the ladies I hadn't seen you yet."

"I was getting ready with some things. But why don't you come with me while the others prepare lunch?"

"I'd love to. We have a lot to talk about."

Patricia and Marisa led the way along another hallway. Marisa opened a large door and smiled at Liz and Angela. "This is the room where we sometimes party."

Angela looked around the room. Red drapes hung from the walls with large paintings set in between. The paintings, she wasn't surprised, consisted of erotic images of nude women and couples. The furniture consisted of lounges and loveseats and a round table in the middle of the room. On the table rested a dark wood box.

"Interesting room and decor." She walked inside and sat. "What is that?" She pointed to the box.

Patricia opened the box and lifted out a crystal roughly cut to look like a couple intertwined with each other. "This is a Mood Figurine, and it has special powers when light touches it."

"What kind of special powers?"

Marisa smiled. "Just wait, you'll know in a few minutes."

Angela looked at Liz, who shared her a puzzled expression. Shed looked around the room again. The décor began to look less exaggerated and more sensual.

Gwyneth opened the door. "Lunch is ready." She gazed at the others. "I see you have discovered the Mood Figurine."

THIRTY-THREE

G ilbert walked into Garnet's Fair Trade Shop. He didn't usually receive the warmest welcome when he came to visit but he had to make a show of being brave this time.

"Hello everybody," he called out.

Heads turned to look at him and a voice called out, "Gilbert!"

Donna hurried to him and gave him a hug. She quickly looked at her father, who stood with a hand on his hip.

Edward took a step toward Gilbert. "What do you wants?"

Gilbert puffed out his chest. "I cames here to invite Donna to a reception." He held up a folded piece of paper.

"What reception be that? I hears of no party."

Gilbert handed the paper to Donna. "This be outside of Vegrandis."

Donna read the invitation. "Papa, Mama, Gilbert be invited Lord Troy Sussex's wedding." She covered her open mouth with her hand.

"What? That cannot be." Edward took the invitation from her hand and held the paper up to the light. "Not a fake," he mumbled.

Gilbert looked at Donna. "So I asks you again, will you go with me?"

"But Gilbert, I not have anything to wear for something this fancy." She took back the invitation from Edward with trembling fingers.

Trudy came from the back of the shop, wiping her hands on her skirt. She peered over Donna's shoulder. "Maybe we can make a nice dress from left over material."

"How much for a good dress?" Gilbert reached into a pocket inside his shirt and pulled out ten silver ferns. "This be enough?"

Edward raised his eyebrows. "Good enough for a fine dress and a woman inside it."

Trudy shoved him on his shoulder. "Papa, watch your mouth." She took the silver ferns from Gilbert's hand. "Come Donna, we got shopping to do."

Edward watched his wife and daughter hurry outside. He thought about the way Gilbert casually pulled out the silver ferns so Donna could have a new dress and the invitation to a lord's wedding. "Gilbert, me good friend, can I offer yous a drink?"

———

Angela filled her plate with a salad and vegetables. The slices of dragon tail did not appeal to her, nor the fish. The fish looked okay, except it still had the head still on the serving plate. She decided to stay vegetarian. She did try the wine, not as flavourful as the ones on Earth, but it certainly seemed to have a high percentage of alcohol in it.

The table, with guests and the servants seated, was decorated with a bright green tablecloth and candles. Several toasts were proposed to the king, various lords and to the bride and groom. Talker ran in and out of the room, occasionally sitting on Liz's lap before leaping down again. Hairy was quiet, sitting on a cushion on a chair. He nibbled at the food on his plate, preferring the dragon tail to the other offerings.

"Everyone can continue to party, but I need to get myself ready." Patricia stood smiling.

Marisa rose. "Juliana and I will help her."

Angela touched Madoc's arm. "What do we do now? Have you finished talking politics? Because if you haven't, I may have to find if there's an unattached knight around here."

He smiled. "There won't be many in Lord Troy's castle, but I'm finished with political discussions for the time being." He escorted her out of the dining room. "Why don't we go for a walk? There's plenty of time for you to get ready."

"Okay. Did you see the flower garden in the back?"

"Yes, I know of it. I want to take you somewhere else."

Angela found the sun strong, but a soft breeze kept her cool. As usual, Madoc said little, but Angela found the silence allowed her to hear insects, birds and other creatures. The brick pathway soon gave way to a worn footpath, obviously used by horses.

They made their way to the top of the hill and there Madoc stopped, pointing to Horstruff spread out below them.

"You can't see the whole town from here but toward the west you can see Lord Perry's castle. The river runs down over there and is the centre of town." He pointed to a different direction. "Do you see the group of six dragons flying just above the horizon?"

"Those are dragons? They look so graceful. I mean the heads are actually pretty ugly but from here with their long tails they look good."

"Perhaps, but they are still just dragons. But what I wanted you to understand that is near where my castle lies."

"Can we go there? I'd love to see it."

"Perhaps tomorrow. It is a long ride by horse or carriage."

"Can't you just zip us there by magic?"

Madoc shook his head. "I could, but to use magic to transfer around for convenience is considered poor taste. If magic is used indiscriminately, it can cause problems with the aether."

"When can I see it? Is it like Lord Troy's castle? Do you have half-naked servants as well?"

Madoc laughed. "No, Lord Troy is unique in that regard. My castle, my home, is looked after by two servants, a married couple to be sure, and my financial matters are looked after by a lady of my acquaintance."

"Oh. Just how much of an acquaintance is she?"

Madoc smiled. "She is part of my past. But she is there and you are here. Shall we return to the castle?"

———

Madoc escorted Angela into the ballroom, one of the biggest she had ever seen or heard of. The room was oval-shaped with the highest part of the dome two stories above. The walls and ceiling were made of white marble with gold trim. Cut into marble in relief were figures of knights, dragons, damsels in distress and nymphs.

"This room is amazing."

Madoc nodded. "It is not unusual for a lord's castle, though most don't have those particular sculptures." He handed her a drink from one of the servants carrying a tray.

Angela saw Juliana was at least wearing a full-length dress, though the scooped neckline didn't hide much of her top. Madoc introduced her to various people, with most of the men dressed in black suits with a small cape at the shoulders while the women wore layered colourful dresses. The women showed curiosity about Angela, Madoc's latest lady friend and her dress. They had never seen a zipper before and were surprised at her shoes.

Almost every woman was interested in the high-heeled shoes, and after wondering out loud how she walked in them, began to consider having them made for themselves.

Nicole smiled. "I lived on Earth at one time and remembered those shoes. I had forgotten about them but now I may try to have a pair made."

"You're from Earth?"

"Oh, yes. Sir Jon and I are very good friends." She looked over where Jon and Liz talked a dozen feet away. "Excuse me, I think I will go over and say hello."

Sir Anthony Graham gave Angela a bow and followed his wife.

Angela looked at Madoc, whispering, "It seems there's some history there between her and Jon."

"There is indeed and also between Lady Elizabeth and Sir Anthony."

"You have to give me the details."

He shook his head. "I do not gossip about people's lives, Angela."

"This isn't gossip. This is information about people we know."

"And gossip is different how?"

Before she could reply, an angry voice boomed out at them, "Council Madoc! What the devil are you doing on Domum?"

Angela looked at the large figure approaching. Next to him, a woman in a yellow dress with blue trim held his arm. Madoc looked shocked at the grim-faced man facing him.

"Lord Perry, I was under the impression…"

Lord Perry burst into a grin. "Relax, I was only joking. How have you been? Things have not been the same since you left Domum."

They exchanged introductions and Lord Perry smiled at Angela. "So you are the young lady I have heard have been keeping company with Council Madoc. He is a lucky man to find a lady as beautiful as you is willing to put up with his behaviour." Lord Perry chuckled again. "I am only jesting. Council Madoc has a fine repu-tation here. In fact, I believe this is as good a time as any to make an announcement. Council Madoc, as of now, your exile has been lifted. You are free to live here on Domum."

Madoc closed his eyes and opened them again slowly. "Thank you, Lord Perry. I—I am speechless."

"Then I shall leave you be in your thoughts. We can talk later about your return here."

Angela looked at Madoc and saw wetness around his eyes. Slowly she took a drink of her wine, wondering what was going happen to them. Gilbert and Donna's arrival diverted her attention.

"Council Madoc, Lady Angela. This be me girlfriend, Donna."

Angela looked at the short but a pretty woman who blushed as she stood just behind Gilbert.

Council Madoc whispered to Angela, "My word, Gilbert is wearing clean clothes. This is indeed a special occasion."

Voices suddenly stopped as horns sounded. Angela turned to see a dozen men, six to a side, had formed a line. They held long curved horns to their mouths. In between, Patricia walked in, escorted by a tall, heavy-set man. She wore what Angela thought was a wedding dress that could be worn on Earth, although it was full of ruffles. The long train had to be carried by Lena and Marisa. "Who's the guy escorting her?"

"That would be Lord Kevin Graham, the father of Anthony Graham. He is actually distantly related to Lord Perry and Lord Troy."

"She looks beautiful. Nice to see she covered herself up for the wedding."

Patricia walked slowly past them. Angela then saw the back of the dress was open, the sides held together by a string that zigzagged between them. "So much for conservative, though it still looks good."

Patricia walked up to the waiting Lord Troy who stood in the centre of the room with an older man who wore a full-length cloak over his suit. The pale-skinned, thin man began to speak.

Angela listened to the words, about love and commitment. It seemed to her the vows were one sided. She had to obey and love him while he only had to provide for her. That was something she would be discussing, she decided, with Madoc if it came to that point in their relationship.

After the kissing of the bride, Angela wandered with Madoc around the room, soon losing track of the people to whom he introduced to her.

"Angela, you know the others," he whispered, "but the gentleman is Sir Keith and his acquaintance, Lady Karla."

She looked at Sir Keith, an overweight, middle-aged man, and Lady Karla, a slim, dark haired woman who eyed her suspiciously.

Lord Perry was speaking, "Of course this means this Sir Nolene has managed to gather a sizable army. It also means he may well have had help from a noble family here in Horstruff in terms of funds and information. I am appalled there is such opposition to our king when the other choice is war and anarchy."

Jon frowned. "I thought the removal of Lord Bennett would bring an end to those who would challenge King Charles."

As Council Madoc answered, Angela was aware how carefully everyone listened to him. She looked at those in the circle and saw the women stood just slightly behind the men, save for herself and Lady Karla, who actually was slightly in front of Sir Keith.

"Lord Bennett was a pawn for others, who stoked his ego into believing other lords would rally behind him to dispose of the king. Alas, they knew he would fail but wanted to see the reaction of the various lords when the king was defied. It gave those others a chance to measure the strength and weakness of the king's subjects."

Sir Keith asked, stuttering slightly, "What are our plans to stop this Sir Nolene? How are we deploying our army to battle him?"

Lord Perry raised his eyebrows. "An interesting question.

However, those decisions are being left to Sir Nathan who is in charge of my army."

Angela saw Lady Karla clench her jaw. There was definitely something about her she did not like. "Look, I know I'm just a woman and I shouldn't be even saying anything, but what's the point of trying to overthrow the king? I mean, would that change anything here? And doesn't the king have a bigger army than anyone else, so you would lose? All this fighting seems a waste of time and just kills a lot of people." She looked at the shocked faces and knew she had stepped outside of bounds by speaking. "Sorry, I guess I wasn't supposed to say anything."

THIRTY-FOUR

L ord Perry smiled and chuckled. "Quite all right, my dear. Sometimes we have to be reminded everyone has an opinion and everyone is affected by the brutalities of war. It is refreshing you spoke up."

Madoc agreed. "It is beneficial to hear all sides before a decision is made. However, to answer your questions, there are those who believe they can gain power under a new king. That could change things, especially if a new king appoints new lords. Laws could be altered, such as allowing increased magic. Taxes could be increased as well. Overall, I believe you are right, Angela. Fighting is a waste of time and people lives."

————

Angela wasn't sure what time she went to bed, but she woke with the sunlight streaming into the room and a dry mouth. She groaned and lifted her head off the pillow. *Damn, he's already up. Probably making me tea. Does he sleep at all?*

She slid out of bed and put on a silk robe left for her on a chair and cautiously opened the door. She heard voices at the end of the hall and ventured to a small dining room overlooking the garden.

Only women sat around the table, drinking tea and eating fruit. Angela recognized the servants, wearing only skirts. Liz and Marisa were also present and like her wore the supplied robes.

Marisa gave her a broad smile. "Good morning, how are you feeling?"

"Not so good. Still tired."

Liz got up, poured her a cup of tea and placed it at an empty spot. "We were just talking about how you spoke up during the discussion on Sir Nolene."

"Oh, I did do that, didn't I? I should have kept my mouth shut."

"We were all proud of you. Women don't normally speak on such matters, but we do have opinions. Of course, it was still a little surprising when you later told Lady Karla to keep her bug eyes to herself."

Angela closed her eyes. "I said that?"

Liz laughed. "Don't worry. None of us likes that witch. She did stop staring at you."

"Madoc must wonder why he brought me to Domum now." She took a tentative drink of her tea. "By the way, where is he?"

"He and all the men have gone to Lord Perry's castle to discuss a course of action. Apparently, one of the king's knights has arrived to update the situation. I don't believe they will be back until this evening," Marisa spoke.

"Great. What do we do until then?"

Alicia laughed. "We'll be fine without the men. After we wake up Patricia and wash up, we will have our own party."

———

"Hello? Is everyone in here?" Lord Troy stepped into the sitting room with Madoc behind him.

Patricia waved at him from her chair. "We're all in here, darling."

"I'm afraid I have some distressing news. King Charles' health has deteriorated to the point where he may not live more than a few weeks. His two sons are currently in a serious battle for the kingdom and their lives. Ladies, it seems the battle for a new king is underway."

Patricia stood. "That is terrible news."

Liz looked at Council Madoc. "Where is Jon?"

Madoc pursed his lips. "It would be preferable for Sir Jon to give you the details, but Sir Jon has volunteered to help organize the battle plans. Lord Perry has accepted his offer."

Liz jumped up. "No, he can't do that! I want him to return home with me."

Lord Troy faced her. "I know what you are thinking but fate has returned Sir Jon just when Domum needs him the most. A man needs to follow his conscience in these matters."

Angela reached for Liz's hand and squeezed it. She looked at Madoc. "And what about you? What happens to us?"

"I do not have a choice in this. I hope you understand but I must return you back to Earth."

———

Liz sat with Angela with her arms crossed in the drawing room. She felt worried and the pit her stomach was growing bigger with the passing time.

They heard a door close and Jon walked in. "Oh, there you are. I have to talk to you about something."

Liz stood up, her hands on her hips. "I heard. You're going to lead an army in battle? What were you thinking?"

"I was thinking someone has to step up in a time of need and do the right thing."

She crossed her arms. "But to lead an army into battle? You're putting your life at risk!"

He shook his head. "I'm not planning to lead the charge or go into battle. I offered to help with the task of planning battle strategies. I'll be safe enough."

Her hands dropped to her sides. "Maybe you'll be safe but shouldn't you have talked to me about this first?"

"He needed someone to stand up and make a commitment. Should I have run back here out of the meeting and tell the lords I first had to talk to you about it?" He raised his eyebrows. "Liz, I had to make a decision when I was with Lord Perry. I hope you understand."

"Yes, of course. I just don't want to lose you now."

"That's okay, love. I'll be safe. Now, I have to go and talk to Lord Troy."

———

Angela faced Madoc in the library. "What do you mean you're sending me back to Earth? Are you dumping me?"

"Dumping you?"

"Getting rid of me. It's an Earth expression you would know if you tried living there long enough and tried to learn the culture. But I forgot you were only visiting there."

"I'm not wanting to get rid of you. I just want you to be safe."

"Maybe you can let me decide where I want to be safe. I am an adult."

Madoc closed his eyes in thought for a moment. "You are quite right. On Domum men make many decisions without consulting women. I forgot our relationship is different. I have an obligation to see this upheaval resolved and thus need to stay here until it is done."

"What does that mean?"

"It means if you wish you may stay at my castle. It also means at the end of this turmoil if you want to return to Earth, I will follow you there."

Angela stared him, her lips trembling. She whispered, "You must really love me then."

He folded his arms around her, squeezing her as he kissed her forehead. "I do love you, Angela, in any world you choose to live in."

THE END

———

Watch for Castle Book 3
The New King
Available Soon

———

**Don't miss out on your next favorite book!
Join the Melange Books mailing list at**
www.melange-books.com/mail.html

THANK YOU FOR READING

Did you enjoy this book?

We invite you to leave a review at the website of your choice, such as Goodreads, Amazon, Barnes & Noble, etc.

DID YOU KNOW THAT LEAVING A REVIEW...

- Helps other readers find books they may enjoy.
- Gives you a chance to let your voice be heard.
- Gives authors recognition for their hard work.
- Doesn't have to be long. A sentence or two about why you liked the book will do.

ALSO BY JH WEAR

Novels

A Taste Of Murder

Play Dead

Witches and Warriors

Shadows And Sensations

A Hole in the Universe (coming soon!)

Castle Series

#1 *Fall to Domum*

#2 *The Curse of the Dacron Gem*

#3 *The New King* (coming soon!)

ABOUT THE AUTHOR

For a few years I wanted to try my hand at writing but too many obstacles prevented me from having the time to do so; three boys and a darling wife that loved home renovations to be more specific. Now the boys have "grown up" and left home I have time to do a bit more what I want to do, such as writing.

My other interests include wine, reading, astronomy, photography and convincing my wife that our home is actually fine the way it is. I have actually lost that battle. She wants our deck replaced; apparently rotten boards isn't considered safe anymore.

www.jhwear.com

 twitter.com/JH_Wear